A Normal Boy

Living in an Asylum

Keating

ISBN: 9781651899380

Any references to historical events, real people, or real places are used fictitiously. Names, characters, and places are products of the author's imagination. Any physical references to the layout of the building are also fictional. Terms such as: retarded, mongoloid, defective, mental, idiot, etc. are used as terms that were considered acceptable in the time period being depicted.

Front cover image by Alamy
Printed by Amazon
Second printing edition 2020.

Published by:
J. L. Keating
Box 63
Kenosee Lake, SK S0C 2S0, Canada

For my family with all my love

Acknowledgements

Jim Keating, my husband. Thank you for your patience and all the hours of proofreading and helpful discussions. You have been a supportive and honest critique that I can always trust.

Tara Keating, my daughter. Thank you for sharing your thoughts as a fellow writer. Your keen eye, years of experience as an editor and grammar skills proved invaluable.

Trenna Keating, my daughter, and twice award-winning playwright. Thank you for the hours of proofreading and for your intelligent questions and insightful suggestions that led me deeper into the story and helped me to enhance the story further.

Anne Macnab – Thank you for your willingness to be one of my first readers. I appreciated your honest opinion and your encouragement to go forward with the story.

Brian Ross – Thank you for your colourfull stories and delightful discussions regarding some of your experiences as an aide during your employment at the hospital.

Preface

The Saskatchewan Hospital officially opened in 1921 and was the largest building in The British Commonwealth and the most expensive building erected in Saskatchewan at that time. In its beginning, the hospital housed 607 patients. Weyburn's hospital was considered on the cutting edge of experimental treatments for people with mental health issues. The facility had a reputation of leading the way in therapeutic programming. At its peak, the facility was home to approximately 2,500 patients. It was officially closed in October of 2006 and demolished in 2009.

The name of the building was originally called the Saskatchewan Hospital, later the Souris Valley Extended Care Hospital, eventually the Souris Valley Regional Care Centre, and finally the Souris Valley Extended Care Centre. Not only did the name go through changes but also the forms of treatment went through many changes. I have made mention in the book about many of the treatments that would have been used from the 1920s to the 1950s.

During the 1950s, Dr. Humphrey Osmond began experimental treatments using lysergic acid diethylamide (LSD). This experimental period does not pertain to the timeline depicted in my book but is certainly worth a mention here as part of the outstanding historical efforts made at this hospital to help find treatments to help the mentally ill.

The hospital played a very important part in our community and offered employment opportunities to many people. A training program for registered psychiatric nursing was implemented and there was a separate building built as the nurses' residence.

Although I was aware that there were some cases of severely mentally challenged children being cared for in the institution, I was not aware that some "normal" children were living as patients in this asylum. My use of the term "normal" is in no way meant to be insulting to anyone who wants to question what is deemed as normal. As you read my story, it becomes apparent at some point why this word is used and why I have chosen it in the title. I would remind the reader that this story depicts events and language of the 1930s to the 1960s.

The fact that there were children, like the subject of this story, who were kept incarcerated for years was not common knowledge. Many wards were not open to visitors in the early years; therefore, this would be easy enough to keep from public awareness.

During the depression, Dirty Thirties and WWII in Saskatchewan, many folks fell on hard times and were desperate for various reasons. During the war, there was a social program called the Home Children that sent children from England overseas to Canada. It struck me as strange that we had children of our own from the prairies that were being dropped off to live in a mental institution and yet, we found homes for immigrant children. This is not to discredit the Home Children in any way. I just wonder why we found homes on farms and in our communities for thousands of immigrant children but we couldn't find suitable homes for our needy children whose parents saw fit to drop them off at the insane asylum.

There were limited social programs; especially,

programs dealing with children. Churches often gave assistance. Placing these children in the one facility available in the region may have seemed the only option. I suspect that some of these cases were considered as temporary. The parents' intent may have been to take custody again once their personal circumstances improved. However, many of these children were never released.

For those children unfortunate enough to fall through the cracks, for whatever reason, ending up in the asylum, I wondered why they were housed in the same quarters as mentally ill adults. Even though there was a problem of over population, it seems so wrong.

I wondered how anyone could possibly see fit to keep a vulnerable, defenseless child in an insane asylum at any time but especially a child who is completely "normal". And this is what has led me to write this book.

Chapter 1

The wind howled and dirt swirled like a dark cloud over the lifeless, ashen-like prairie. Wooden shingles lifted from the outbuildings and flew across the yard like blades cutting anything in their path. Tumble weeds rolled and danced their way like bouncing beach balls across the fields to far-away places. Mother had gone into labour and was about to give birth to her fourth child—me, Donald Johanson. It was July 1, 1931.

Under normal circumstances, when a child is born it is supposed to be a time of celebration. In my parents' generation, it was particularly a time for celebration when you were blessed with the first son. I came into a loving family with two nurturing parents, three doting, older sisters and grandparents to boot. So, it would seem I had the ideal recipe for a happy childhood. I had no way of knowing that life was going to interrupt my blissful childhood and take me into the bowels of hell. I was going to be uprooted by the Devil himself and he was going to have his way with my soul.

A popular quotation used today regarding the upbringing of children is: "It takes a village to raise a child." Well, I walked along a very long and lonely path and there was no village there to rescue me from the depths of hell on earth. It amazes me that over time I've seen people protesting and crusading for women's rights, gay rights, abortion, racism, and every other thing imaginable. Good causes? Perhaps, but where in God's name were the village and the protesters when innocent, normal children were placed in mental asylums?

Shame on those who knew, but did nothing about it. They saw me and they saw many just like me. They chose to remain silent and look the other way. Many law-abiding, church-going citizens who worked in the mental health system knew there were children like myself—children with no known or proven mental illness or mental disability—incarcerated in an asylum that was ill equipped, to say the least, to keep such children imprisoned, and yet, none of them raised issue about this. In fact, they cooperated to help keep us children hidden from the public.

People at the top certainly weren't doing anything to investigate or rescue such children from this situation and people at the bottom would shrug shoulders and say, "What can we do? We have no authority." It strikes me odd that those unionized people have authority and great strength in numbers and the backing of their unions when they want to vie for higher wages or better working conditions or benefits. They aren't shy about speaking up if it benefits them.

No one combined their efforts or united with the use of their power in their union to raise questions or concerns about keeping normal children locked up with mentally ill adults. Come along into my world and let me tell you what it's like to be a boy abandoned and forgotten, living in an asylum.

&)Q

My parents, Charles and Anna Johanson, lived on a homestead farm near the agricultural city of Weyburn, Saskatchewan, Canada. I was the youngest of four children and was the only son. I guess you could say I was the "after thought" of the family—the "unplanned" one. It seemed, however, that my parents were very pleased to have a son, at last, after having three daughters. The plan had been to have the baby delivered in the hospital but the dirt was blowing into deep drifts and you couldn't see across the yard let alone see the road. So my sister, Ethel, assisted mother. It was too risky to go into town and our neighbour, Irma McDougal, could not come through the storm to our farm to help. It was the Dirty Thirties.

&)Q

Ethel was the eldest child. She had naturally-curly, red hair, big blue eyes and freckles across her rosy cheeks and nose. She laughed like a screech owl. She was nearly always cheerful. When she laughed she got the hiccups. You could hear her hiccupping all through the house. It seemed there was only one level of sound for Ethel and that was "full volume".

Clara was blond and—as curly as Ethel's hair was—Clara's was poker straight. She had soft blonde hair to her shoulders and it always reminded me of corn silk. Clara, or Cev, as she was affectionately referred to, was dainty and had the face of an angel. The other sisters sometimes called her, "Queenie" and she didn't seem to care. She just flipped her blonde hair with the back of her hand and stuck her nose in the air and then flashed her big beautiful smile as if to say, "You two are jealous and I love it!" She had the same big blue eyes as Ethel and she knew just how to use them to get her way. She would lower her chin and tilt her head to one side and look up through those long eyelashes and my father was putty in her hands!

Doris was the youngest of the three girls. She had thick, wavy, chocolate-brown hair and dark eyebrows to match. She had a few freckles like Ethel and the same big saucer-shaped, blue eyes that the other two had but she was somehow a little less feminine than her older sisters. Doris was a bit of a Tom-boy. She was quiet and more serious than the other sisters. That is not to say she didn't have a sense of humour because she did. She'd throw her head back and hold her stomach and have a good laugh along with anyone who told a joke but it didn't happen too often.

She was less interested in fussing about stylish clothes and never put that nail varnish on her fingernails that Clara loved to use. No frills for Doris; just comfortable and practical clothing that suited farm life. She would be more apt to be found helping Father to build something out of wood or help him in the barn if she could get out of household duties. She also loved to help Mother in the garden and I think Mother enjoyed the time to have one daughter all to herself.

My father, Charles Johanson, came to Canada from Sweden with his immigrant parents in the early 1900s. My grandparents staked a claim for land and began their farm life with a sod hut until they had enough saved to erect a proper wooden structure for a house. They raised seven children, including my father. They were proud to be Canadians and Grandfather insisted they would speak English at home as much as possible to learn the language and assimilate to their new country and customs.

Grandmother learned new recipes for the prairie farm life she now lived. She found wild Saskatoon berries, wild raspberries and choke cherries, for instance. These were a good source of vitamin C and Grandmother heard that they helped prevent scurvy. She soon learned to make jams, jellies or pies from these berries. Dandelions were also picked and the greens were used in salads and there was a dandelion wine that she learned to make as well. Nothing that grew wild or that was planted went to waste if it was edible at all. She still did her best to keep some traditional Swedish recipes for special holidays.

Life for my ancestors was not always easy. There were droughts and insect infestations and crop failures along with diseases affecting the livestock but somehow they always survived. When one thing failed, it seemed that another came through. Grandmother always said that when God closes a door, He opens a window somewhere. She was an eternal optimist or maybe it was her strong faith in God that made her have that optimism.

In 1928, they had a bumper crop and things had improved greatly. My father told me that the family always prayed and went to church on Sundays. He said his parents insisted on the children learning to put God first. They kept the Sabbath holy, meaning it was considered "a day of rest". The only chores done on Sundays were things that were necessary—such as feeding the livestock. However, if it was harvest time, they would be expected to be in the field day and night even on a Sunday.

During harvest, Grandpa figured the Lord would expect them to get a good crop off the land since the Lord was good enough to provide a bountiful crop. He said only a fool would waste valuable harvest time. The Lord would not smile upon such a fool.

My grandfather and his sons were hard-working farmers. They raised cattle, pigs, chickens and geese. There were a couple of horses but they were just work horses. My father and his siblings would often hitch up a horse and take a wagon to school. Sometimes, they walked and sometimes they might ride the horses bare back to school but most times they walked as Grandfather would have need of the horses himself.

My grandmother planted a large garden which produced vegetables that were carefully preserved and stored in the cool basement for the long prairie winters. She also had a root cellar dug into the earth where many preserves and root vegetables were kept cool all summer, thanks to Grandpa and his sons hauling large blocks of ice which they cut from the dugout and layered with sawdust to keep them from melting.

As the family grew and moved to other parts of Canada and United States, my father was the only one left to take over the farm. When Grandma passed away and Grandpa retired from farming and moved into town, Charles found the farm a lonely place and began looking for a wife. That's when he met Anna, a beautiful slender, blonde girl (of

Norwegian background) who worked as a domestic at a neighbouring farm.

Anna and Charles married and began their family. Life continued much the same as the generation before. My father thought it was time to build an even larger house more suitable for his growing family so they built the two-story house where I was born. It was a beautiful home—well built and with all the modern conveniences of the time.

The ground floor consisted of a roomy back porch, large kitchen, living room, dining room, music/library room and built-in veranda across the front of the living room. The second floor had four bedrooms and a large bathroom. In the wide upstairs hallway, there was a staircase that led to the attic. That was where I had my room. The girls and my parents had the bedrooms on the second floor.

I loved my bedroom with the dormer window. I could lie in bed and see the stars twinkling in the night sky. I particularly loved hearing the rain falling on the roof when we got a good prairie down pour. My father would say that it was like "pennies from Heaven". I didn't realize it then but he meant that the rain was good for the crops; which, in turn was financially good for us. Not only was it good for the crops and Mother's garden but we collected rain water in a reservoir that was stored in the basement and could be pumped up to the kitchen or wash room.

The kitchen was one of my favorite rooms of the house. It was a large open room with the table in the very center. Mother liked to display a bright gingham or floral tablecloth that she had embroidered herself. She liked things to look presentable because you never knew when a neighbour or the minister might drop by. There was a large bow-window facing southwest that let a lot of warm sunlight in which added a bright warm glow to the room. Mother used an old wood-burning cook stove and every Saturday she baked bread that would fill the house with the most wonderful aroma. I loved the way she brushed the buns with a sugar and egg glaze that turned the buns shiny on top. She was always baking or cooking something to feed our family. The kitchen was the busiest room of the house because everyone passed through it to get to any other room. One door led from the kitchen to the dining room and another door led to the hallway that led to the stairway and also connected to the front parlor.

The walls had 9-foot ceilings with wooden beams running across the width of the room. The doorways and windows were cased with dark oak wood trim to match the beams. The dining room had a built-in china cabinet where Mother kept her special set of dishes brought over from the old country. There was a large oak dining room table and chair set that sat proudly in the middle of the dining room. On this table, mother placed a large lace tablecloth that she had crocheted. A fireplace flanked one wall in the living room. Mother and my sisters kept everything spotless. The rooms smelled of lemon furniture oil and Johnson's paste floor wax.

I thought my mother was the most beautiful person in the world. I remember sitting on her bed and watching her brush her golden auburn hair. She was always well groomed and smelled clean and fresh. She was a quiet reserved woman who always seemed to look as though she was holding some thoughts back from those around her. She was not stern or unkind—just busy with her daily chores and perhaps a little tired of raising children by the time I came along.

I tended to follow my father around and leave the house to my mother and sisters. My favorite times were when Father was working on a piece of farm machinery. He would explain things to me as he was taking a machine apart and greasing parts up and restoring things. He believed in doing repairs after harvest and would check things out again way before spring seeding. He wanted things "oiled up and working smoothly when needed", as he would say. I took a keen interest in this type of activity on the farm. I was always eager to help but I'm sure that most of the time, I was more of a hindrance with continually asking questions. However, Father never made me feel that way. He was always so positive about how pleased he was to have my company. He talked to me like I was an adult rather than like I was a child. He seemed to expect that I had the intelligence to comprehend what he was teaching me. He would let me sit on his lap while he made the rounds in the field with the tractor or combine. He would allow me to do the steering sometimes. I actually believed I was driving the machine.

Farm life required that certain tasks be done daily and some more than once a day, like the milking of the cows. Father usually did the early morning and evening milking and sometimes I went along. I was not good at milking but I would fetch pails for him and help to load them onto my wagon and take them to the house. Mother and my sisters would operate the cream separator which we kept in the back porch. The cream was separated from the milk. The cream was saved and sold to the Co-Op Creamery in town. Clabber was what resulted when the thickened raw milk turned sour.

This was very much like buttermilk and Mother would use this clabber in her baking to help to make things "fluffy", as she put it. The cleaning of this machine was serious business. My mother insisted that it be cleaned after every use and all the parts had to be washed and then rinsed in boiling water and then set on a wire rack to be steamed.

Everyone understood very early in life, without having it even explained, that jobs needed to be done for us to eat and survive the winters. Food was a constant effort to grow and eventually reap or butcher and preserve. I helped Mother every day to gather eggs. My sisters looked after the geese. I was always thankful that I didn't have too much to do with the geese because they could be mean at times. They would run after me in the farm yard at times honking and flapping their wings and they scared the daylights out of me. More than once they managed to take a nip at me.

When Father and I came in from the field during seeding or harvest, I would do my best to imitate all my father's actions. We had a pump and washstand in the back entry porch and Father always washed up here before entering the house. He would take off his overalls and hang them on a wooden peg. He had put a peg on the wall down low for me so I could reach to hang up my overalls too. Mother insisted on no barn clothes to be worn in the house.

Father would roll up his sleeves and work up a lather of soap all the way up to his elbows. He would scrub his fingernails and knuckles with a brush and so I would copy him. I remember how the brush used to make my skin feel rather sore and tingly and how pink my arms would look when I was finished but I insisted on following this procedure to the letter. To me, anything my father did or said was perfect and that is exactly how I wanted to be.

Father was more outgoing than Mother. He loved to tease her and he could make her smile and blush even after all those years of marriage. Whatever her inner thoughts were, she could let loose and have a laugh when Father cajoled her. There were some tender moments when he would come up behind her at the kitchen sink and put his hands on her hips and kiss the back of her neck. Then he'd whisper something in her ear and she would blush and say, "Charlie! The boy is watching!" as she slapped his hands and pushed him away.

I didn't mind. I was happy to see my mother smiling. I would giggle as Father gave me a wink and a smile and tickled me as he passed by. Then, I'd follow him into the living room and we'd wrestle until my face was red and I was all hot and sweaty. Finally, Father would say in a good natured tone, "OK Donnie! That's enough, Son. It's time to settle down."

I loved that physical interaction between us. He told me he would teach me to box one day. I knew he was going to make me strong like him.

Chapter 2

I often wonder what life would have been like for me had circumstances been different. But it wasn't to be; tragedy struck when Father was attacked one morning by a bull. In that terrible instant, our whole world as we knew it changed. There was no way to see it coming or to prevent it from happening. I remember Mother running from her garden to the bullpen. I remember her screams for help and the hired man running to assist her. I saw Mother holding Father's head and wailing, "Charlie, don't leave me! Hang on Charlie, Frank's gone to get the truck. Charlie, Charlie, I love you darling! Please help us God!"

The rest is a blur in my mind—blood, so much blood. I know Father was taken to the hospital but he hemorrhaged badly and passed away that night.

The house seemed so empty and still after that. No one wanted to talk it seemed. It was as though if we spoke we would start to cry; and what could we say to one another anyway? We were numb and maybe that was the best way to be at that time. I saw mother's apron still crimson with Father's blood soaking in the washroom. I looked at Father's leather work boots by the washstand. The day he was killed, he had been wearing his rubber boots so his leather work boots remained intact. No blood. How I longed to see him sit down on the wooden bench and pull on those boots. I sat on the bench and put my feet into his boots. I reached up and touched his work overalls and put my face into the worn denim, faded and smeared with grass stains and dirt.

I needed to touch something of his to feel close to him. I inhaled as long and as hard as I could to bring the smell of my father into me. I felt hot tears begin to stream from my eyes uncontrollably. I had not intended to cry. It just came and I let the river flow for a few moments. I could almost hear my father saying softly, "Come on now Donnie—you've got to buck up Son; boys don't cry, you know."

Words he would say to me in the past if we were outside and I got upset over some small thing and began to cry, hoping to get some sympathy. He was trying to teach me that boys don't cry like girls. I always thought that was odd that girls could pull that off and boys were expected not to go down that path. It was difficult but it would come to serve me in days ahead. Learning to keep my emotions in check was a valuable lesson in life.

It was a terrible time in those first few weeks. Life was a painful place of dark unknowns. I fretted over how our family was going to manage. Neighbours dropped by with pies, casseroles, fresh fruit and homemade buns. Ladies from the church stopped in as well and I remember Irma

McDougal putting her arms around Mother's shoulders one day as Mother wept softly.

"You go right ahead and have a little cry, dear," said Irma in her comforting voice that seemed so soothing to Mother but also to me. "I'm going to make us a cup of tea and I'll help you get supper started before I leave. Donnie, you can help me set the table for your mother," she added as she stood up from crouching beside Mother. She patted Mother on the back and then put the kettle on the stove. We all had a cup of tea and I even saw Mother smile and that made me smile too. I wondered if it was OK that we were smiling and enjoying a moment with Irma when Father had suffered a terrible death. I wondered if God would disapprove of our smiling. Would I be punished for laughing and smiling one day?

Mother fell into a deep depression and my sisters had to take over the chores and do the cooking and cleaning as best they could. However, even though Mother moved about like a robot, she made herself get up and start her day by working in her garden and gathering the eggs from the chicken coop. She would have to work hard and the girls weren't going to be able to do much because they had school.

As depressed as Mother was, she insisted the girls not let their studies suffer. I was too young to do a man's job but I could help her with gathering eggs, milking cows, cleaning the barn and picking peas in her garden. As much as we all tried to do what we could, it wasn't enough and we all knew we would need to rely more on our hired hand.

Frank Schmidt was a muscular, rugged German with blonde curly hair and cold steel coloured hazel eyes. My father was also a fair-haired man but he was taller and slimmer than Frank. Frank was always edgy and seemed to be in a rush to do a job and seemed rather impatient. He didn't seem to smile much or have much of a sense of humour, compared to my Dad. He was always in a serious mood, it seemed. Frank had never paid any attention to me or my sisters in the past. He rarely ever spoke to us unless we spoke to him first and then it would be little more than a grunt from him.

I guess we had no reason to care much about that until after my Father died. His attention certainly took a new focus on my mother after Father died. He worked round the clock that August during harvest. There wasn't much of a crop due to the drought. Wheat was dropping in price so mother was worried and stressed all the time. No matter how much I grew to dislike him later, I cannot say Frank was lazy. He treated the machinery and the livestock as if they were his own. His efforts were appreciated by all; especially, it seemed, by Mother. She would sit up waiting for him to come in from the field and she would have a meal waiting for him. Or, she would be busy making something appetizing to take out to him in the field during the day.

I could hear them talking sometimes late at night when I was in bed. I couldn't always hear their words but I would hear them laugh and then I would hear the soft conversation and I knew my mother was probably blushing like she had when Father teased and whispered to her. I felt anger over this and buried my head in my pillow and sobbed. Why couldn't Father come back and make Frank stick to tending to chores?

At first they were discreet but soon afterwards they became more open about their attraction to one another.

Harvest was over and I guess they were celebrating a little and Frank had been drinking liquor from my Father's cupboard. He grabbed Mother as she began to clear the supper dishes and pulled her onto his lap. He growled at my sisters and me to get busy and clean up the kitchen. We looked at one another but quickly did as he bade us. We were not used to such behaviour and certainly did not like him speaking to us in this manner; however, Mother was not about to take our side in this and it was abundantly clear from that moment on that Mother was allowing Frank to become head of our household.

ℰℭ

The seasons came and went. Thanksgiving was not a time to give thanks as far as I was concerned. My father was never coming back and my mother didn't seem to even care or miss him. She was too busy darning socks and doing laundry for Frank. I hated to see her smiling now and walking around the house like she had some joyful secret. What right did anyone have to feel happy—especially her? Mother had put all Father's belongings in boxes and taken them to the Salvation Army and given some things to friends and neighbours. Before anyone else noticed, I picked up Father's work boots from beside the bench and hid them away in a back corner of my closet in my bedroom. No one was going to touch those boots. I would be the only man to wear them one day!

Christmas was the worst time without Father. At least when it was harvest time, Frank was outside and working long hours. Now he was in the house more. Before Father's death, he had lived in the old original farmhouse built by my grandparents across the yard. But now, he had moved into one of my older sister's bedrooms upstairs across the hall from Mother's room.

I heard footsteps in the middle of the night on more than one occasion back and forth between those two rooms. I didn't know anything about sex in those days other than what I saw the farm animals doing. But I didn't know what people did. I only knew that it didn't feel good having Frank in our house. He didn't belong there. Little did I know that I was about to find out who belonged and who didn't belong in that house.

Chapter 3

It was summer and it was stifling hot. There had been hardly a drop of rain. We'd had an infestation of grasshoppers and I wondered if we'd ever get a day without wind, dust or bugs. Mother would often lay wet towels along the window sills and at the door threshold to keep the dust from filtering into the house. She was fussy about keeping her house clean.

Frank had proposed to Mother and she had accepted. This was going to make his status in our home official. Frank's proposal had come with conditions. One night I could hear them talking in the living room downstairs. There was a grate in the floor in the upstairs hallway to let the heat from the lower level come upstairs and I used to lie on my stomach and peek through the grill to watch and listen to Mother and Frank. It wasn't easy to hear as they were talking rather low but I picked up bits of their conversation. Mother sat with her head resting on Frank's shoulder and he was looking straight ahead when he said, "Anna, I've told you from the beginning that I don't like kids."

"I know, Frank," she replied as she sat up straight now, looking downward, afraid to make eye contact with Frank, "but, I just thought that one day . . ." she seemed almost to be pleading now.

"No, it's either him or me—that's the deal—take it or leave it. I can go my way and you can go your way; or, I'll live here under my terms and if you agree, you'll never have to worry or work hard again. I'll see to it that you are looked after properly."

I wanted to listen more but my stomach was beginning to hurt from being in that position. I was afraid I might make the floor boards squeak. They might hear me and I'd be discovered. I was supposed to be in bed. As I tiptoed to my room, I tried to figure out who Frank was talking about when he said, "It's either *him* or me . . ."

℅ℂℜ

"Girls, Donald! Come here, please! Mother called to us. Ethel was puttering in the kitchen as Cev chattered about some boy in school who she was sure fancied her.

"Doris! Where are you? Mothered called up the stairwell as Ethel and Cev came into the living room.

"I'm coming Mother!" shouted Doris. "Can't a person have a quiet moment to do my homework? What's the big deal?"

"Sit down children. I've got something serious to discuss with you." Mother seemed intense as she twisted her hands and then smoothed her apron. A lock of her hair fell in front of her eye and she blew it out of her face and then smoothed it back and pinned it with one of her bobby pins. I thought I rather liked the look she had with that lock of hair falling in front of her eye like that—a beautiful auburn curl that bounced softly. It reminded me of a movie star.

Mother was very slim and not heavy in the bosom like so many movie stars were. Not that I had seen movies much let alone movies with voluptuous women. But, Father had some magazines in the little bedside table and I would sneak into their bedroom on more than one occasion to look at those pretty ladies in the magazines. Mother's eyes were beautiful too. They seemed to sparkle when she laughed. I hadn't seen that sparkle for some time and now, if I did see it, it was usually when I walked into a room when she had been giggling like a teenager over something Frank had obviously said. I didn't want to see her eyes sparkle around Frank. As I was about to day dream myself punching Frank right in the kisser, I was snapped back to earth by mother's voice. She was talking in a serious tone.

"Children, I know it has been a difficult time since we lost your father. I appreciate what you have done to try to help me but I think you all know that I cannot run this farm alone and I will be alone when time comes that you all grow up and leave here. As you also know, Frank has become more to me recently than just the hired hand. He has become a special and kind friend that I can rely on. You girls are old enough now to move out of the house and find work. You've had some high school education by now and girls don't need much education." Mother looked at each of us nervously trying to get a read from our shocked expressions.

"But Mother! I love school and I'm not going to get as much education as Ethel and Cev!" Doris began to cry. "I don't think Father would be very happy about this carrying on you are doing with Frank either!" She jumped up and left the room crying.

"Don't you dare Doris!" mother retorted defensively. "I have a right to a life of my own and you girls will soon be off getting married anyway. As far as education goes, you all have more schooling than I ever got and girls don't need much schooling. They just get married and have babies anyway. For the time being you can likely get work on the neighbouring farms doing housework and baby-sitting. It will do until something better comes up."

She added that if they wanted more education, it would be up to them to pay for it. After all, they couldn't expect Frank to foot the bills for them now. I sat there with my mouth and eyes wide open. I wasn't getting the full thrust of this conversation. I was stunned and confused. I think I was in shock.

Ethel sat looking at her hands, holding back the tears. "I'd better go see if Doris is alright."

"Sit down Ethel—I'm not finished and you need to hear this." Mother collected herself and began again in an attempt to sound calm.

"Frank is different than your father. I loved your father and he was a good husband and father. Frank is a good man too in his own way. He works very hard. It's just that he never developed any affection toward children."

She explained that this was especially true in our case since none of us were his "real children". All I remember thinking was that I was glad to not be Frank's son. I was glad to have experienced the love of my "real father". I would rather have lost my father at a young age than to never have known him. Frank wasn't good enough to clean my father's boots let alone live in his house. Of course, I kept that thought to myself. I could see I'd get no where trying to say that out loud to my mother.

I sat fidgeting around and looking out the window as we sat there. I was thinking that I wanted to be out in the yard on the tire swing. It was such a beautiful day. For once the wind wasn't so bad. School was out now for the summer and I wanted to ride my bike or go climb trees and pretend I was a pirate on a ship looking out to sea. I couldn't seem to focus on the depth of what Mother was explaining. I didn't like seeing my sisters crying but I didn't realize how all this drama was going to impact my life. I knew I had better pay attention. I sat up and leaned forward to stare at my mother as she talked.

She turned to me with a forced smile on her face that seemed like a feeble attempt to sound like she had something special in mind for me that I would like.

"Donnie, you will get a chance to go to a summer farm camp where there will be lots of animals and other boys to play with."

I heard the words but couldn't comprehend. I don't remember asking any questions. But it was simple and straight forward—Frank belonged in the house—my sisters and I did not.

෨෬

Moving day came for my sisters before it came for me. The girls were sad and Mother seemed sad too. She had raised good girls who had been a great help to her in the home. They had made the house lively with all their teenage chatter. If I thought the house was empty and quiet after Father's death, it was even more so now that the girls were gone. Just as I had longed for Father and had needed to touch something of his to feel close to him, I had that same feeling about my sisters now that they had moved out.

One day, feeling particularly lonely and blue, I had slipped into the bedroom shared by Cev and Doris. Most of their things were still there as they had only taken their clothing with them. Ethel and Cev went to neighbouring farms to do domestic work. Doris was sent to our maternal grandmother's place. Grandmother said if Doris helped her at home on weekends, then Grandmother would pay for one more year of school.

I looked around the room and my eyes fell on a doll crib in front of the window. I went over and picked up one of the dolls and sat down on the floor and just held the doll for a moment. I felt the hot tears well up in my eyes and run down my cheeks and splash onto my shirt. I hugged the doll tight, trying to gain some sort of comfort. I needed to hold something and I needed something or someone to hold me. I felt as though I wanted to scream but all I could do was sob in silence. It was only a moment and then I gathered myself and wiped my tears.

I put the doll back in the crib and stood up and turned around. That's when I saw him watching me. Frank stood there in the doorway. He didn't say a word but he didn't have to. I saw the look of disgust and hate in his eyes as they seemed to burn right through my very soul. As brief as that moment was, it would have a great impact on my destiny. How little we sometimes realize that a small action, as innocent as it may seem, can determine the direction of a life.

 හ⭕ଓ

The next day, I was on a journey to what would become my new home. Frank, Mother and I were traveling to Weyburn in our half-ton truck. Mother had packed me a small suitcase with a few things. Two pair of pants and three short-sleeved tee-shirts, one long-sleeved flannelette plaid shirt, some socks, a denim jacket and a woolen sweater that Mother had knit me for Christmas, a couple of comic books and my two most treasured possessions—my father's pocket watch and a small photo of my mother in an ornate silver frame. She had also packaged up a few homemade peanut butter cookies for me (my favorite cookies). But there was no sign of my father's boots.

"Oh well," I thought, "I'll be coming home soon enough and I have to grow some anyway before they will fit properly."

They told me it would be like going to summer camp. That didn't help me to picture things too well since I had never been to a summer camp and didn't know what any kind of camp was like. I thought if I'm going to camp, I'm at least thankful it is "summer camp" because I couldn't quite imagine what a "winter camp" might be like but I figured it would be less desirable for sure. I decided we were on an adventure and I was quite enjoying the drive looking at all the farms, the crops and the livestock. I hadn't been far from the farm before, other than trips into town for groceries, supplies or doctor appointments. And as far as I knew, I was going to visit a farm where there were going to be lots of boys to play with and I loved farms so that didn't sound too bad. I don't think I was old enough to understand that I wasn't coming home again—I was nine years of age.

Chapter 4

I don't remember much conversation as we traveled along the dusty gravel road into town. Weyburn was a nice enough city at this time of year. Things were pretty dry and lacking much green but I could smell lilacs through the open window of the truck. There was a big ball diamond and the fair grounds that we passed coming into town. Frank pulled into a gas station. While he filled up the truck, he told Mother to go get me a treat. It was the first and last time that Frank did anything kind toward me. I was surprised but beamed from ear to ear as I hurriedly jumped out of the truck. Mother got me a bottle of Orange Crush and a bag of licorice babies and some jaw breakers! Wow! This was my day!

Then we headed down this long road that was treed on both sides with branches that seemed to form an arch over the road. I thought what a lovely shady lane this was on a scorching hot summer day. The road opened up to a huge red brick building with manicured lawns adorned with abundant colours of mixed flowers and more lilac bushes. The air was sweet with floral perfume. A perfect summer day and now we were entering this massive building that smelled of antiseptic and floor wax. The floors shone like mirrors. Our footsteps were making loud clacking sounds that echoed and seemed even louder. The ceilings were higher than anywhere I'd ever seen. This seemed more like a palace than a farm. There was a beautiful winding staircase at the end of the entrance hall with a golden railing! This was like nothing I could ever imagine.

We walked up to an opening in the wall where there was a woman on the other side of the counter. She wore her hair in a bun or French roll. I'm not sure but my sisters did their hair up like that so I had heard the terms. She wore black-rimmed eyeglasses that made her look like she had cat eyes. I watched her lips and was sure I'd never seen lips that colour before. They were orange! Mother told her we were here to see the Superintendent, Mr. Anderson. The lady with the orange lips told us to follow her and we all went into this office with a desk and leather chairs in it and books on the wall. Mr. Anderson shook hands with Mother and Frank and then smiled down at me.

"Hello Donald. Would you like to take a seat outside my office for a while? Later, we'll take you out to see the animals in the barn."

I sat on a wooden armchair against the wall outside the office and swung my feet back and forth while I enjoyed a few more candies. Mother wouldn't let me bring the Orange Crush into the building. I wondered if the barn was going to be as big as our barn. I hoped they had horses. Maybe I could learn to ride while I stayed at this summer camp. Before too long, Mother and Frank came out and Mr. Anderson escorted us out of the building and we walked a short distance to the barn. It was huge! I was very impressed and thought this was going to be fun to run around this place on all that grass and to play in this barn. All of a sudden Mother put her hands on my shoulders and leaned down to look me in the face.

"Donnie, I have to go now and I want you to be a good boy. Remember you have those peanut butter cookies if you get hungry but don't eat them all at once or you might get a tummy ache. Mind your manners and eat all the food they put before you at meal time. Don't forget to brush your teeth and wash your face. Don't forget to wash behind your ears now too."

"Oh—for God's sake Anna! That's enough instructions now. We need to get going. I've got supplies to pick up and chores waiting back home," Frank barked. He quickly shook Mr. Anderson's hand and tugged at Mother's elbow. She followed but she turned and looked back at me one more time over her shoulder. She wore a blue suit with a fitted jacket and a little hat to match with white gloves. I wanted her to stay with me. I felt my lip start to quiver. She broke from Frank's grasp and ran back to me and bent down and gave me a quick hug and a kiss. She took her glove off and licked her fingers and swept my hair back and another kiss on my forehead. Then she ran back to Frank.

"But Mother," I called, "When will you come back to get me? Where will I sleep?" I began to panic and started to run after her but Mr. Anderson grabbed me and held me back.

"Now Donald, you stay here young man. We'll get you settled in. It will be alright. You'll see."

Mr. Anderson took me back into his office and asked the lady with the orange lips to have someone come to get me. Soon a guy in a white jacket came in and I was told his name was Nurse Jerry McCarron. I thought there must be some mistake because I never knew a man could be a nurse.

"Jerry will take you now, Donald. Jerry, show the boy around, please." And away we went up that beautiful stairway with the golden railing. We stopped at a door that Jerry had to unlock. He had a lot of big keys on a ring that jangled when he pulled them out of his crisp white jacket pocket. Once we entered, he stopped to lock the door again. Then a smell hit me that made my stomach wretch. I felt light headed but maybe I was just getting hungry. "No," I thought, "I'm not hungry; I feel sick and I smell urine."

Jerry (I never could bring myself to call him "nurse" McCarron) stepped out of the hallway into a side room that was full of beds lined up along both sides of the room. The beds were so close together that it would be very difficult to walk between them. Jerry was rather nice looking, I guess. He had black curly hair that was really shiny and almost dripping with hair grease. Probably that oily stuff that comes in a tube, called Brylcreem. It makes your hair shiny but I really didn't know why anyone would want to put that stuff in his hair. He was kind of bony and had a big Adams apple in his throat that moved up and down when he talked. He smelled not too bad and it was a relief to my nostrils to smell his aftershave cologne compared to that smell of urine that was burning my eyes and nose.

"This is where you'll sleep tonight and you can give me that suitcase. No one has personal items in here. The staff will keep your clothes locked up and you'll get what they give you to wear in the mornings. Your job will be to take the sheets off all these beds first thing every morning and

30

you'll help the nurses put clean sheets on after that. You may be assigned other duties to help out as well. Just do whatever anyone tells you to do and you won't get in any trouble. This is your home now and we are like your parents from now on. Oh, and you won't have a bed of your own for now. Sorry, but we're really crowded here and you'll have to learn to share. As soon as a bed is available, we'll assign one to you."

"Follow me now and I'll take you to supper." I looked at the clock in the dining hall and saw it was not quite 4 o'clock in the afternoon. I wondered why they ate supper that early at this camp. There were long tables in this large room and huge windows with small panes of glass. I wondered why the windows were so high and I was way too short to be able to see out. But, I could see the sky and some leaves dancing in the breeze of the perfect summer day outside. Gosh, I wanted to be out in that day instead of in this smelly place.

People started coming into the dining hall and they seemed to be mostly adults and they were strange. They were all sizes and shapes and some walked funny with their heads down. Nurses walked holding hands with some guiding them to the table. One man had no teeth and I wondered how in the world he was going to chew his food. I hoped he was not going to be sitting across from me. I was told to sit down beside an elderly woman.

Jerry said, "This is Mary and she will keep an eye on you so you better behave at the table."

I looked up at Mary and she smiled a toothless smile at me. Well, she did have a few teeth and her eyes twinkled at me when she smiled. Oddly, she had some hairs growing out of her chin. I'd never seen a woman with whiskers before.

31

She had gray hair tied back in a bun but there were strands of hair dangling down both sides of her face and it didn't seem to bother her at all that sometimes they got stuck in the corners of her mouth when she talked. She talked while she chewed her food and sometimes bits of kernel corn dropped out while she talked and that didn't bother her either. Mary seemed nice enough. She asked me my name.

"I'm Donald Johanson. I'm going to stay in the summer camp here."

She didn't seem to hear me or care what I said so I just tried to eat my food and be the good boy that my mother had said to be. The food was pale in colour; a piece of pale white chicken breast with mashed potatoes and kernel corn. The potatoes had lumps in them. My mother's mashed potatoes were always smooth and served hot with gravy. No gravy with these; just some insipid, colourless margarine. The margarine wouldn't melt into the potatoes because they were already cold. There was bread pudding for dessert with a bit of warm milk and cinnamon sprinkled on top. Again— it wasn't as good as Mother's pudding, but not bad. I had to remember that this was camp life now.

After supper people seemed to move to different places. There was a large room that they called the "Day Room" and you could sit in there if you wanted. There were big leather chairs that you could sit in to read. There were magazines and some books with nice coloured pictures of birds of the prairies that I liked. There were tables with some board games and cards where some people played cribbage and smoked. There were spittoons on the floor and some cigarette butts as well.

One man caught my eye because he had red hair like my sister, Ethel. He was a large man with the biggest hands I'd ever seen. He wore a beanie hat that had a lot of badges pinned onto it. I wanted to touch that hat and look at all the badges he had but I didn't think I'd better be so bold. I heard someone call to him from across the room.

"Hey Big Red! Where were you today?" a man wearing pajamas and slippers asked. I wondered why he was already wearing pajamas and I also wondered when I was going to see the boys my age in this camp.

"I had work to do downtown at the Legion," answered Big Red. "I can't sit around here all day because I have a job at the Legion you know."

So, I wondered was this man's name really "Big Red"? Who names their child a name like that?

No, I thought, *that has to be a nickname like Cev or Queenie for my sister Clara.* All of a sudden thinking about Clara made me think of Ethel and Doris and my lip started to quiver and my eyes welled up with pools of hot tears again and I tried to find a place to get away from all these people around me. I ran into the hallway and tried to see my way to that room that I was told to sleep in but my eyes were blurry with tears. I rubbed my knuckles into my eyes to wipe the tears away when a nurse came toward me.

"What's wrong little fellow?" she asked as she gently put her hand on my shoulder and knelt down in front of me.

"I want to go home!" I shouted. "I don't like it here at camp." I started coughing and choking and she pulled me to her and patted me on the back.

"There, there now. Don't cry. Is this your first day? I haven't seen you before. You must be new. What's your name, dear?"

"D-on-ald," I stammered as I snorted snot and tears onto her sweater.

"OK, Donald, let's go see if we can find you a glass of juice and maybe a piece of apple before bed. That might be nice or maybe we'll get you a cookie. Would you like that?"

"I have my own cookies. My Mother made me some peanut butter cookies but Jerry took my suitcase away." The thought of my mother's homemade peanut butter cookies started me bawling all over again and I was now shaking like a leaf.

"Oh my—peanut butter cookies from your mother, eh? Well, that is very special and you are a lucky boy because I have the key to the cupboard where your suitcase is stashed and we are going to go get you one of those cookies right now. What do you say to that?"

Nurse Edna Beattie took me by my sweaty hand and led me to my cupboard. As promised, she let me help myself to a cookie and then she winked at me and put the suitcase back.

"This will be our secret and you will get a cookie whenever I can get one for you."

Nurse Beattie (I learned that no one called anyone on staff by their first name—last names only) was younger than Jerry I figured. But, she must be a little older than my sisters. She could be around Ethel's age which would be 19. She had blonde hair and smooth, milky white skin with soft pink cheeks. Her lips were rather thin but not severe by any means.

She wore no lipstick and I liked that. She just seemed scrubbed and simple, like my mother. She was like an angel sent to me that first day. I hoped I could be near her again. She let me eat my cookie and she got me a glass of milk. She said that juice is not as good with a peanut butter cookie as a glass of milk. I had to agree.

She took me to the bathroom after my snack and helped me out of my clothes and put me into a warm bath. She washed my hair and I took the facecloth from her hands and washed my own face and made sure to scrub behind my ears to try to do what would please my mother. I will never forget this warm bath and the kindness of Nurse Beattie that night because I came to find out later that no one gets a bath whenever they like. Baths were generally taken only once a week and the tubs were not used for bathing. Instead, there were large shower stalls used for bathing—"gang showers" is what they were called. No privacy there. Several people would shower beside one another. There was no privacy. The tubs were metal and there were big blankets of brown canvas covers that snapped to fit these tubs. I would find out later what that was all about.

I was to the point of thinking that I was ready for bed but I wondered who I was going to share the bed with. Maybe I would finally meet a boy my age to share my bed. Nurse Beattie got me into my pajamas and I felt clean. I loved the smell of my mother's Ivory detergent and the smell of fresh air on my clean pajamas. Mother had hung them with her laundry on her clothesline out by her garden. I started to feel those tears wanting to come again but I was determined not to let Nurse Beattie see me crying again after all she had gone through to help me.

"Alright little man, let's get you tucked into bed. You'll be up at six o'clock tomorrow morning so you'd better get to sleep." With that she turned and whisked away into the night. I wondered as I was drifting off to sleep why they needed nurses at a camp for boys. I had a lot to learn about camp I guessed. Indeed.

Chapter 5

"What's happening?" I woke to my own voice crying. It was pitch black. Why am I face-down trying to breathe? Someone was on top of me squashing the air out of my lungs! I tried to move and push him off but I couldn't move. He was too heavy. What was happening? Mother! Mother! . . . .pain, ripping pain, burning pain. I'm face down, crying but more than crying, I was trying to scream and I made guttural sounds like an animal. I turned my head to the side to gulp in some air and a big, hot, smelly hand clamped down over my mouth.

He hissed in my ear, "Shut up you little shit or I'll smother you to death. You make one more sound and I'll punch your lights out." Then, he heaved and humped his body into mine. I felt the burning pain and then he slumped and let out a big sigh and I could smell his onion breath. He took his hand away and rolled over. I was too frightened to move. I lay frozen long into the night before I finally drifted off again. I didn't look at him. I didn't want to.

"Good morning gentlemen—wake up!" I opened my eyes and saw the male attendant actually walking on top of the beds from one bed to the next waking men up as he went. The beds were so close together that I guess it was the only way to do it quickly. I tried to sit up but was quickly reminded of the episode during the night by the pain in my behind. I felt so sore like the time I fell on my bike and smacked my bum and private parts on the bike bar—same kind of pain. I felt immediate shame and embarrassment because my pajama bottoms were missing. I felt around under the sheets to the bottom of the bed and quickly retrieved them and jumped into them. I hoped no one had noticed my little white ass. I turned around and saw this fat man that had been my bed partner last night. He let a big fart rip and stood up scratching his hairy belly. I looked away from his droopy eyes and hoped he would leave me alone.

"What's your name?" he asked with a bit of a lisp. I just looked at him and looked away again. "Hey! Look at me boy. I'm talk'n to ya. Cat got your tongue kid?"

I looked back at his fat, unshaven, stubble-haired face and stuck my chin out to stand up to him as best as I could muster.

"My name is Donald Johanson and my Dad can box and he taught me to box and you'd better leave me alone because I can punch your face in!" Of course this was a lie. My father wasn't a boxer although he did tell me he'd teach me some boxing tips one day—we just hadn't quite had that chance before he was killed by the bull. But I didn't want this fat pig to know that I didn't have some protector that would beat him up if he touched me again.

Some of the men nearby started to laugh and then the male attendant came up to me.

"You came in yesterday, I see from the charts. Name is Donald? That right?"

"Yes" I answered as I looked down at my bare feet and wondered where my shoes were.

"Well, Donald—you can start stripping sheets off these beds and put them in this laundry bin over here. Hurry up so you can get ready for breakfast. You'll be great at this because you're almost skinny enough to fit between the beds. You can help the nurses to put the clean sheets on. See that bucket over there? You can wash the mattresses off with that soapy water. There are some rubber gloves there too. Better get at it!" and he turned and started helping some of the men get dressed. I couldn't believe that grown men didn't seem to know how to put their clothes on. I quickly pulled on my jeans and tee-shirt from last night that I'd folded and placed on the floor under my bed.

I started with the sheets from my bed and noticed there was blood on my side. I grabbed them up quickly and rolled the blood up inside out of sight. Again, I was embarrassed and didn't want anyone to see my shame.

There was that smell again! Piss! God—so many of the beds were soiled and I could see now why the guy told me I'd have to wash the mattresses down. They all had rubber sheets on them so they wiped up easily enough. Thank god for the rubber gloves even though they were way too big for my hands.

꿍ꞇꙅ

Breakfast was noisy as people filed into the dining hall, chatting, coughing and scraping chairs over the floor to get seated. I saw a couple of kids this time and hoped I could get to talk to them. They must be in the same camp as me. But one was a girl. Mother had only said there would be boys to play with at this camp.

All of a sudden someone screamed and most people didn't seem to stop eating or take much notice but I jumped out of my chair and could see that a woman had fallen to the floor and she was vibrating and started foaming from her mouth. A nurse came running and grabbed a towel from the table and shoved it into the woman's mouth. She held her head so she wouldn't keep banging it on the floor. Someone else in the room laughed like they had just heard a great joke. Soon, the male attendant came along and carried the young woman away.

"What the heck happened to that lady?" I asked into the air to anyone who cared to answer.

"She's got epilepsy. She takes fits." The woman across the table who spoke without lifting her head up and looking at me. Her hair was brushed and hung prettily around her oval face in soft curls. She had bobby pins holding a lock of hair on one side which seemed very stylish. Her fingernails were painted with red nail varnish like my sister's. She wore a red dress that matched her nails and a pair of black pumps. She even had stockings on with the seam up the back.

"Happens fairly often—but she'll be alright in no time. What's your name?"

I wondered if she worked here or if she was a visitor but she was eating at the same table as me so I figured she must live here like me.

"Don Johanson," I answered as I pushed my spoon aimlessly around my bowl of cream of wheat. "What's your name?" I tried to sound polite.

"Miriam." She dropped her eyes to her food again. "I'm here because my mother thinks I'm too boy crazy. I had a boyfriend and wanted to run away with him to get hitched but my mother put me in here to break us up." She pushed her chair back from the table and lit up a cigarette. She closed her eyes and put her head back as she blew out a stream of smoke. She sat with her legs crossed and kicked her foot up and down just enough to make her beautiful legs more noticeable. There was something very graceful about a woman's leg with a black patent, high-heeled shoe bobbing up and down. I'd never noticed a woman like this before.

Somehow, I was able to eat some cold toast with strawberry jam but I couldn't stand to eat the pale colourless cream of wheat. I hated cream of wheat. I would much prefer porridge with brown sugar and cinnamon like Mother gave me at home. I drank my orange juice and then wondered what was next. I also wondered about Miriam and why her mother would want to make her come to this camp.

I was beginning to realize that it was something more than just a boys' camp. There was a whole lot more going on and a lot more people here than what I would imagine would be at a boys' camp. But, I had never been anywhere away from home and what did I know about such things?

Chapter 6

It was September now and I had pretty much learned the daily routine of this "camp". The days were long and boring because I didn't get to play outside much. I did really like it when I was allowed to go out to the barn though. If there was a job to do out there that they thought a kid could handle, they sometimes took me along. That was where I saw Big Red again. He could throw bales of hay up way over his head and make it look like he was tossing a feather into the air. His big hands were rough and calloused. His skin was tanned from working outside so much. But his face was more pink and freckled than tanned like his arms. He seemed to know everyone and everyone knew him. If I didn't know better, I would have thought he owned the barn and all the animals in it! It was a dairy farm with cows that gave milk and all the dairy products like milk, cream, butter and cheese were made right on site in the big brick building.

Big Red, or Red as many called him for short, had a very large wooden wagon that he pulled behind him when he walked to town to go to work for the Legion. He picked up empty beer and pop bottles from the roadside as he walked to and from the big brick building. He was proud of his job even though he didn't really work every day; just mostly one or two days a week. But, he got paid for what he did and he made money off the bottles he collected so he had money and could buy candy and comics or a new badge for his beanie whenever he wanted.

One day not long after I had been brought to this camp, I overheard Jerry McCarron talking to another one of the male attendants. They were talking about Big Red and the male attendant asked Jerry if it was true that Big Red was born in the hospital.

"Nah," answered Jerry, "That's a tale that got started but the real story is that he didn't move here until he was two years old. His mother had a break down and had to be brought in and there was no one around to look after Red. The father took off with another woman and left the mother and she couldn't cope. Couldn't look after herself let alone look after a toddler. Neighbours complained and the church stepped up to get some help. The mother committed suicide after she was here for a short time. She hung herself in the bowling alley in the basement of the building.

So, Red has lived here all his life. I don't think he's really as simple minded as everyone thinks. No one ever bothered to spend any time with him to bring him up normal and teach him any social graces. He's had no schooling either so he sounds simple just because he never learned proper English. Anything he knows is just what he picked up living here spending time around the farm. He has the strength of an ox and sometimes people take advantage of him."

"Well," said the other male attendant, "He seems to have a lot of freedom to come and go as he pleases."

"He's got a home here and he doesn't know anything else. He has nothing to run away from and he is harmless to society. He likes people and people in the community like him. He helps set up tables at the Legion for banquettes, weddings, dances and such. They give him a little money so he's happy. Sometimes I think he's the lucky one because he doesn't know anything else and has never had any worries in life. No one dares to pick on the guy because he could eat you for breakfast if he'd a mind to." They laughed in agreement over that statement.

I wondered if anyone picked on Big Red at bedtime. I wished at that moment that I was his size so I could beat the crap out of the guys that were rubbing their hands all over me in bed at night. I'd been there for months by then and three or four nights a week, someone would try to touch me where they had no business touching me. I had never been in a situation like this before but now it was a common occurrence it seemed. Even though I had managed to get a bed to myself (someone either died or was able to leave one way or another—lucky them!), there was always someone wanting to come to bother me in the dark.

I didn't know what oral sex was and I didn't know anything about sex or what a pedophile was but I knew what they were doing to me was wrong and I knew I couldn't talk about it. I wanted to write a letter to Mother but I found out that mail was intercepted and read and I couldn't let anyone know my shame. You weren't allowed to use the phone and that wasn't much help anyway as Mother didn't have a phone.

I decided to keep busy as much as I could because that helped me to forget the other stuff.

I was sweeping the floors in the dining room one morning when a nurse approached me. She was young and I thought she was very pretty.

"Donald? Or do you like Don or Donnie better?"

"Uh, I like Don and Donnie is OK too. Usually my mother calls me Donnie and if I'm in trouble or she is mad for some reason, then she calls me Donald."

"OK, then Donnie—my name is Nurse Berk. Actually, I'm still in training so you can just call me Susan if you like. Seems less formal don't you think? Anyway, I'm here to take you to school this morning. Follow me, please."

School? I wondered. *What the heck was going on here? I thought if summer was over and school was starting then my mother should be taking me back home by now.*

"What do you mean? My mother should be getting me soon to start school back home."

"Well, this will keep you up with things and help you out until she does come for you."

School was not in a separate building like I expected. It was just a room in the big brick building. Susan led me into a room that was similar to my dormitory where my bed was but this room had tables and chairs instead of the usual desks like in my old school. There was a chalk board along the wall at one side of the room. There was a map of Canada on the other wall across the room and there was the Union Jack flag beside it. There was a picture of Queen Victoria and another big photo of King George beside the flag. So, it looked like a classroom. There were book shelves and a desk at the wall in front of the windows where the teacher would sit.

And there sat the teacher, Mrs. Barkley . . . red frizzy hair, round glasses that were thick and made her eyes seem even bigger than they were. She reminded me of a frog with those big eyes. She had a skinny narrow nose with a bump in the middle of it and a mole on the one cheek beside the corner of her mouth. She wore a gray suit with a white silk blouse and a cameo broach at her neck. Her legs were rather thick compared to her fine facial features and she wore ugly thick-soled oxfords.

Susan spoke to the teacher and then left me with a pat on the shoulder.

"Welcome Donald. You can have a seat at the table over here beside Martha and Joe. Martha, will you please get a scribbler from the shelf and a pencil and eraser for Donald. Oh, and bring a reader over as well."

I felt my cheeks turning red as I felt the eyes of all the other students on me. I squeezed into my place between Martha and Joe. I was glad there was one boy beside me instead of being between two girls. Martha brought me the books and gave me a smile as she put them in front of me. Joe looked at me and smiled too. I felt a little better already.

There were about a dozen kids in that class and I wondered why I was only seeing them now. Class was fine that day and I actually found myself very interested and happy to be using my mind again, especially on math. I loved math and I liked looking at the map of Canada and the globe of the world with all the countries and all the oceans. English grammar was not too interesting, but just the same, it felt rather good to be in a classroom again and with some kids.

In the afternoon for recess, I had chance to play and run around and smell the crisp fall air. We kicked a ball around and that was great fun. I think I was pretty good at that and the other boys seemed to accept me, I hoped.

Before we went back to class, Joe came to me and tapped me on the shoulder.

"Hey Donnie, I think I saw you in the dining hall one day but you were across the room from me." He asked me why I was there and I told him I was dropped off to stay in camp on the farm but I was waiting for my mother to come soon to pick me up because I had a school back home. I told him I lived on a farm and went to a country school.

"What are you talking about Donnie?" he asked as he screwed up his face and his freckles bounced across his wrinkled-up nose. His sandy coloured hair was curly and looked like he hadn't combed it that morning and his ears seemed to stick out from his head. He was shorter than me but had a good sturdy looking body. I sized him up as a tough guy that I wouldn't want to scrap with.

"You aren't in a camp! You are in a mental hospital. This is the insane asylum for loonies. You ain't goin home no time soon likely. People come here and they stay here!"

"You liar!" I spat back at him. "That can't be true." I felt myself break into an immediate sweat and the back of my shirt felt damp from running around. Beads of sweat began to trickle down my back. I was about to grab him by the collar and shake him.

"Yes it is true" interrupted Martha who had just come up to stand beside us. "I'm sorry Donnie, but us kids are stuck here for whatever reason and we gotta make the best of it. There are some nice things though and you'll see it will be OK. We have picnics and get gifts at Christmas. Christmas is really a nice time with music and dances in the auditorium. We will be your friends and we can have fun together. Don't worry."

I knew in my heart that what they were saying was probably the truth. It was all making sense to me now and I hated to admit it but I had to. It was time to realize that Mother was not coming—at least not any time soon. Maybe I had a different reason than the others for being there and maybe my time wouldn't be as long as they were saying. I didn't want to believe I was never going home. But, I decided not to pick a fight over it with the only kids I'd finally met and maybe had a chance at making them my friends.

When class finished that afternoon, I walked with Martha. She had silky soft long blonde hair like spun gold. She had blue eyes with long eyelashes and dimples in her cheeks when she smiled. "Where do you live here and where do Joe and the other kids all live? How come I haven't seen you at meal time or anywhere?

"I'm in 3C and Joe is in 4C. They've got kids spread all out and the girls are mixed in with the women's units and you boys are in the men's units. I've had chicken pox and so I was under quarantine for a while but I'll be able to eat in the dining hall again now. And at least we get together in school," she smiled. "But you and Joe are on the same floor, just around the corner from one another so you might manage to bump into one another sometimes. I think there are other boys you will see too, maybe."

"Are all the kids kind of crazy here? 'Cause I'm not, you're not and Joe doesn't seem to be."

"No, most of us are like you. We have a couple of [1] mongoloids that you might have noticed. One is that Chinese girl, her name is Lily but she can't say Lily. She calls herself, Lulu. I quite like her even though she's different. She's very sweet and always happy, it seems."

"Royden is kind of different too. He will remember any date you ever tell him. If you tell him your birthday, he will always remember and tell you every time he sees you that you were born on such and such a date. He knows what the weather was like the day you were born too. Mrs. Barkley called him an [2] idiot savant—whatever that means. Then, we have another boy in a wheelchair that was born with spina bifida and he's pretty nice but his parents can't look after him. There are one or two kids that are, what they call, "emotionally disturbed" and they get out of control sometimes and that gets them into a lot of trouble."

"How did you come to be here, Martha?"

She stopped short and looked down at the floor.

"It's kind of a long story but my mummy died when I was four and my daddy drank a lot. He left me alone one time and I wandered out into the yard and a neighbour found me. She called the police and they brought me here. I've been here ever since and my daddy has never come to get me. I guess he must still be drinking too much and that is where all his money and energy goes. But I like to believe he will stop the drink one day and come for me."

---

[1] Although considered dated now, it was the appropriate word to describe someone with Down Syndrome in the time depicted.

[2] Someone who has a mental disability but who is very good at doing a particular thing.

"Sounds like your story is a bit worse than mine. I had a great father and I love my mother too but Father died and Mother is going to marry the hired hand. His name is Frank and he doesn't like kids so I have to live here. But, I don't think I'll be here forever. Do you?"

She smiled and lifted her head again.

"I have to go this way now. I'll see you tomorrow, Donnie!" and she turned and hurried off. I thought that it was nice to actually talk to someone my own age for a change. I felt like I now had a friend, even if she was only a girl. I hoped I'd get to pal with Joe too if he wanted me for a friend. Maybe I shouldn't have called him a liar. I hoped he'd forgive me.

Chapter 7

Seasons came and went. School was the best thing in my life for the next couple of years. I was 12 now and hadn't had a birthday party since I left home. Nurse Beattie had kept our secret and had doled out my peanut butter cookies until the last crumb was gone. That seemed like a long time ago now but she kept the secret going and brought me cookies at night from the kitchen before bed whenever she could. Sometimes she had a comic book for me or a bit of candy. There was a canteen where you could buy things like that but I didn't have any money like Big Red.

It was supper time and Nurse Beattie came and stood beside me before dessert was being dished up.

"So, a little birdie told me that it is your birthday today, Donnie." She winked and brought out a little cupcake with chocolate icing and a candle on top from behind her back.

"Surprise!" She placed it on the table in front of me and pulled out a lighter and lit the candle. She started singing

"Happy Birthday to you" and other people at the table joined in.

"Now make a wish Donnie and blow out the candle." I closed my eyes and silently wished that God would take me from this place before my next birthday.

Nurse Beattie had a small package in her pocket that she handed me. It was tied up in a pretty blue ribbon and attached was a tiny Canadian Red Ensign flag.

"I thought you'd like the little flag because your birthday is on Dominion Day so that makes it extra special. You and the country share the same birthday—except, of course, you are much younger!" she giggled.

I didn't know what to say but I opened the gift and to my delight there was a rabbit foot on a little chain.

"You can attach this to your belt loop or through one of your button holes on your shirt and it is supposed to bring you good luck."

I couldn't speak so I just reached out and gave her a hug around her waist. Someone cared about me. It lifted my spirits and I thanked her and then quickly left the dining hall before I might start to cry. I was 12 now and I was not about to let anyone see me cry. My father's words still meant a lot to me and I knew I had to "buck up" as he would say.

I had long outgrown my denim jeans that I had when I first arrived so I had to wear the clothing that they provided. My pajamas with that lovely fresh smell of Mother's laundry soap were long gone. They went to the laundry one day and I never saw them again. Much to my disappointment, I was given a night shirt to sleep in like all the other guys on my ward. I hated those things because they left me all the more vulnerable for others to grab at my private parts. Also, the night shirts got all twisted in the middle of the night and ended up around my belly.

I did have a belt and belt loops so I fastened my rabbit foot and let it hide under my shirt in case anyone else decided they wanted it. The belt I wore was one I made myself in the activity room. This was part of "Activity Treatment" as they called it. I got to learn how to do leather tooling and the belt was my first accomplishment. Some of the people made wallets and handbags and did beautiful designs on the leather.

ೞೞ

One afternoon in August, Mrs. Barkley decided to take us out for a picnic on the lawn. We had peanut butter and banana sandwiches made up by the kitchen staff and there were apples as well. We were all having a wonderful time. The girls were sitting making bracelets with long coloured strings of wool and beads and the boys were running around kicking the soccer ball after lunch. Mrs. Barkley had told us many times not to go beyond the ball diamond. I was extremely curious to see what lay beyond that ball diamond. I wondered a short distance from the other kids and I climbed a tree. I thought I might see farther if I got up high enough.

"Donald! Get down out of that tree this instant!" Mrs. Barkley was stomping toward me and her fists were clenched and she seemed to have steam coming out of her ears. I felt like a raging bull was coming for me.

"You are going inside right this minute. This is the thanks you give me for letting you have a picnic!"

"I'm sorry," I stammered as I almost tumbled to the ground. "I didn't mean to do anything wrong. What did I do?" I whimpered, as she grabbed me by my ear and then slapped the back of my head. I didn't know why she was being so mean. I thought nothing of climbing a tree. I did that all the time on the farm and no one ever cared about it.

"I'm going to write up a report on this and you will learn your lesson." She did write a report and I received a serious punishment. If I thought life was difficult to this point, I had a great shock in front of me yet. I was going to need my rabbit foot!

૎ૐ

Once breakfast was over and my bed-stripping duties were completed, a male attendant came for me.

"Come on kid, follow me." He looked almost sad as he led me down to the basement. I'd never been down there before. We came to a locked door and as soon as he opened that door, my eyes saw things that I'll never forget.

"Welcome to the Snake Pit, kid."

He opened the door and pushed me forward. There was a naked man; in fact, there were a lot of naked men. Some sat or lay on the floor. One fellow was naked and harnessed into a large walker, similar to a baby walker. He leapt toward me in this contraption and screamed at me like a banshee. I grabbed onto the attendant and hung on for dear life.

There was another man lying on the floor and his head was huge like a beach ball. He had no hair and there was a little crack on the side of his head where blood trickled from. A nurse was kneeling down putting a diaper on him.

"What's wrong with that guy's head?" I whispered to the attendant

"He's a hydrocephalic—water on the brain. He was born with it and you can't do anything about it," he answered as if he were talking about changing a tire or some other mundane thing. "This is 2A where we keep the [3]Defectives or the 'Little Boys' as we like to call them. Once you get to know them, you get kind of attached to them like you would a puppy dog, I guess. They are brought here in most cases straight from birth. They've never seen the light of day other than in this room and the bit of space between it and the place they came from. We do try to put clothes on them but they live in soft pajamas with only elastic waistbands. No belts, buttons, strings or anything they can put in their mouths that might choke them."

There was urine and feces on the floor and it stank like a barn. It gagged me and I could see why they called it the snake pit. Grown men slithered around on the floor because they never learned how to walk. It was the longest walk I had ever endured as we walked slowly to the other end of the ward, skirting around crawling, slithering bodies. Many of the "little boys" came up to us and touched us. One wanted to touch my hair and I pulled away.

One man had a huge growth on the side of his cheek and it was almost as big as his head. It had the look of boils on it and the attendant told me it was a cancerous growth of some sort and they would squeeze puss out of it and it stank the whole ward up. I didn't think it could smell any worse than it did that day. The poor man, I thought and I wondered if he was in a lot of pain. I asked, "Is he in pain? It looks like it must be really awfully sore."

---

[3]Term used correctly in time depicted to describe someone with low mental abilities.

"Ah, who knows? No sense, no feeling I figure."

I was beginning to feel very dizzy and then everything went black. I had fainted and hit the floor. I didn't feel anything. It was just blackness that came after being dizzy and feeling sick to my stomach. When I woke up, I was laying on a bed with an ice pack on my forehead. I had a large goose egg swelling there. I was in another dormitory but it didn't have as many beds in it as the one I had been sleeping in. A nurse came in and asked me how I felt. She told me to sit up and have a sip of water. Her name was Nurse Brown.

"You fainted. It happens down here sometimes. You'll get used to it because you are going to be put to work down here. You're safe in this part because the Defectives are in their own ward and you came through it and now you are on the other side of that ward. You must have done something pretty bad. This is where they send patients who act up sometimes."

"How long will I have to be down here?" I sat up rubbing my head.

"You'll be with us in the Refractory Ward for likely about three weeks" she answered with no sign of feeling the least bit sorry for me. She was all matter of fact and all business like in her manner. But, maybe if I worked down in this snake pit like she and others did, maybe I'd have no feelings or compassion left to spare either.

So for the next three weeks, it was one of my duties to put on a pair of rubber boots that came up to my knees and were way too large for me but that was all I was given to wear. I had to take a hose and spray the cement floors down in 2A Snake Pit. There were drains in the floor that I directed all the mess toward and down it went. I actually got so I kind of enjoyed it. Strangely, I felt like I was doing something good for those poor defectives—the "Little Boys". They couldn't help themselves and so it was up to others to clean their space for them. I also did it for my own good to get rid of the stench that made me feel sick.

I wasn't allowed to feed the little boys but I was told to clean up the dirty trays and take them away to be washed. I brought in cleaning towels and stacks of laundered pajama clothing and took the dirty soiled things away. I had to get an attendant to unlock the doors on both sides. Sometimes they were too busy so I had to wait.

I had sights and odours burned into my nostrils and my brain. I wondered if I was in hell. I decided that it must not be the real hell because I'd heard that there were flames in hell and so far I hadn't seen any evidence of that. But, whatever this place was, it sure was not anywhere I had ever imagined I'd be one day.

Where was God? Why did He allow this? What could His plan be for these little boys? What was His plan for me?

I thought that darn rabbit foot was not helping me much!

Chapter 8

There were stretches in time when I had chance to explore. I wandered down the hall from my dormitory and found a room with a sign on the door that said, Research Lab. I looked both ways and tried the door and oddly, it opened. I'd never seen such a room as this before. There were high desks with stools around them. There were test tubes everywhere and beaker jars, rubber tubes and bottles full of all sorts of chemicals. There were shelves with big black binders full of typewritten and hand-written notes. I wanted to snoop around more but I figured someone would catch me. I'd love to see an experiment in progress. Maybe I'd get chance to pop in again later. I wondered what sort of experiments they would be doing in a mental hospital.

The Snake Pit had something rather astonishing. There were several murals painted by one of the male patients in the basement. I was in awe of the colours and the crowd scenes of people protesting and waving banners printed with: We Want a Vote. I was told by Nurse Brown that the artist was obsessed with painting and painted so much he exhausted himself and his family had him placed in the asylum. He remained there until he died. *Gosh*, I thought to myself, *I'd better remember never to show too much interest in pursuing art like that if I ever want to get out of this place.*

As I walked down the hallway, I noticed doors with little rectangular window slots in them. I stopped at one door and stretched up onto my tiptoes and my nose and eyes just barely reached the window. I looked in and there was a guy sitting in the corner on the floor. The walls of the room were padded and there was only a mattress on the floor. He rocked back and forth hitting his head on the padded walls. He was wearing a jacket that kept his arms crossed over his stomach and the arms seemed to be belted so he couldn't use his hands. Every now and then he threw his head back and howled like a wolf howling at the moon followed by a shrill scream that pierced my eardrums.

Across the hallway, I peeked into another room and there was a woman just standing looking up at the window which she was way too short to be able to see out. She wore a pale blue denim sack dress and was barefoot. Her hair was long and matted. She twisted a strand of hair around her finger and then as if she sensed I was watching her, she suddenly turned and she caught sight of me. She ran to the door and threw herself at the window and banged her fists on the door. She clenched her teeth and growled at me and her eyes looked like a crazed animal.

I fell back onto the floor and got up just in time as a nurse was coming down the hall with trays of food. It was Nurse Susan Berk, the nurse in training. She looked nervous. I stepped aside as she rolled the food trolley close to the door where the woman had now gone quiet. When Susan opened the door, the woman jumped onto Susan's back and started pulling her around the room by her hair. Susan screamed and I yelled, "Help—somebody help!"

All of a sudden Jerry came flying down the hall and bolted into the room to save Susan. He got behind the crazy woman and pulled her off Nurse Susan. The woman screamed and kicked but Jerry managed to toss her aside and help Nurse Susan to her feet. Jerry backed out of the cell room away from the woman and Nurse Susan scurried out into the hallway. She was shaken but gathered herself as she adjusted her white apron and tried to tidy her hair back up into a bun. Jerry locked the door quickly and the woman came to the window and cried, "I'm sorry! I thought you were that other nurse—Bitch Brown. I didn't mean to hurt you!" As she broke down crying, I couldn't help but feel sorry for her.

"Are you OK nurse?"

"Yes, thank you. I'm fine."

"I'll be back in a minute." He skipped off down the hallway and then came back in an instant carrying a broom.

"Come over here and I'll show you how we do this down here." Then, he took a plate of food from the trolley. The plates were metal pie plates down here rather than the usual china ones like we had upstairs in our dining hall. Jerry set one plate of food on the floor outside the crazy woman's door and then used the broom to push the plate under the doorway. The doors were just high enough off the floor that you could get the plates to slide under. They were made that way so you could hose the floors to clean them. I ran and got another broom and came back to help Nurse Susan finish the job. Things went smoothly from that point and she was happy to have me there to assist her.

"You know," she spoke openly to me, "the head nurse sent me down here and told me if I could stand to work on this ward, I could work anywhere after this without any problem. I hope I can get through this and prove to her and all the others that I can do it."

"Yeah, I got sent down here too and it's really scary but after a while I guess you can get used to anything if you have to. I think you will be a very good nurse and you will prove you can do anything they give you to do. Hey, why does that man have on a funny jacket and why does that lady have on a funny sack dress?"

"Oh, the man is wearing what they call a straight jacket. It looks terrible but it's for his own protection. He may hurt himself and he will need that restraining device for a while. But don't worry, they'll take it off later. And the sack dress is simple clothing that is made here in the hospital. It is made from heavy denim which is very durable. It has to be a strong fabric to stand up to frequent washings. There can't be buttons or ties or belts because these things may just get pulled off or the patients might even use a belt or tie to harm themselves. People have been known to hang themselves with such things. People who are in constant distress or who are sometimes violent will often tear at their clothing or even their own hair and flesh. A pretty cotton dress would get torn to shreds by the likes of that woman in there!" Nurse Susan chuckled.

I was relieved to see she had calmed herself now to the point that she could smile and have a little laugh. I was glad that Jerry had come to the rescue.

Chapter 9

Another day when I had some time to explore, I found a large side room that had a boxing ring in it. There was a punching bag and boxing gloves on a shelf all lined up neatly. There was a sign on the wall that read: Hank's Boxing Class – Saturdays 9:00 – 12:00 noon and 1:00 – 4:00 pm. Oh, my heart started to pound in my chest and my palms got sweaty with nervous excitement. I had nothing to do on Saturdays so I was going to make sure to check this out. I did get to check it out but, of course, I had no money to sign up for a class. But, the coach, Hank, was really nice and he let me sit and watch the guys working out and boxing the punching bags and then sparring in the ring. They wore head protectors and had shiny satin shorts and special leather shoes. They looked swell to me. They were all muscled up. I wanted to look like them when I grew up.

One day I stopped by while Hank was having his lunch between classes.

"Hey sport!" he called to me as he munched on his sandwich. "What's up with you? You must be helping out down here eh?"

"Yup, that's right. Got myself into trouble for climbing a tree and now I'm here. I want to learn to box one day. My father said he'd teach me to box but then he died before we could do it," I told him.

"Shucks, kid, that's too bad. Listen, I have a few minutes now. Do you want a few tips?" He stood up and walked over to grab some boxing gloves. "Here, put these on."

"Wow—you mean it?" I grabbed the gloves and put them on and he laced them up for me. Then he showed me how to keep one hand up to protect my face and keep the other one lower ready to punch. He showed me how to bounce around from side to side to get a spring-like movement in my step. Probably the best thing he taught me was how to duck quickly to miss an opponent's jabs. He gave me a few basics and then said he'd better get ready for his next class and I had to get back to my duties. I was thrilled because, I thought, someday I might have a better chance to defend myself against those creeps that wanted to have their way with me in bed.

Finally the three weeks came to an end and I was led back upstairs to my ward. The one thing that I had taken great comfort in, about being in the basement, was that no one down there had tried to put their hands on me in the middle of the night. I had slept alone and in peace . . . but I was back now. Nothing changed. It was more of the same groping and touching and forcing me to perform oral sex week in and week out.

It wasn't just mentally ill male patients who took advantage of me. There were a couple of male attendants who were pedophiles as well. I was pretty sure that the one guy was drinking on the job as I could smell whiskey on his breath. My only hope was to grow up and get strong enough to defend myself and now with some tips from Hank, I felt one day I might turn the tables. I wasn't quite there yet at the age of 12.

ഇര

The bedtime call would come like an order from an army sergeant. A male staff attendant would shout, "Bedtime gentlemen" and there would be two nurses at each end of the ward. Clothing came off and bed shirts would be put on. Fights and hair pulling often ensued as some patients were like zombies and would sit or stand by their bed. They didn't know enough to follow orders to get undressed. Others wanted nothing to do with being undressed and they would fight anyone who came near them to help them undress. I didn't mind seeing them smack one another or sucker punch someone out. Most of them had done something to me at one time or another so I was fine with them hurting one another.

Now that I had completed grade six, my days were very long. I missed being in school. The cut off was grade six. There was no further formal education beyond that point. We children always hated weekends and holidays because that meant no school and less contact with one another. School had offered the only social and interactive part of our day for us kids that we could really enjoy. Some of us truly would have loved to have more education but that was all we were going to get. I guess we were lucky that much was offered to us. Big Red never got that chance because it wasn't offered when he was growing up.

Religion was something that was also offered due to the different ministers from Weyburn volunteering to give a service in the auditorium. There was a woman who played the organ. She was a patient and she seemed perfectly normal. She was British and still had a lovely soft English accent when she spoke. Her name was Catherine and she wore her soft gray hair wound into a sculptural shaped bun that had an interesting twist to it. I assumed she did her own hair into that shape and I thought she likely had been doing it since she was a young woman. Catherine's only problem seemed that she had a problem with her memory. She thought she was actually working for the church. She probably did work for a church at one time. The thing that was puzzling for me was how she could play that organ and the piano, often with no music and yet, she didn't remember anything else for two minutes.

Hymn books were handed out at the door as you came into the room. I went in sometimes just because it was something to do. I didn't feel that there was much in the sermons that helped me or fit into my life as I was living it. I actually felt doubly abandoned, not only by my mother but also by God. I didn't blame my mother as much as I blamed God. I felt that Mother would never have left me here if it hadn't been for Frank's influence. But when it came to God—well, I figured the rabbit foot I got from Nurse Beattie was probably doing as much good as God was lately.

But, I did go to listen to the music because some of the hymns were quite joyful and sometimes people would clap and sway to the music. I looked upon it as another source of entertainment, if nothing else. There wasn't much else to do on weekends. No school, no crafts or activities.

There was one man who always dressed in a scout's uniform and his name was Benson. I don't know if that was his last name or his first name but that was all I ever heard anyone call him. He never missed church or any event where the Lord's prayer or national anthem would be sung. He was the most patriotic man I had ever come to know. I think it was due to the war going on and he wanted to show his alliance with his country.

One day, during a church service, he stood at the entrance to the hall in his scout uniform. He had a brown paper bag over his head and he stood at attention for the longest time. I don't know quite what he was thinking about using the paper bag unless he thought if he couldn't see anyone, then they couldn't see him. He was keeping his identity a secret, he figured.

After the minister had finished his sermon, Benson took off the paper bag with a flourish and flung it into the air and marched to the front of the hall and saluted the minister and then turned about face and marched back out!

The minister smiled and said, "Thank you Benson for your patriotism."

ॐ

Another opportunity that I was pleased about was to learn the game of chess. There was a brilliant man, named Jock, who taught me to play. The only problem with this was that

Jock was a catatonic patient. There would be weeks and months go by and Jock would be immobile in an almost statue position. The nurses would move his arms and legs into positions for him when sitting or laying down. They tried to move his limbs often during the day to help him with his circulation. He would stay in the position they placed him in for hours and, in fact, if they didn't move him, he'd most likely stay in that position for days and weeks. But every so often, Jock would become normal and when he did, he loved to play chess. Doctors and orderlies and other patients would gladly challenge him to see if they could beat him at his game and also to engage the man and give him something to enjoy. Rarely could anyone beat him.

I would practice the game with other patients and anyone else who wished to play a game with me. I practiced so I would be in better shape to challenge Jock when he was "awake", as we referred to his good moments of being mobile. I was never able to win a game against Jock. But, I was OK with that because it was the one and only thing Jock had that he enjoyed and that engaged him with other human beings. I was fine with him winning. In fact, I think most people were happy that he was so good at the game even though he only got to play it sporadically.

Chapter 10

Because I was bored, I asked nurses to give me jobs of any sort just to have something to occupy myself. There were lots of things I could do such as: sweep or mop a floor, empty bedpans, pick up food trays, clean the barn, work in the gardens, fold laundry or even my old job of changing bed sheets. Working in the gardens and helping weed flower beds was a job I particularly enjoyed because it got me outside in the fresh air.

I discovered that there were some patients who had built little huts in the trees. They used any sort of cardboard, wood or metal scrap that they could find and kept themselves busy building and adding on over time. These huts were an escape for some patients who had become trusted enough to not roam too far. They found privacy and refuge in these huts. A place of solace where they felt they had a little more control over their life day to day. They would store food, books, bits of small furniture, pieces of linoleum or an old rug to cover some of the ground so they had a place to have a nap or just be away from others.

I knew the feeling of wanting to be away from others at times. People interested me and there were plenty of interesting people to observe; however, there were times when I wished I could be completely on my own. I tried to remember what it was like to be able to eat or sleep or move from room to room without feeling like I was part of a crowd. On one of those days that I had that feeling I had been walking in the hallway—just walking and thinking. One of the male attendants, named Art, ordered me to come into the Day Room. I'm not sure what the reason was but he seemed bothered by my walking back and forth in the hallway.

"Don!" he barked down the hallway to me. I stopped and turned around to face him.

"Get back here to the Day Room."

"No thanks. I'd rather just walk out here for now." I was not trying to be defiant. I simply wanted to walk and be alone in my thoughts. However, Art took my response to be in defiance of his order. He started walking—almost running toward me and I could see the veins in his neck standing out and his temples pulsing with every step.

"I said get back here and I'm not telling you again. You will do as I say!" he hissed, as he grabbed me by my arm. I instinctively pulled away from him. I instantly felt that I could not put up with one more adult person touching me or grabbing me for any reason again. I'd had enough.

"Let go of me!" I retaliated. This was probably not the smartest thing I'd done but I seemed to be on autopilot and there was no turning back now. His face was brilliant red now and he pushed me in the chest knocking me backwards off my feet and down I went with a thud onto my back and I couldn't breathe. The wind was knocked out of me. I froze in pain trying to catch my breath and that pause gave him ample time to kick me. He gave me a couple of swift kicks to my ribs and I rolled over to protect myself as best as I could and then he pounded on my buttocks and my back with his fists. I felt the sharp cut to my flesh from his ring as he pounded me with his fists. Finally, he grabbed me by my shirt and pulled me up and started dragging me to the Day Room.

All of a sudden his grasp on me let go and I dropped to the floor again. As I turned my head around and began to try to get up on my hands and knees, I saw Joe. He had run head long into Art from behind as if making a football tackle. He managed to knock Art off his feet. His fists were clenched and he stood there with his feet apart in a stance showing he was ready to fight.

"Leave him alone!" shouted Joe. "He ain't done noth'n you need to be hit'n him for."

"Oh so you want some of the action too, hey? You little shit—I'll give you some action alright!" and Art jumped to his feet and I wanted to help Joe but my ribs were sore and I had trouble getting up. I watched in fear and could see that Joe was scared too but he was not backing down.

Art came at Joe with a vengeance and although Joe made a gallant attempt to get a couple of swings and punches in, he was no match for "Mr. Muscle Man". Art made a right upper cut and caught Joe on the chin. His head went back and he followed his head down hard onto the concrete floor. He lay there motionless, blood streaming from his chin. He'd hit his head so hard that he was unconscious.

Art turned to me and grabbed me again and dragged me into the Day Room. He threw me into a chair and then gave me one final smack on the back of my head just to finish things off before walking away. I hung my head and fought back the tears. I was 14 now and was beginning to feel like I needed to stand up for myself but Art was still too much for me to over power. I could feel everyone in the room looking at me but no one dared step in to comfort or help me out. They all knew better. Maybe some of them had met with Art's wrath before too.

When I looked up and was watching Art walk toward the door, I saw Big Red. He had Joe cradled in his arms! Joe hung there lifeless, still unconscious and bloody. Big Red filled the doorway with his bulkiness and with Joe sprawled in his arms. Art stopped short in his tracks.

"Somebody hurt this boy for some reason? Would that be you, Art?" Big Red looked angry and his jaw was clenched and he gritted his teeth and looked down at Art.

"Nobody should be hitt'n on these boys. It's not nice for big guys to pick on little guys you know Art. I'm a lot bigger than you and you don't want me to hit you—do you? I don't think you do. Now, I'm gonna carry this boy into the bathroom and then I'm gonna get him looked at by a nurse and you ain't gonna do noth'n to stop me, you hear?"

Then Big Red motioned to me with a nod to come with him, "Come on here Donnie. You come along with me. Nobody gonna hurt you." He gave Art a dirty last look and waited for me to get up and waited until I was safely in front of him. He stayed between me and Art.

Art stood there, dumbfounded with his mouth gaping open, small and helpless compared to Red. He was a bully but he'd be no match for Big Red and he knew it. He knew better than to challenge this friendly giant who may not have had an education but he had more common sense and decency in his little finger than Art had in his whole body. Art was smart enough to know that people respected Big Red and that he would tell the truth. He may have been considered simple in intelligence but no one would ever accuse him of being a liar. Art knew he had to concede to the giant.

Art would have gotten away with his beating on me that day if it hadn't been for the fact that one of the doctors happened to be doing some rounds before bed and saw me take off my shirt. He stopped and walked over to me.

"What the heck did you do, Son, to get the bruises? Turn around and let me see. You've got some nasty welts and cuts here on your back."

I winced with pain as he pressed lightly on my rib cage as he was examining me. I told him about the incident with Art and I wondered if it was any use. Would he believe me? But I found out later that the doctor had given Art a stern warning. Apparently, staff members were never supposed to use violence or force that would injure a patient. It was grounds for immediate dismissal. From things that I witnessed, it might have been a good idea to make that rule clear more often. But at least Art left me and Joe alone after that.

ଛୋଡ଼

As I sat reading in the Day Room one afternoon, I noticed a woman that looked slightly familiar. She sat slumped in a chair smoking a cigarette. Her fingers were all yellow from smoking so much and her fingernails had chipped red nail varnish on them. Her hair hung limply but one side was pinned back with a bobby pin.

"Oh my gosh!" I rose from my chair and walked over to her. "Miriam, is that you?" I asked—my voice cracking. I hated it when my voice cracked just at a time when I most wanted to sound grown up. It seemed to happen a lot lately.

She really didn't respond but kept smoking and seemed to be in a world of her own. She seemed detached from anything going on around her.

"That's right," spoke a voice from another woman sitting next to her. "This is Miriam alright—what's left of her after they gave her that lobotomy. Drilled holes in her head and now she doesn't care about anything anymore. Actually, maybe that's not such a bad thing—all things considered," she chuckled.

"But, why? What did she do to make them do that to her?" I asked in utter shock and bewilderment.

"Well, she kept on about her boyfriend and how much she loved him and she kept herself all prettied up for him too. She went home for a visit over a weekend to her mother's home and she tried to meet the boyfriend and was going to run off with him. Her mother caught her sneaking out of the house and had her brought back in here. Miriam put up a real fight like a cat—scratching and kicking. Since she'd had shock treatments in the past and they thought it hadn't settled her down enough, they gave her a lobotomy. Well, that worked as you can see. She's calm now and she isn't looking for her man anymore. I'm her friend and we used to share secrets but now we just sit and I keep her company while she smokes."

I was glad Miriam had a friend even though she seemed rather unaware of the woman's company. Everybody needs a friend; someone who is willing to be with you—even when you aren't at your best. I thought about my friends Joe and Martha. Joe was there for me and he put himself in harm's way to try to help me. It was a good thing indeed to have a true friend like him.

SO CR

I hadn't seen Nurse Beattie around for some time. When I saw Nurse Susan Berk, I asked her about Nurse Beattie.

"I shouldn't really be discussing Nurse Beattie's private life with you but just don't tell anyone who you heard this from, OK?" Susan was taking a break so she seemed willing to talk to me.

"Sure, I won't say anything to anyone about it. Is something wrong?"

"Nurse Beattie's husband fell down a well and was killed a couple of weeks ago. She's gone to stay with relatives for a while."

"Oh, gosh, I'm so sorry to hear that. I didn't actually even know she was married," I confessed.

"They were married for about three years, I think. They were happy and wanted to start a family. It's so sad. But, she'll be back and you can count on her because she's a strong person."

I didn't doubt that at all. I pondered on this for the rest of the afternoon. It seemed that I had been living here so long that I was unaware about much life outside this place. The people who lived here and the people who worked here were just part of my world. They were characters and I watched their drama and viewed them from a distance at times. Some of them affected me or had a direct connection or influence on my life here; but, until now, I had not thought much of the fact that the people who worked here had personal lives out there—beyond here.

It was hard to imagine Nurse Beattie being married and having a desire to have a child. She was just "Nurse Beattie" and I liked her very much but that was all she had been to me until now. It was about what she could do for me in here. I was glad I had her as a wonderful and caring nurse but now, I realized that was rather thoughtless and ignorant of me to not realize she and others here were real people who had real lives.

I made a mental note to remember this in future. I thought I could work on this flaw in my own character and it was actually a bit of fun after this awakening because every time I came upon one of the staff, I found myself now wondering about their personal lives.

I wondered about Art and tried to imagine what might be happening in his life that made him a bully. This didn't make me like him or want to befriend him. But, I at least could now rationalize that there might possibly be something that made him behave the way he did. It also made sense to me to avoid people like him. There was something about people like this that raised the hairs on the back of my neck.

It almost became like a little game to me to try to learn more about people. I started asking questions like: are you married? How many children do you have? Did you go to high school? That was a favourite question for me because I wanted to know what high school was like.

Some staff were very patient and answered my questions and one day a patient overheard me asking about high school. His name was Arnold and he told me he was a lawyer but that he had suffered a nervous breakdown. He said he was feeling much better and expected that he would soon be returning home. He asked me if I liked reading.

"Yes, I really do like to read."

"What kind of books do you like?"

"I like the Life magazines and the National Geographic magazines a lot."

"That's good. You should keep reading every day. Look at the newspapers too and I've got a couple of books I'll lend to you. You seem like a bright boy to me and you should be in school."

"I wish I could go to school and learn more but they don't have any more classes here after grade 6, you know."

"Do you like math and geography?"

"I like math but what is geography?"

"Geography is the study of the physical features of the earth. It's about the distribution of people and resources and all sorts of things about the use of land and even industries."

"What are resources and industries?"

He reached into a cloth drawstring bag that he had at his side. He pulled out a large black covered book.

"This is my father's Webster's Dictionary. I keep it with me all the time because it helps me feel close to him. He was a very good man and he was instrumental in my becoming a lawyer. He never got the education that he wanted as a youngster. It was so important to him that I get a good education. This book was what he carried with him and it was like an encyclopedia."

"What's an encyclopedia?"

"Well, here, I'll show you how to look that word up in this book. You can look up the meaning for resources and industries while you are at it." He showed me how to use the dictionary.

"This book is not just a dictionary. It has lots of other interesting things in it as well. Look here in the back part of the book. See, this part is all about the etiquette of the day. Etiquette is all about "manners". You already have some good manners but you can read about the proper manners that were used before our time. You'll get a kick out of it. See this paragraph here—they talk all about the proper time of day to call on a person and how to leave a calling card and even what type of stationery you should use. Do you know what stationery is? It is paper! See, just in a few minutes, we are learning some fun things. Some things still apply to today so you will learn many new things. And, look at this part— it shows you how to write a business letter, in fact, many kinds of business letters."

"Gee, this is a great book. It's got so much inside it. It's like many books in one," I flipped through more pages and was amazed.

"If you ever want to read this book you can have it for an afternoon. I'll share it with you but only when we are in the Day Room together. I'll read one of my other books and you can sit and look at this book. I won't let it out of my sight but I'm willing to share it with you."

"Gosh, thanks Arnold. I'll be careful with it. Can we take it to the Day Room now?"

"Sure and maybe one day you will get your own book like this. Books are very important and can open up new adventures for you. You learn what you can from any book you can get your hands on in this place and it will help you one day. Reading and learning will make good use of the time you spend in here. I have a feeling that you won't always live in this place."

"I hope you're right."

After that day, Arnold suggested that I get a scribbler and make notes for myself from his book. I loved it and it gave me something to do and he would sit nearby so I could use his book and ask him questions. He knew the answers to all my questions and he was always patient with me.

The day did come that he was released. He had to take his book, of course, but I had made so many notes that I felt like I had a great book of my own from it. Before he left he gave me a couple of his novels. I read *For Whom the Bell Tolls*, by Ernest Hemmingway three times. The other book was *The Diary of a Young Girl*, by Anne Frank. I realized that I had very little knowledge of the world out there and I vowed that I would try to learn more about it. I was hungry to learn now.

Arnold had given me a great gift. Reading was like an escape from my world and the more I read, the more I wanted to read.

One day, I got a real surprise. Nurse Jerry brought me a parcel and I could see it had already been opened and then re-wrapped. This was because all mail was opened and monitored before giving it to the patients. I tore the paper off and there was a Webster's Dictionary! Inside the cover was a note from Arnold: *Dear Don; This is a newer edition and, although it doesn't have all the etiquette things in it, it does have a lot of useful information. Keep reading and learning. Sincerely, your friend, Arnold*

I treasured this book and never forgot Arnold's kind gesture.

Chapter 11

It was winter of 1948. That was the year that a special volunteer program got started by a group of concerned women from Regina. They came and toured the hospital and made reports and decided where they felt they wanted to put their energy and money as far as helping out. They would come to visit and spent time with elderly patients and people who were not very mobile. They were kind and they wanted to help but as far as I could see, there was not much they could do to help the situation even with the best intentions.

One day I witnessed a rather nice thing with one of the volunteers. She went over to talk to a patient that had been mute for as long as I'd been there. The patient, Joyce, was lying on a lounge chair. The volunteer went and sat beside her, touched her shoulder and spoke softly to her. After the volunteer had chatted for a while (no one knew what she said), Joyce actually turned her head toward the volunteer, smiled and said, "Thank you. You are very kind."

It was amazing! I don't think the volunteer had any idea what she had just accomplished. A nurse explained that

Joyce had not spoken for years. The volunteer was beaming and vowed she'd come back again next month.

The volunteers donated a lot of materials to the activity therapy group. They would box up gifts for patients for Christmas. However, I don't think they were ever told that there were now 17 children in this place. They were only allowed to see what was deemed appropriate by the administration. So, I doubt that the kids got much more than perhaps woolen scarves, sweaters, slippers or something that would do as a gift. I'm sure if those women had known, they would have made an effort to see that there were some dolls or toys for kids that were age appropriate. However, there were some toys that were donated either from staff or perhaps the Salvation Army. Nothing much was new and sharing meant nothing really belonged to an individual. You never had anything that you could really call your own possession.

This was the same year that I turned 17. I had been in [4]"the Mental", by this time, for eight years and not one phone call or visit from anyone who knew me. I knew I didn't belong there because I knew there was nothing wrong with my mental capacity. Although, it did seem that the longer one stayed in this place, the more you might begin to act crazy. Even some staff members were affected by this place and it took its toll on even the most intelligent people.

There was one psychiatrist, named Dr. Edward Finklestein. He was a young man and I think this hospital was probably his first experience as a psychiatric doctor. According to hospital rumours, he became unable to tolerate

---

[4]Commonly used and considered appropriate during the time depicted as a quick reference to the asylum by the community.

the possibility of picking up germs from patients. He began to believe that if he did, he would become infected with mental illness or some disease. He would wipe the door knob on his office door after anyone else touched it. He wiped the chair in his office after a patient sat on it. It became almost impossible for him to even leave his office for fear of someone touching him as he would try to make his way to the exit to leave the building. He had to completely disrobe when he got home and wanted his wife to immediately sterilize his clothing in boiling water and he would have to wash his vehicle steering wheel and seat off so it would be sanitized for the next day.

This extreme phobia of his began to interfere with his ability to focus on his duties. His mental state was duly noted and, eventually, the very thing he most feared came true. He became so ill that he had to be placed on a ward and he was given shock treatments for a few months and then he was able to leave the hospital but he never worked there again. Perhaps the stigma was too much even for a medical person once they were labeled, "mentally ill".

Shock treatments were given once a day for several weeks and eventually, a patient with high anxiety would seem to calm down. I determined after seeing this treatment used on people that I would have to be very guarded about my behaviour. It was one thing to be sent to the "Snake Pit" but if a person acted too crazy or threw any sort of an angry fit, they would be held down and have electrodes attached to their temples and a rubber mouth guard placed between their teeth and then hit with a bolt of electric current that made the body writhe and bounce right off the gurney.

My friend, Art, the attendant that laced me that day for disrespecting his orders to get into the Day Room, was one of the attendants that always seemed to be holding someone down for a shock treatment. He looked over his shoulder one day as he was holding a patient down, strapping the kicking man to the gurney.

"You want to be next?" he grinned with a taunting leer at me.

I stepped back and knew better than to even speak to him. No sense giving him any ammunition to come after me and I sure as hell had no desire to be strapped to one of those gurneys! Or end up getting a lobotomy like poor Miriam.

ℰᏀᏅ

Perhaps Dr. Finklestein's phobia about germs was not completely unfounded. There was a serious concern with the disease, tuberculosis. It had reached such high levels in Saskatchewan (more than any other province in Canada) that an annex to the Mental Hospital had to be built and if a patient or staff member got the disease, he or she would be cared for in the annex. It was easy to contract this disease due to the crowded living conditions.

Unfortunately, my pal Joe became ill and coughed up some blood one day. The nurse immediately sent Joe for an X-ray of his lungs and the condition was confirmed. Martha and I tried to cheer ourselves up by promising that we'd try to visit Joe if we could. After about five months, we were allowed a short visit to try to lift Joe's spirits a little.

"I'm kind of scared, Don." Martha confessed as we walked toward Joe's room. "I hope we don't catch the germs here."

"Nah—we'll be fine, Martha," I tried to sound convincing but I really had no idea. "We aren't gonna kiss him—or were you planning to?" I teased her.

"No way!" she blushed and pushed me lightly on the shoulder. "I'm not even going to touch him. But, I am going to try to make him feel like we care about him. I'm going to give him this book to read. It has coloured pictures of animals and people from Africa. It's a National Geographic magazine."

"Yeah, yeah, of course."

We found our way to his room. There was old Joe, alright—beaming at us from ear to ear. He had quite a scar on his chin which would be a constant reminder of his day with Mr. Muscle Man, Art.

"Hey, Joe! How you doing buddy?" I asked. Martha broke her word and did touch him but only on his knee as he was covered up to his chin in blankets.

"You guys are a sight for sore eyes! I'd love to sit up and give you a hug, Martha, but I'm not allowed to lift my head off this pillow."

"Oh, Joe—don't try moving if you aren't supposed to. It's so nice to see you again. We've worried about you, haven't we, Don? We sure miss having you around. When will you be coming back?"

"They tell me it won't be for a couple of months yet. I have to build my strength back up first. They wheel me out into a veranda every day to soak up as much fresh air as possible. This is every day! no matter what the weather is like. If it is winter, they just bundle us up with more blankets and keep us warm as possible but we must breathe fresh air in slowly every day. I'm not allowed to try to walk yet but if my next chest X-ray is good, I'll be allowed to start sitting up and eventually, I will get back on my feet. I get better food in here than in the loonie bin. It is the doctor's orders that we get nutritious, fresh food as part of the treatment, so that's a bonus." Joe laughed, trying to sound cheerful. He was the last person who would want any pity coming from either of us.

He went on to tell us that there was a ward for [5]retarded children in the annex and that he felt sorry for them because they didn't get outside very often and there was no school class for them either. So, there were even more kids in this place than I realized. But, at least if they were retarded, they had a reason to be there. I had no reason to be there and neither did Martha or Joe—other than for the reason of his tuberculosis, of course.

---

[5]Retarded (outdated term) was an acceptable term used in the time being depicted to describe a person less advanced in mental, physical, or social development than is usual for one's age.

Chapter 12

I always knew I wanted to leave from the moment I spent my first night there but I had always wanted to believe that, one day, someone from my family was going to come to get me. Now that I had come to realize this was unlikely, I began to think I may need to find a way to escape.

It was summer—the flowers were in full bloom and the aroma of their sweet scent was intoxicating. The Caragana bushes had tiny yellow flowers that we would pick and eat. I loved the sweetness in them. I had been helping in the gardens and, as I walked back toward the main building, I couldn't resist taking a moment to lie down on the freshly mown grass. It filled my nostrils with that fresh green, clean smell. I inhaled it hoping to cleanse my head and body of the stench within those confining walls. It reminded me of the farm and the smell of freshly mown hay. I stared up into the blue sky at the soft cotton-like clouds and let myself daydream of freedom . . .

People escaped more often than I would have thought possible. For a short time, I was sent on errands to the laundry building to help fold bedding to be brought back into the main building. This was where I met John Keating who was the head of the laundry department. John seemed to take a liking to me for some reason. Maybe it was because he said he had a grandson about my age.

One time, we sat for a break in the coffee room and he told me of an interesting incident that had happened there. People who worked in the laundry building would bring their lunches, packed into empty jam pails and store them in the coffee room cupboard. Lunch pails started going missing and staff members were beginning to suspect one another of stealing. After a few rude accusations, and arguments back and forth, tension was building.

Then one day, John explained, he was sitting having a smoke when suddenly he heard something overhead in the building. He knew it wasn't a mouse or rat because it was a heavy, slow sound of footsteps rather than a scurrying sound from a mouse or rat.

He grabbed a flashlight and began the climb up the ladder to an attic opening in the ceiling. He opened the attic door slowly and held the flashlight above his head as he peered into the dark room. It took a few minutes, even with the flashlight, for his eyes to adjust in the dim and dusty room. He shone the light around the room and could make out the form of a heap of blankets on the floor in a corner. It looked suspiciously like someone was using this as a place to sleep. There, on the floor, beside the pile of bedding were stacks of empty jam pails!

All of a sudden a moving form bolted from a dark corner, ran across the room and jumped out a window.

"Help!" hollered John. "Somebody jumped out the attic window. Run outside and catch him!"

Workers dropped what they were doing and scrambled out the back door and, after somewhat of a chase, they managed to capture the culprit. He was a patient that had gone missing months ago. He had been living in the attic of the laundry during the day and was stealing lunches to live off. He wandered about outside during the nights.

When I heard this story, soon after the capture of the guy, I started thinking—if he could do that, maybe I could do it too.

ℰᏅ

A few days later, I saw an opportunity. A doctor had left his white coat hanging on a coat tree in his office. The door to his office was open and I was mopping floors so I had an excuse to be in his office. I looked around and no one was in sight so I went into his office and quickly felt inside the coat. I knew doctors always carried a set of master keys in their coats. Sure enough! I removed the master key from the ring and slipped it into my pocket and mopped my way out of the office.

I was so excited by my actions that my heart was pounding. I had never stolen anything before in my life but I was definitely stealing this key and I was happy to be doing it. I had no guilt about it at all. *The Lord helps those who help themselves*, I thought.

The only problem was I didn't really know what I was going to do next. I knew I'd have to wait until night time until after the last nurse or orderly had made their rounds to get everyone ready for bed.

I was afraid to leave the key in my pocket for fear that someone might pick up my blue jeans and the key might fall out. I came up with what I thought was a brilliant idea to hide the key. I took an orange at supper time and placed it on my bed-side table. I shoved the key into the orange and got into bed and kept my eye on that orange. After lights were out and people started snoring, I slipped quietly out of my bed and put my clothes back on. I kept the key hidden in the orange in case I got stopped. If I were to be caught, I feared they would check my pockets. At least that way I'd be able to keep the key concealed in case I had to try this again some other time.

I made my way down the dimly lit hallway; no one was stirring anywhere. I could hear the nurses chatting in the nurses' station. They were deep into a conversation about crafts and the one nurse was knitting something. She was showing the other nurse the pattern she was making as a gift for a child in her family. I ducked down low and crawled on all fours past the counter that surrounded the nurses' station. That was easy enough.

I got to the locked door at the end of the corridor and took another look over my shoulder as I put the key in the lock. Safe! I opened the door only as far as I needed to slip my body out and locked it behind me. I didn't use the elevator for fear of meeting someone. I quietly crept down the staircase and found my way out of a side door. I was free!

I had no plan and no intentions of an actual "escape". After all, I had nowhere to go and no one to run to—I couldn't go home. There wasn't any place for me to hide and I only had the clothes on my back. But, I was on a little adventure and I was going to explore. All I wanted was to be out of the building by myself and feel what it might be like to be a normal teenage boy allowed to walk the streets on my own.

I walked downtown and saw other teens out in cars. Boys in cars whistled at girls walking by, trying to entice the girls to come along for a ride. Most times, the girls pretended not to notice the boys and would stick their noses in the air or giggle and whisper to one another. But, sometimes the girls would hop in a car and ride off with boys. I noticed teens coming and going from the Club Café. It was a Chinese café and it seemed like a popular spot for teenagers. I promised myself that if I had some money one day, I'd come back and go inside. I could imagine myself sitting down in a booth with a girlfriend and sipping on a milkshake together.

The night was warm and people cruised by in cars up and down the main drag. At one street corner, motors revved and two carloads of teens took off in a race right down Main Street. I thought how lucky these boys and girls were to be having such a good time. I did think that if I ever got a car I'd be apt to take much better care of it than to race with it. But just the same, it did seem quite thrilling and they all seemed to be laughing and enjoying themselves. It made me feel lonely and like a freak from some other planet.

I walked by the Soo Theatre and read the posters advertising the movies being shown. I thought it would be great to take in a movie but I had no money so I moved along. I found a billiards room and stepped inside to watch some of the men playing a game of pool. I didn't stay long as I didn't want to draw too much attention. No one seemed to notice me. They were intent on their games. The room was filled with smoke and not all the people were older. Some looked like they were about my age. They were smoking cigarettes just like the men. I wondered what it must feel like to have money and to be able to hang out with a gang of guys my own age.

After satisfying myself that I had seen what downtown Weyburn looked like at night, I headed back to my "real world".

Chapter 13

I bolted awake in the middle of the night to a blood curdling scream. It wasn't odd to hear someone scream or yell during the night or anytime during the day but this was something horrific. It reminded me of the scream from my mother when my father lay bloody in her arms in the bull pen on that tragic day.

I jumped out of bed; I had to see what was going on. I went out into the hallway and saw nurses around a woman on the floor. Male orderlies were running from everywhere. Patients were moving from their beds into the hallway to see what was happening. I moved closer and looked at the woman as orderlies held her down. Nurses were scrambling for bandages and someone was giving her an injection.

She screamed and thrashed around. I could see that she had bloody hands and then I got a glimpse of her face. One eyeball was hanging from a string of flesh from her eye socket. A nurse told the orderlies and other nurses that she had plucked her own eye out!

I ran to the nearest toilet and vomited. I shook and trembled as I sat in a cubical weeping. For the first time in a

95

long time I broke down and sobbed. My body broke out in a cold sweat and I wretched again. Waking in the middle of the night to this was worse than any nightmare I could have had. The reality in my life was so much worse than what I could imagine or dream in a nightmare. The sorrow that I experienced for this poor woman, and even for the nurses and others who witnessed her tragedy, was just too much.

How do human beings reach such a low point in their own minds that they can tear at their own flesh hurting themselves or others in such a way? Where is God? Is He watching? Why doesn't He intercede and save people from their own destructive ways? I needed to leave this place . . .

ഇൻൻ

I found out the next day that the woman, named Gertie, had been admitted during the night and was distraught. She complained of a severe headache was rocking back and forth, banging her head on the wall. Apparently, she had seen her three-year old daughter get attacked by a neighbour's dog earlier that week. The little girl had been playing in a paddling pool in the back yard. Gertie had momentarily gone into the house to bring out cookies and lemonade. She was very quick and had kept her eye on the child from the kitchen window while getting the snack ready.

The neighbour's dog from across the street got off its leash and attacked the child. Gertie ran outside immediately but she couldn't catch the dog before he had mangled the little girl's face and nearly ripped off her little arm. The dog ran around the back yard dragging and shaking the child like a rag doll. A man from next door heard the screams from Gertie and ran to assist and brought a shovel with him to hit the dog. Sadly, the child's jugular vein had been severely punctured and torn open. She couldn't survive the attack. She was pronounced dead on arrival to the hospital.

Gertie had not slept and was not eating. She had been hysterical all week. She blamed herself for going into the house and leaving the child unattended, but truth be known, it may have happened in spite of this. She cried, "I don't want my eyes! I don't want to see anymore!"

ꙮꙮ

Martha was busy pulling weeds in a flower bed one day and I was hoeing the chunks of dry earth between the flowers. Martha had a bad experience a few days before this and she was still not over it. She was weeding and working; not saying much. Earlier that week, she had been sexually attacked by a male orderly. He had pulled her into a room where linens were stored and had molested her. She managed to break free at one point and she ran frantically down the hallway screaming hysterically. Two male attendants came running after her and wouldn't you know it—one of them was my friend, "Mr. Muscle Man," Art. As the men tried to restrain her from running, she went even crazier on them.

"Get your filthy hands off me you big apes!"

She tried biting their strong hands and scratched at their faces. She tried kicking them and slapping at them. They got on each side of her and one of them kicked her feet out from under her. She hit the floor and they carried her into the bathroom. They stripped off her clothing, forced her into one of the metal tubs and secured the canvas tarp over her so that only her head stuck out. She continued kicking and screaming as they filled the tub with cold water. She cried and screamed and kicked in that tub until she played herself out completely. She was left there for hours until she was subdued to the point of being limp and lifeless as a corpse.

This treatment, called Hydrotherapy Treatment, was used to calm a hysterical patient. The water temperature would be very cold which slowed the blood flow to the brain, decreasing mental and physical activity. Patients could be left in these "continuous baths" for hours. Of course, no one bothered to ask Martha what had brought on her hysteria. Even if she had tried to tell them, they would likely never believe her.

"OK, Martha. Let's get you out of the tub now and get you dressed for bed."

Art was back to lift her out of the tub. He sat her on a chair because she was too limp and exhausted to be able to stand. He began rubbing her dry with a towel and then he came around behind her and draped the towel over her shoulders. As he did so, he slipped his hands down and began caressing her bare breasts. She didn't fight. She had no fight left in her. She seemed to be in a trance, unable to make any sound. She had no voice left from all the screaming she had done earlier.

"What's going on in here, Art?" It was Nurse Beattie. She put her hands on her hips and said, "I think I will take it from here, if you don't mind. You can tend to the men down the hall. Some of them are going at it with getting ready for bed. You're needed there more than you are here."

Art jumped wrapped the towel around Martha covering her exposed breasts and walked out of the room quickly. Nurse Beattie continued to stand with her hands on her hips and watched his backside and then slammed the door behind him. Martha sat motionless but tears streamed down her cheeks.

"Come on sweetheart. Let's get you into a nice nightie now and tuck you into bed. You've had a rough day. I'll get you a little cup of tea too. There now, hold up your arms while I slip you into your nightie. There's a good girl." Nurse Beattie was an angel to Martha just as she had been to me many years before.

The word was spread from one patient to another and when I learned of this, I was angry, sick and tormented. I felt all the more determined that I was going to get out of this place for good this time. I had to try and if Martha would come, I would take her with me.

$\omega\alpha$

"Martha!" I half whispered to her as she knelt in the dirt picking tiny weeds. "Martha, look at me—we have to talk about something." She stopped and looked up with an expressionless, glazed look in her eyes.

"I can get us out of here." I kept hoeing while I spoke. There were other patients working in the flower beds but they were not really close enough to overhear me as long as I spoke in a low voice. But where there were patients, there would also be one or two staff members.

"What?" she asked as she tilted her head back to stare up at me. Her face looked so beautiful with a few freckles and a blush of pink from the sun on her nose and cheeks. "What are you saying, Don? Are you nuts?"

I almost laughed out loud at that question but I had to be serious.

"I've got a plan, Martha, and I'm going one way or the other and I'm going soon. I want to take you with me to get us both free of this hell hole. But, I'm not going to force you. You don't deserve to be here and neither do I. This is all wrong and no one is coming for us so we've got to take matters into our own hands. Trust me Martha. You are my best friend in the world and I would never hurt you. I only want to help you to get away from here. What do you think?"

"But how, Donnie?" she whispered back. "If they catch us, what will happen?"

"Keep weeding Martha." I turned my back from her for a minute and looked around to make sure no one was watching or listening to us. It seemed clear.

"We won't get caught and anyway, if they did catch us—what the hell more can they do to us that they haven't already done?"

"I trust you Donnie. I truly do. You're my best friend too and if you have a plan, I'm willing to give it a go. Let's do it!" she smiled up at me and wiped the little beads of sweat from her forehead with the back of her hand, leaving a streak of dirt on her face.

I felt good to see her smiling again. Having seen her so lifeless and so quiet had me worried. I wanted to wipe the dirt from her face and put my arms around her. I wanted to tell her we were going to be fine but I didn't dare. The less attention we drew to ourselves, the better.

I still had the master key which I kept hidden either in my underwear, or in my sock, or in an orange. I kept a guard on it day and night. Escape might be possible when we were already outside but we were closely supervised at most times when outdoors. I would wait and think. I'd try to formulate a plan for us. Stepping out on my own for an evening stroll was one thing but taking Martha with me and not coming back was going to be something else.

Chapter 14

Nurse Beattie smiled at me as she came toward me in the hallway on the way to lunch. She had been back to work now for a long time since the death of her husband. I had talked to her one day about her loss. I tried to give her my condolences. I remember, I had asked her how she managed to go on after such a devastating loss and how she managed to keep her composure through all the difficult things that happened on the wards day in and day out. What she told me was another one of life's little lessons.

"It helps keep my mind off my own troubles when I'm busy. I'd rather be here with you, the other patients and my coworkers than sitting at home doing nothing. It's always a good thing to keep one's mind occupied and your hands busy."

"Do you mean like the [6] Work Therapy for the patients?" I asked her.

---

[6] A form of treatment used to keep patients in the fresh air, engaged physically so they would eat and sleep well and to give a sense of purpose or self-worth. This treatment was eventually discontinued.

"Yes—exactly like that. And furthermore, I don't feel like I'm the one doing so much for others here as they are doing for me," she added.

"What does that mean? I'm sorry I don't get it," I answered. "How could people in this place possibly be helping you?"

"It's like this—I have come to learn a long time ago that by giving service to others I get so much more in return. When I help someone who is ill or unable to help themselves in some way, I feel good about myself. Have you ever heard that phrase, *there but for the grace of God, go I*?"

"No, I don't think I have," I replied.

"Well, it means that when you see someone who is less fortunate than you, has less than you, is hurting, is sick, or handicapped in any way—that could be you someday. You could be in that same condition or situation in your life and it is only by God's grace or his will that you—or any of us—manage to escape it. Do you see now?" she smiled.

"I'm not exactly sure but does that mean that God wanted me to end up in here even though I am not insane or retarded? Because I think about that quite a bit and I don't think I like God if He wants me stuck here."

"No, I don't think it is that God wants you stuck here Don. I think He may be trying to help you since you are here. God gave men and women the right to think for themselves. That's why we have a brain. Of course, we know there are some poor souls in here that have lost the ability to think and their brains are severely affected, but maybe that is why God wanted us to have a place like this so we can help to look after those poor folks. For the rest of us who have the ability to use our brains, we can make decisions—but, sometimes we make the wrong decisions. But, rest assured, He knows where you are and He may have a reason for what has happened. Perhaps your Mother used her mind but she was weak and she made a bad decision. Try thinking of it this way—if you had stayed with your Mother and her new husband—I'm sorry, I forget what his name is," she paused.

"Frank."

"Oh yes—Frank," she continued. "If you had ended up living with your Mother and Frank, it might have been worse for you in the end to be subjected every day to a man who hated children so much. So maybe think about it this way; maybe God did protect you from your Mother's poor decision and from a life that would have hurt you even worse than the bad days you've had here."

"I guess maybe but I think I wish God would have found a little better place to stick me than this place." I looked down at my feet because I had difficulty looking her in the eye with my statement. I felt a little guilty questioning God's will for me.

"I chose this place to do my work, Don. This is a vocation for me rather than just a job."

"What's a vocation? Oh, never mind, I can look that up later in my Webster's Dictionary."

"I could have chosen to be a secretary or a clerk in a store. I chose this very place as my special place to work. I wanted to help people. I wanted to learn about mental illnesses and to see if I could make a difference in someone's life, even in a small way. I am not knocking anyone for wanting to be a secretary—don't get me wrong. But, you see, I knew I would receive something special by working in a place like this. People here need others like me to look after them. This place is where you live for now and I'm here with you. Maybe God is watching us both and He wants us to have this discussion. I like to think that God has a reason for everything and He is always watching us from above, from behind and from below. He's got a protective shield, so to speak, all around us. I think He wanted me to be here today so we could have this little chat. But, I should get going back to work. Are you going to the dance tomorrow, Donnie?"

"I didn't know there was a dance. I'm not very good at dancing but I like music."

"I think you should attend. You'll like this music. My younger brother, Doug Beattie, and his Vagabonds are playing. That's the name of his band. They have a great saxophone player and a vocalist. They play old time music like polkas and fox trots but they have some more modern pieces, too, which I like. They play at the Legion most weekends and at Club 13. You should definitely come."

"Yeah—I probably will. It's not like I have anything better to do!" I laughed. "Thanks for letting me know. It will be interesting to see what your brother and his band sound like. That's great that you have a brother who has a band."

I walked away from her and didn't think too much more about our conversation because my thoughts had suddenly turned to an exciting idea. This was it! The chance I had been waiting for—the dance would give us the opportunity for our escape. I was planning it in my mind as I walked to the dining hall. I found my way to a table where Martha was already eating her lunch. I sat beside her.

"Mm, you'll love lunch today, Donnie. It's one of our favorites! Macaroni with wieners and tomatoes and cheese, melted on top just the way we like it!"

"Well, eat lots because it might be a while until our next meal".

"What do you mean? Oh, and hey—did you hear about the dance today?"

"I mean, we are leaving here and, yes—I heard about the dance. We're going to leave while that dance is on and everyone is there."

"Oh, my gosh, Donnie—are you serious?"

"Yes, I've got a master key and we are going to walk out of here from the dance."

"A master key—how did you find that?"

"I'll explain that later. After lunch wait around here for a few minutes to give me time to run over to the laundry building. Then just walk slowly to the Day Room and go in and pick up a magazine. Don't get into any board games or any conversations with anyone. Just sit and wait. When you see me come into the Day Room, you get up and leave and go to the linen closet just down the hall from there. I'll meet you there but we can't walk together. If someone comes along, just turn around and walk back to the Day Room. Don't let anyone see you going into the linen closet. We'll just watch and we'll meet at the linen closet when the coast is clear. You got it?"

"OK, Donnie—got it!"

I made my way to the laundry building but I tried to walk at a normal pace rather than hurry too much. I didn't want to draw any attention to myself. I grabbed a linen trolley and no one suspected anything as I was already accepted as a helper in the laundry department at times. Of course, I did have to get an attendant to unlock the door for me so I could leave and go over to the laundry building but that was easy enough.

"Hey, Donnie—how's it going, son?" John waved a friendly welcome to me as I started unloading dirty laundry bins. "There are some clean things over there for you to take back with you."

"OK, John!"

I found exactly what I was looking for. I grabbed a clean nurse's apron and cap and shoved them in between two sheets. I stacked up my bins with clean linens and quickly headed back to the main building. I loaded the shelves in the linen closet with the clean linens and made sure to push the special items behind another stack. I didn't want anyone to come in and take that nurse's apron and cap before I could meet here again with Martha, as planned.

I walked quickly to the Day Room. Martha looked up from her magazine. Luckily, there were very few patients in the room and no nurses. I grabbed a newspaper and sat down. Martha got up and walked calmly out of the room, just the way I'd instructed her. She walked down the hallway toward the linen closet. I waited a few minutes to see if she had to turn around to come back. She didn't so I figured the coast was clear. I left the room and followed. No one was coming so we managed to meet in the linen closet. I felt a little tingly inside with nervous excitement that our "plan" was now in motion!

"Here, Martha!" I grabbed the clean nurse's apron and cap. "Put this inside your dress and it is good you have a sweater on. Do the same thing tonight before the dance. If you have a belt, maybe wear that as well to make sure nothing falls down while we dance or when you walk. Can you do your hair up like the nurses wear their hair?"

"Sure, Donnie—I was going to do my hair up today anyway to look pretty and it is so hot out that I thought it would be nice. When and how am I going to get the nurse's apron and cap on?"

"OK, listen—after we have a dance or two and I think things look safe, I'll let you know and you go to the bathroom and get into it there. Just stay in one of the toilet stalls until you are pretty sure there's no one else in there and then walk out as normal and calm as you can. I'll leave a little after you and meet you in the hallway. I'm hoping most people will be in the auditorium. If we have a big problem, just turn around and go back to the bathroom and take the stuff off and come back to the dance."

"Oh Donnie, I'm praying for us."

"Well, that's a nice thing to do Martha. You do that for us and I'll make a wish on my rabbit foot and we'll hope both things work for us!"

I stuck my head out of the linen closet and then signaled to Martha that is was clear to follow me out. I went one direction and she hurried off in the opposite direction.

Chapter 15

I want some red roses for a blue lady. Mister Florist, take my order please. We had a silly quarrel the other day—I hope these pretty flowers, chase her blues away! . . .

The vocalist was singing out to the music of the band as I walked into the auditorium. Wow! They sounded great. It was a swell song and I was half wishing I could stay for the whole dance to listen to them but I knew we had to stick to our plan. It was only about three o'clock in the afternoon. Seemed a bit odd maybe to be having a dance in the afternoon but everything had to be on a tight time frame to accommodate shift changes and so that supper and bed time regime was kept on schedule.

"You made it Donnie! How do you like my brother's band?" Nurse Beattie beamed.

"They're really sounding great. Which one is your brother?"

"The fellow on the right playing the accordion; he plays violin and keyboard as well but he's best known for his accordion music."

"Ah, I see. He's got dark hair but you are blonde. But, I think you have the same facial features," I tried to sound interested but, really, I was scanning the room to see if Martha was there yet.

"Well, I'd better go get some punch Nurse Beattie. I hope you have a nice time at the dance and thanks again for telling me about it. The music sounds great!"

Martha was waiting at a table and she was sitting beside Miriam and her friend. Miriam was smoking but at least her hair was neat and someone had bothered to paint her nails for her. She had on a nice dress with polka dots on it. Sadly, her expression was still vacant and she seemed to care less about the music or the chatter from her friend.

I set a glass of punch down in front of Martha and one for myself.

"Hello, ladies. I hope you are enjoying the music. Did you know the band leader is a brother to our Nurse Beattie?" I patted Martha on the leg under the table because I wanted to assure her all was well.

"Thanks for the punch Donnie. The music does sound very professional. Do you like dancing?' Martha took a sip of her punch.

"Well, I am not very good but I'll try if you want to give it a go."

Martha stood up and it was just now that I had chance to notice her dress. She wore a simple blue cotton dress with a flared skirt and a white lace Peter Pan collar. She had a wide, blue-satin ribbon tied in a bow around her slim waistline. She also wore a thin white cardigan sweater which she wore open so you could see the front of her dress. Her hair was done up in a neat French roll. I had never seen her look so lovely. She looked grown up and like a real woman instead of like the little girl that I'd first met. She was 16 now and I was a year older.

We had a dance to the tune "Buttons and Bows". The saxophone player announced that this was a Dinah Shore song that was a popular tune on the radio. I liked it and Martha seemed to know a few steps and tried to help me out. I told her that we needed to stay a while and enjoy the dance for a bit. I didn't want to make our move too soon. I thought we should wait until there were a lot of people on the dance floor.

"Where did you manage to hide the apron and cap, Martha? I can't see any bulge in the front of your dress."

"I had to stuff it in the back and tuck it into my under panties. With the sweater just loose, I figured it doesn't show. I snitched the blue ribbon from the Activity Room supplies to tie around my waist. I think it makes a pretty belt and it holds things pretty securely."

"God, you are smart, girl! Good for you. And you look very pretty in that dress. You did your hair up so nicely. I've never seen anybody look nicer than you do tonight."

"Gee, thanks Donnie. You look nice too".

"Oops—sorry!" I accidentally bumped her toes. I was trying to follow to the music but I was awkward.

"That's OK. Don't worry. Lots of people here don't know how to dance real well either. I'm just happy that you are trying."

When that song ended the band started with a slower song which was a waltz called, the "Tennessee Waltz". Boy that guy on the saxophone made that instrument sing in that number. I managed to follow Martha on that one a little better.

I watched some of the other dancers and tried my best to imitate the body movement to the time of the music. When the song ended, we went over to the food table and I whispered to Martha to take a good-sized helping of snacks in case it was a while until we would be able to eat again.

"Well, I'm not really very hungry but I will take a few of those fresh strawberries and a piece of that delicious looking watermelon. It seems I'm a bit too nervous to have much appetite."

"Hey, everybody—let's polka!" shouted the band leader. "Everybody up!" and the music started. The floor flooded fast as patients and staff mingled to the lively tune of "Roll Out the Barrel". This was our cue and I told Martha to head to the bathroom and I would follow shortly.

I got a kick out of watching people do the polka. I laughed out loud seeing Nurse Beattie bouncing around with Big Red on the dance floor. For someone as big as he was, he seemed light and nimble on his feet. A gentle giant and a tiny nurse—quite the sight!

I worked my way through the crowded dance floor to the door and slipped out into the hallway before the polka was over. It was clear and Martha was walking toward me with her white nurse's apron and cap on and looked perfect. I turned and walked ahead of her so that if someone did come along it wouldn't seem that we were together. Luckily, we made it to the door unnoticed.

I put the master key into the lock and opened the door quickly. I felt a rush as we were making our plan a reality.

Chapter 16

The day was just beginning to cool down. Although we'd just left a dance, it wasn't dark yet. We'd managed to get outside and I gulped in the fresh air and breathed a sigh of relief as we had succeeded in getting out of the building. I tugged gently on Martha's elbow and nodded for her to head toward the side to get away from the front of the building. We walked to the Caragana bushes along the pathway past the tennis courts where the trees were thicker and we were out of sight from the main building. We hurried along the footpath and through an open meadow area until we came to the river side. We crossed the wooden walking bridge to the other side and entered a bushy area where I told Martha to leave the nurse's apron and cap under a bush.

It was July 4 and although my birthday had gone unnoticed this year, I felt like today was my day! The circus was in town and you could hear the music of the carousel.

"Let's go to the Circus, Martha!"

"But we don't have any money, Donnie."

"I know, we'll think of something."

We needn't have worried because a sign was posted telling people to come in. They were still setting some things up and so they weren't charging at the gate and you could walk around the mid-way free of charge. I had only been to one circus before with my parents and sisters a long time ago. The sights were amazing to me and Martha had never been to a circus before so it was fun to watch her eyes light up and her mouth open in a perpetual smile. We both laughed and giggled and I took her by the hand for the first time.

"Hey buddy! Bring your girlfriend over here! I'll give you a free throw. Come on—win your girlfriend a free teddy bear!" one of the carnies called to me. He looked like he was probably only about my age.

"What do I have to do?"

"It's easy, my friend! Just throw one of these baseballs at the puppets and knock them down. If you can knock three of them over, I'll give your girl a nice big teddy bear."

I looked at Martha and she smiled back at me and I just had to try for her. She'd never had a teddy bear and I knew she wanted me to try.

"Go on Donnie. I bet you can do it," she urged me. I smiled back and gave her a wink.

"OK, here we go." I picked up one of the balls and cupped it into my fingers. I took a step back from the booth, steadied my eyes on the target of one puppet and held my left arm out at shoulder height and drew back my right arm and threw the ball. Dead on! I hit the puppet and knocked it down. Martha squealed with glee and clapped her hands. Then, I picked up another ball and Martha clasped her hands under her chin and squinted her eyes afraid to look.

Wham! Down went another puppet!

"Look here folks! We might have a winner here!" the carnie yelled trying to drum up more interest from passers-by.

"Come on over and watch this young man win a teddy bear. You could win one too folks, come on over."

People gathered to watch. Parents with kids and teenagers out on the town—little did they realize they were watching an escaped mental patient. But right now, in my head, I was a normal teenage boy out with his best friend and I was going to win that damn teddy bear! I held myself steady and wound up again. Bam! I did it! All those years of skipping rocks across the water in the dugout and knocking tin cans off fence posts had paid off.

"See folks! He's a winner! Try your luck out, folks. Three throws for 50 cents. You saw how easy it was for this guy. You can be a winner too!" He handed Martha a fluffy teddy bear. She nuzzled her nose into the soft pink furry bear and smiled from ear to ear. I put my arm around her shoulders and we continued around the mid-way.

There was a piece of paper on the ground that caught my eye. I bent to pick it up and realized it wasn't just a piece of paper; it was a five-dollar bill! I quickly tucked it into my pocket and looked around but no one even noticed. I didn't feel like it was stealing but, if someone nearby had claimed it I would have had to give it up to them for sure. This just seemed like a "rabbit foot" at work!

"Come on, Martha. Let's get something to eat."

Martha wanted to have a shiny red candied apple. She had never tasted one before and we giggled as she tried biting into it and had trouble sinking her teeth through the candied surface. I had pink cotton candy on a paper cone. We walked around nibbling on our treats, sharing bites with one another and enjoying the sights of the rides. We went into the big top tent. We didn't get to see an actual show but they were rehearsing and preparing for the big show so we got to watch the elephants moving around in the centre ring. There were five of them and they moved in sync with one another and the trainer had a stick in his hand and would raise the stick and the elephants would raise their trunks in unison as they each placed one front foot on a drum type stand. Then, the trainer would waive the stick in a circle above his head and the elephants would stand up on their hind legs and turn in circles.

There were four trapeze artists that climbed up a rope ladder to a very high height. There were two men and two women. The women were dressed scantily and in the most revealing costumes I'd ever seen on anyone. I looked at Martha and she winked back at me. The trapeze artists were amazing as they would do all sorts of somersaults in the air from one swing to another. There was a huge net under them so if they did happen to fall, they wouldn't kill themselves but when the real show would be performed, there would be no net. We were only there for a few minutes; I would have liked to stay longer because Martha was enjoying it so much but I knew we had a lot of walking ahead of us.

"We'd better get going, Martha."

ℰℂℛ

We continued along the railway tracks. I knew this rail line was in the direction of Regina and if we followed it and kept off the road, we could get far enough out before we started hitchhiking. We'd walk as far as possible before it was dark and then get on the road. I hoped to be riding in a car by the time it was dark.

We didn't have to stay on the railway track as long as we kept it in our sight and went the same direction. We were safer to be in the fields we hoped. I couldn't believe how wonderful it was to be walking in a field of wheat with the sun on my face and a beautiful summer breeze blowing through my hair and the smell of earth and wheat.

Red-winged black birds perched on the bulrushes in the ditch and butterflies all seemed to be happy to see us. One landed right on Martha's shoulder which made her very happy. She said that if a yellow butterfly lands on you or flies close to you, it is a sign that a departed loved one is coming to say "hello" to you. She thought this must be her mother who was coming to say hello and to wish us good luck. Dragon flies swarmed about eating mosquitoes—thank heaven for that! It reminded me of my carefree days back home on our farm.

I took Martha by the hand again as the ground was a bit uneven. It was so nice to hold her hand and show her that I would take care of her.

"Donnie, can we get to Regina today?"

"Well, if we can hitch a ride along the way, I think it is very possible. I just don't want to try hitching a ride until we put a bit more distance between us and the hospital in case someone from there has missed us and is driving around looking for us."

"What can we do once we get to Regina?"

"We'll figure that out as we go. Just concentrate on walking now and thinking about how great it is to have this day of freedom."

There was a cloud building and it was extremely humid. Martha had taken her sweater off and wrapped it around her waist. I unbuttoned my shirt a bit and we trudged on. In some places it was easier to walk alongside the road in the ditches but the grass and weeds were high enough that we were not too easily seen from the cars passing by. There were wild roses and black-eyed Susan wild flowers growing along the road. Martha stopped to take some dirt out of her shoe and I quickly picked a little bouquet for her. I used to do that in the summer for my mother and I wondered if I'd be able to bring flowers to my mother again one day now that I was free.

"I've never been to Regina. What do you want to be when we get to Regina?" Martha asked as she sniffed the bouquet of flowers.

"Well, I haven't given that much thought up to this point. But, I guess I like farming and I think that is what my father would have liked me to do. I suppose that is kind of a lost dream now though. If Father had lived, I likely would have been taking over the farm. So, I guess I'll just have to wait and see what the future brings me. What do you want to be Martha?"

"I am not sure but I know I love younger children. I'm already missing Lily, or "Lulu", as she calls herself. I feel sort of bad taking off and leaving her. Now who is going to brush her hair for her and watch out for her? So, anyway, I wonder if I could ever be a teacher. I suppose that is a ridiculous thing to think of ever happening."

"Why do you say that? Of course it is possible. You are smart enough and you should believe that you can do it one day. I think you'd make a wonderful teacher. You love little kids and you are always patient and kind to them. In fact, you are kind to everyone."

I put my arm around her shoulder and she laid her head on my shoulder and we were completely happy in that moment. We were friends and we were enjoying our freedom. We were sharing our thoughts and it was so nice to be able to talk without worrying that we were being watched. We could hold hands and not feel like we were being watched by disapproving eyes. I had never felt so close to another human being.

I know I loved my parents and my sisters but this was different. Martha had lived what I had lived. She had been raped and beaten and abandoned as I had been. We knew without words what each had suffered. We held one another up sharing this beautiful moment of freedom. We were one in spirit.

Chapter 17

I don't know how far we had walked but it was beginning to get really black with that heavy cloud cover. It started spitting big heavy droplets of rain and the wind got stronger. The air had turned really cold suddenly. Martha quickly put her sweater back on and buttoned it up. There was a crack of thunder and then, off in the not too far distance, a bolt of fork lightening struck. It reached from the heavens down to the earth like a big hand ready to grab us.

"Oh Donnie—I'm scared of lightening!"

"Run Martha! There is a farm up there and we can maybe get some shelter there until it stops raining."

We ran to what seemed to be an outbuilding maybe used for storing farm machinery. But it was locked. Now, it started to hail. I figured we had better just run up to the house to see if someone was home to let us in for a short while.

We knocked frantically on the door; the door opened and there stood Mrs. Barkley, our former teacher! I felt a sudden surge of panic and wanted to run for it but I knew there was no use in trying to run in this weather and she'd already seen and recognized us both.

"What on earth! Where did you two come from?" She seemed as shocked as we were.

"Hello Mrs. Barkley. We're sorry to barge in like this but we need a little shelter until this storm blows over. Could we come in for a little while? We won't be any bother to you," I implored. I hoped she wouldn't ask too many questions and I hoped the storm would stop soon.

"Well, you better come in hadn't you now. Come in quickly before you get hit on the head with that hail. My hollyhocks are being pulverized out there."

The house was cool. The curtains were drawn to keep the scorching sun out that had been so hot earlier. There was an oscillating fan humming in the kitchen blowing the scent of some baking into our nostrils. It smelled delicious.

"I've been baking buns today so the kitchen is in a bit of a mess. I've got a roast beef in the oven so you might as well stay for supper."

"That is so kind of you Mrs. Barkley." Martha unbuttoned her sweater and sat demurely on the sofa in the living room.

"Well, we really should get back on the road but I guess if it is going to be hailing out, we might as well stay. Thank you Mrs. Barkley for your kind offer." I took my shoes off and walked over to sit beside Martha.

"My husband went into Weyburn for parts for the combine today but he'll be along for supper any minute now. You two must be hungry."

"Well, we stopped at the circus in town and had a treat but your supper smells delicious," complimented Martha.

"The circus?" she put her hands on her hips and looked at us with suspicion. I'd seen that look from her many times in class. "How'd you two manage to get to a circus and how's it that you landed way out here in the countryside?"

"Well, uh, you see they did an assessment on us last week. Yeah, and they found that there wasn't anything wrong with our mental capacity so they had no choice but to let us go free. We're going to hitch a ride to Regina and go stay with Martha's grandmother there until we can get jobs. I guess you could say we're kind of treating it like a holiday because we've never been to Regina before," I lied through my teeth, trying to keep an honest looking expression on my face.

"Oh, here's Henry coming into the yard now. I hope the truck doesn't get hail damage. Well, if it does it will be one thing but if the crop is ruined that will be another thing!"

Mr. Barkley was a rather stout man with a balding head. He had a bulbous nose and rosy red cheeks. He wore a plaid shirt and the buttons were straining to hold together over his huge stomach. He wore blue jeans that were a little too short and he had a red handkerchief hanging out of his back pocket. He rolled up his shirt sleeves, washed his hands and combed what little hair he had as he came to the table. He seemed comfortable with having two strangers at his supper table as if this was a common occurrence.

The table was set with elegant womanly touches like my mother would have done. There was a floral center piece and a water jug with ice cubes and sliced lemons. There was a small silver butter plate with a little butter spreader knife and salt and pepper shakers at each end of the table so no one had to reach far to get the seasonings. There were steaming hot vegetables in serving bowls, and linen napkins at each place setting. I pulled out a chair for Martha and then sat beside her. I knew we were both nervous.

Conversation seemed pleasant enough in spite of my nervousness. Mrs. Barkley didn't ask questions much to my relief and Mr. Barkley just chatted about the hail and the crops and the price of wheat, etc. I tried to sound interested and make the odd comment but I really was not there. My mind was elsewhere. I knew by the sounds of the weather outside that the hail had stopped. The rain was letting up so I was anxious to get out again but Mrs. Barkley was now in the kitchen cutting apple pie for dessert.

Knock! Knock! There was a loud thumping on the door. Mrs. Barkley hurried to open the door. In walked two policemen in full uniform. My heart sank.

"In here officers," Mrs. Barkley motioned and led the policemen into the dining room where we sat frozen to our chairs.

"I phoned the police on you two and I don't want any trouble so you get up now and go with them to their car. You two are in a lot of hot water and, Donald, you are just a little liar telling me that story about being set free of the hospital. I know better than that!"

We did as she told us and what else could we do? We were caught; there was no point in trying to run or fight. I should have known we would never be allowed to leave on our own from Mrs. Barkley's home. That woman had never liked me for some unknown reason. She was the one responsible for sending me to the Snake Pit. She had always disliked me from the start. My hope had been that she might take pity on us; especially, because she had to know in her mind that we were not mentally ill or violent. We were "normal".

"We'll take it from here, Ma'am. Thank you for calling us and you folks have a nice evening now."

The officer grabbed me by my arm. I felt his strength immediately and knew there was not going to be any resistance on my part. They handcuffed each of us once we were outside the house and put us in the back seat of the squad car. Martha's eyes filled with tears. She dropped her head and the tears rolled down her cheeks and splashed onto her sweater.

"Don't cry, Martha," I whispered to her. "It will be alright. We had a great day and no one can take that away from us—ever!" I felt sorry for her and knew that I was responsible for getting her into this situation. I knew there would be consequences but I prayed that no serious harm would come to Martha. She didn't deserve any more than she had already suffered.

They took us to the police station. I didn't understand why they didn't just take us back to the Mental Hospital.

"Sit down here young man. We have some questions for you," the big burly officer motioned me to a chair. Martha was taken to another room to be questioned separately.

"So, you have been on an adventure today, eh?" he leaned back and balanced on the two back legs of his chair.

"Yes sir."

"Uh-huh. And you and this girl are sweethearts—correct?"

"Well, not exactly sir. We are best friends though."

"You ran away from the Mental Hospital and have spent the day together out there in the bushes. I'm thinking you probably had a little hanky-panky time together, right?"

"No sir, nothing like that!" I wanted to tell him that we both got enough of that sort of thing in the hell hole we escaped from and we didn't need any more of that from one another. We were satisfied with just being friends. But, of course, I didn't dare.

"You sure now? She's a mighty pretty young thing. You'd be a fool not to want to get some of that. You can tell me if you did. It would be understandable. You're a normal red-blooded young man so I'm sure you must have had a piece of her."

"No sir—absolutely not!" I was disgusted at his insinuations.

"We are just friends and I respect and care about Martha and I've never done anything like that to her and never will. She has had enough trouble and doesn't need that from me or anyone else!"

"Well, if you ask me, [7]Tommy Douglas should never have backed down on his original idea to sterilize you subnormal types. Too bad he changed his mind on eugenics after he became Premier of the province. We don't need your type having a bunch of babies and bringing any more retards into this world to feed."

I felt my face burning and I wanted to reach across the table and choke the life out of this prick. I had no idea who Tommy Douglas was and I had never heard the word

---

[7]Wikipedia – Tommy Douglas – MA Thesis on Eugenics

[8]eugenics before but I knew that I didn't like what this cop was saying.

Why did it seem that nearly every adult in my life in the past eight years thought they either had to have sex with me, smack me around or falsely accuse me? As far as "sub-normal" intelligence went, I was wondering about this cop and his mental capacity but I didn't dare say what I really thought. There was nothing to do but sit there and take it. Any response from me would have been used against me. I worried about Martha in the other room and what they were asking her.

After about two hours of this insanity, Martha was brought out looking pale and worn out. She was carrying the pink teddy bear I'd won for her at the Circus. She hung her head in utter defeat and had that glazed over look in her eyes again. Now it was my turn to feel defeated too. I'd led her to this and I had failed her.

---

[8]The science of improving a human population by controlled breeding to increase the occurrence of desirable heritable characteristics. Developed largely by Francis Galton as a method of improving the human race, it fell into disfavor only after the perversion of its doctrines by the Nazis. (Oxford)

Chapter 18

The rain ran down the window panes in blurry sheets that distorted everything in view outside. It seemed in sync with my distorted view on my life on the inside. Thunder rolled in the distance. The skies seemed to open up and it was as if everything I'd just gone through was being washed away down the river to the end of the earth. For the first time, I really felt like I was doomed and would never get out of the place. All the hopes and dreams of freedom and being a hero for Martha were being washed down into the gutters and out to the river into never-never land.

"Hi Donnie, what's the long face about?"

It was Joe standing there looking more like a man than a boy and smiling that big stupid grin at me.

"Joe! You're back? Man, you look good," I lied to him. He looked way too skinny and he was quite pale faced. "Are you feeling OK now buddy?" I almost started to cry at the very sight of my best friend. Here he was again coming to me at my lowest time. He seemed to have a way of showing up just when I could use a friend.

"Yeah—I'm practically as good as new. I'm just back today and they've put me in the same dormitory as you."

"Gee, that is great news. Martha will be happy to see you and she can use some cheering up. In fact, I can use some cheering up too."

We sat in the Day Room and I explained what had happened to Martha and me. It felt good to be able to talk about it with someone who wouldn't judge.

"God, that is crazy! Oops, I shouldn't use that word in here. But you guys really busted out of this place and got that far? Wow! I wish I could have been with you. If I hadn't had to stay in the TB annex, I'd have run away with you. You would have made it if it hadn't been for the storm likely. And can you believe the bad luck of landing in at Mrs. Barkley's place. That old bag! She just can't stand to see someone happy it seems. Just think, by now you would be living in sin in Regina together!" he laughed out loud.

"It's not like that between Martha and me, Joe. We have a special friendship and I care about her and I don't like people saying things like that about us. So, put a lid on it OK, buddy. It's not funny."

"OK, I'm sorry. I get it. Anyway, I'm kind of glad you didn't make it but I say that only because I just got out of the long ordeal in the TB centre and I'd be really lonely without you and Martha. You two are my only friends in the whole world. I've never had friends before I met you guys."

"Thanks Joe, Martha and I feel the same about you too. I'm glad you are back and we'll be the three amigos again—right?"

"That's us! The three amigos! I like that—uh, what's an amigo anyway?"

ജ്ഞ

Life returned to the same daily routine. I was like a robot doing chores as I was told but my mind was elsewhere. I kept replaying the scene of the escape into the countryside. I imagined I could feel the same breezes and sunshine on my face. I remembered the sweet smell of the wheat fields. I replayed it in my mind over and over and tried to imagine the same scene without the storm that had led us to the trap at Mrs. Barkley's farm. Who could have imagined for one minute that we'd have the misfortune of having Mrs. Barkley be the one to be living there. If it had been someone else, maybe they would never have called the police. If only we had not had to stop there. I chastised myself for taking precious time to stop at the circus. But on the other hand, that was one of the happiest moments in our lives and we both had something great to remember because of it. If only, if only . . .

Martha was not the same. She was too quiet and I understood why and I felt like it was my fault. She would never have had the courage to do this on her own. I had dragged her into it and now look at her. She was limp and lifeless. She was nice to me but she was distant.

"Martha, did you know Joe is back?" I wanted to bring her the good news.

"Yes, I saw him yesterday. He seems healthy again even though he seems pretty thin. I'm glad for him. I think he got pretty bored and lonely being in there all this time."

"Me too—he is in my dormitory now so that is good."

"Oh, I'm glad to hear."

"Listen, Martha—I am so sorry that things went the way they did. I feel terrible and I hope you aren't mad at me."

"Oh, no Donnie—I could never be mad at you. You haven't done anything wrong. I'm just sad that we didn't make it all the way. We nearly did it. It is just that now that I know how great it feels to be out of here, I hate it here all the more. But, I don't blame you. I thank you for showing me something wonderful. I had a day like nothing I've ever experienced before and that is worth a lot to me."

"Thanks—you mean everything to me. I feel I can face anything as long as I know we're still friends. I've been wondering and worrying about us."

"Donnie, you are still my best friend. I think we are just both a bit depressed after all we've been through."

"Ssh! be careful about using the word 'depressed', Martha. Don't ever tell anyone in here that you are feeling that way. We have to buck up and try to be strong. If they think we are moping around too much, they might give us shock treatment, God forbid. So, put a smile on your face and pretend if you have to at least until you can smile for real again. I hope that will happen for you soon."

"I know—or one of those ice baths! I don't ever want to have another one of those. I'll make sure I don't let anyone see me moping around. Thanks for the good advice. You are still my best friend," she reached for my hand and we had a brief moment of the innocent touch that sealed our bond.

We were back to having to be most careful not to be seen touching for fear it would be misinterpreted. If they thought we were being sexual with one another, we'd be separated for sure. It was as if our lives depended on one another. We both understood the importance of being careful not to jeopardize things by being seen together too often. I made a point of not sitting with her at meal time. I would sit with Joe. Having a friend in this place meant everything. It was like a lifeline.

ॐ

Having Joe in my dormitory was great. We managed to get beds next to one another and we protected one another from any sexual predators that came at us. We were teenagers now and we were stronger than many of the patients in our ward. Together, we were a force to be reckoned with.

Before I had the backing of Joe, I had found ways to avoid things during the night. I sometimes took a blanket and my pillow and hid under my bed once lights were out and people started snoring. I found that if I huddled up on the floor, against the wall, under the head of the bed, people couldn't see me as they walked by the foot of the bed. This worked best when I was younger and not so tall, of course.

One night I awoke to find one of the male orderlies lying beside me. He startled me and I tried to sit up. He patted me on my shoulder and told me to lie down. He said he was just so tired and he needed to catch a nap and then he'd leave. He didn't bother me that night. However, another night, I awoke to the realization that he was fondling me. I reached under my pillow and felt for my rabbit foot. I jammed the claws on the foot into his eye and he shrieked and rolled off the bed. He ran off to the bathroom holding his bleeding eye. He never bothered me again after that night. I think he was afraid of me and I felt empowered. I realized I had the ability now to defend myself.

After that incident, I kept my rabbit foot and my leather belt under my pillow every night. One night when a groper tried to molest Joe, I grabbed my belt and hit the culprit with the buckle end. I strapped him with all my might and sent him running to his bed. Joe sat up and looked at me and we both burst into laughter. We had to bury our faces in our pillows because we couldn't stop laughing.

Chapter 19

That autumn, I was allowed to take a wood working class as part of my Activity Treatment. There was a wonderful guy named Pete who was the instructor and main carpenter. He was a big man with broad shoulders and big strong hands that were calloused and rugged from all the rough treatment they received handing wood, sandpaper, metal and glue. Pete had twinkling eyes and a smile that went from ear to ear. He never lost his patience with anyone and that was a good thing because many of the patients that he had in his shop couldn't follow instructions worth a darn.

There were some, however, who did manage well and they were mostly guys who had been tradesmen or farmers before they came to the hospital. They already had some skills and were competent at handling some of the tools. I, on the other hand, had to start at square one and had everything to learn. My father was handy with making things and using tools and I remembered how much I loved sitting on the floor in his workshop watching him tinker on a machine or build something.

I managed to make a little table and chair set for children. Pete took orders for furniture items from the community. Sometimes there would be a church wanting some little chairs for the children's Sunday school classes or someone wanting wooden benches or tables for halls or a park. Pete would try to fill whatever orders came in and that kept him busy training patients to do the work. I was pretty proud of the job I had done. Pete was kind and showed me every step of the way what to do with all the tools.

"Make sure you always take good care of the tools, Son. They are expensive and will last a long time if we take good care of them. I expect you to put each tool up on that work bench or on the wall there where you get them from. I like everything put back in place when you are finished using a tool. That way you can always find them or if the next guy needs a tool, he doesn't have to go searching for it. Get it?"

"Yes, sir; my father had a lot of tools in his workshop on the farm and he was like that too. He was teaching me to use some things and how to keep things oiled up and running but that was a long time ago now. He died when I was eight."

"Oh, that's too bad. I'm sure he would be pleased to see you working so hard at building some nice furniture."

"Yes, I think so too. He liked to use scraps up and not waste materials. He never threw anything away. I remember that for sure."

"I think your father was a smart farmer and you are pretty smart too. I don't understand why you are in here. Did you do something or have nerve problems? You don't seem emotionally disturbed to me."

"No, nothing like that—it's a mystery to me too. All I know is that my mother married the hired hand after my father died. His name is Frank and he doesn't like kids and so now I'm here."

"Well, you are doing fine in my class and you are learning something that you will never regret learning. Maybe it will come in handy one day for you."

"Thanks Pete. I hope so too."

Joe was also in the class and he seemed to be a real natural with all the tools and he was eager to learn everything. We had fun working on projects together and we felt like men rather than boys. We were treated with such kindness and respect from Pete. We forgot everything else when we were working with our hands and learning neat things from Pete.

I thought back to my conversation with Nurse Beattie that day when she had told me how important it is to be busy and that busy hands helped to make you feel useful. I was beginning to understand this now as I worked in Pete's shop.

I remembered her explanation about how God might have had a plan for me; how He may have been saving me from having to live with Frank and my mother. Maybe if I had been living under one roof with Frank, I would never have had the chance to learn how to use these wood working tools. Somehow I doubted very much that Frank would have had the patience or the inclination to try to teach me to work with wood or to use tools. I couldn't picture us working together on anything.

If I hadn't ended up in this place, I would never have met Joe who stood up for me putting himself in danger against a bully like Art. I would have missed meeting Martha and all our heart-to-heart talks. I wouldn't have met a kind nurse like Nurse Beattie to talk to me about God, or Hank who kindly showed me some boxing tips. I would have missed Arnold who gave me the gift of the Webster's Dictionary and the even greater gift of an appreciation for reading and learning. And now, Pete, who was teaching me something useful.

Maybe God was watching after all. . .

ဢဢ

"Wake up gentlemen! Time to rise and shine! Don, get dressed and come with me." It was Nurse Jerry McCarron.

I wondered what trouble I had got myself into now and wondered what this was going to lead to. I pulled my shirt and pants on and sat down to lace up my shoes.

"Where am I going, Jerry?"

"We're going to see Superintendent Anderson. That's all I know."

I'd had very little to do with Mr. Anderson over the years other than to see him at some of the dances and picnic days. I had no idea what to expect.

Jerry knocked on the Superintendent's door and Mr. Anderson told us to come in. He greeted me with a smile and gestured for me to sit in the chair in front of his desk. Jerry sat in the chair beside me.

"Well, Donald, I have some good and bad news for you. The bad news is that your grandfather is dying. I'm sorry. The good news is that he has made a request from his death bed that his final wishes be carried out. He has made the statement that you should be set free from here. He believes you never should have been brought here. He has further stated that your sisters are prepared to take legal action on his behalf to see that you are released immediately.

Seems your grandfather never agreed with your mother placing you in here."

I couldn't speak. I was numb and had an out-of-body experience at that moment. Who was this man with his lips moving and what was he saying to me? I felt faint and my palms turned cold and clammy.

"Here, Don, have a glass of water. You have turned pale. I know this is a lot to comprehend. You are nearly 18 years of age now and you don't seem to have any real disability mentally so we think you should be given this chance to make it on the outside."

I sipped the water and wiped the sweat from my palms on the knees of my pants.

"Uh, I'm not sure I quite understand—uh, I'm sorry. Wh-at, I mean, where and when?" I stammered.

"Well, it's up to you but you can leave very soon— but there is a catch. You must have a job within a week of leaving here. I'll give you some money to get you started. I can make arrangements with the YMCA in Regina to give you a room for the week and that is it. No job, you come back here. I can't allow you to just wander the streets in Regina so that's the deal."

"But, how?"

"I will get you a ride from here to Regina. You'll stand a greater chance of finding employment there than you will here in Weyburn and I think a fresh start away from here might be advisable for you. I'll arrange for a ride for you right to the YMCA. That is no problem. But, I can't stress it enough, Don—you must get work and be able to support yourself. Once I'm convinced that is happening, you will be allowed to continue your life as you see fit. I truly wish you all the best and you can let me know how soon you want to go. I can have arrangements made for tomorrow if you like."

"Uh, yeah, I'd like to say good-bye to some people before then. But, yeah—tomorrow is good, I guess. Thanks."

I know I got back to my dormitory but I don't remember walking back. I was in a daze and still feeling that out-of-body experience. Was this really happening? It was so unexpected. It was all happening so fast but I went along with it willingly because I was afraid something might happen and the Superintendent might end up changing his mind. Tomorrow would be fine.

৪৩৫৪

I knew I had to tell Martha first but I wasn't sure how I was going to tell her. I knew I didn't want to tell her in front of anyone else. I waited until supper was over. I spotted her across the room. I waited until people began to leave the dining hall and then I approached her.

"Martha," I whispered, "Go to the linen room and I'll meet you there in a minute."

She looked startled but got up and headed out without any questions.

I followed and made sure there was no one around at the moment I ducked into the linen room.

"We don't have a lot of time Martha. But, I have something important to tell you. I don't know how to say it any other way than to just tell you—I'm being released tomorrow. The Superintendent is having me driven to Regina and I will be staying at the YMCA until I find a job. He's giving me a week to find a job. If I don't get one, he's having me brought back here."

"Well, I—what? I mean what the—how did this happen so fast?"

"It didn't happen fast enough," I tried to make a little joke. She wasn't smiling.

"My grandfather is dying and it is his final wish that I be set free because he knows I'm not crazy and I don't belong in here. I wish he would have done something before now for me but then I wouldn't have met you. So, I'm glad I met you Martha and I hope we can meet again one day."

"But, Donnie, how am I going to be able to live in here without you anymore," she broke down.

"I'm so sorry, Martha. If I could, you know I'd take you with me but I won't be allowed. I am not even sure I can make it work to keep myself out of here."

I hugged her to me and she cried quietly with her head against my shoulder. I kissed her forehead and then her cheek. She lifted her face to me and I kissed her on her lips. I couldn't let her go without at least that one kiss. It was sweet and innocent and so was she.

"You'll get out one day too Martha. We'll hope and pray to meet again. You know Joe will still be here and he's your friend too. He'll watch out for you."

"I know Don, but Joe's not you."

Chapter 20

The night before my release, I explained what was happening to Joe before bed. He sat beside me on my bed. He took the news with quiet resignation. He wanted to be happy for me but, like Martha, he was having separation anxiety with my departure.

"I'm sorry, buddy. I want to be happy for you but this is just such a sudden shock to me. I am going to miss you." Joe looked down at his hands. He couldn't look me in the eye. I understood.

"I know. It's a shock to me too. I don't know what to expect. I don't know if I'll make it. Maybe I'll be back in a few days if I can't land a job of some sort."

"Well, I'm sure you will survive. If anyone can do it, you can."

"Thanks Joe. I hope you'll get some good luck too and find your way out of here one way or another. Here, I want you to have this. It might bring you some good luck." I handed him my rabbit foot.

"Thanks pal. I'll hang on to it and hope it brings us together again someday." Joe patted me on the back and I gave him a hug. I was thankful for all the times Joe had been there for me. He was being as supportive now as possible. I knew we'd miss each other but I was glad he would be there for Martha.

☙੨☙

Jerry came to help me get ready to leave the next morning. He unlocked the cupboard and got out my suitcase that he had put in that same cupboard the day I first arrived. He laid it on the bed for me.

"Go ahead kid and open it and make sure your things are in there."

Well, the clothes I'd brought were all gone except the sweater that my mother had knit for me. It was still there but, of course, it was way too small for me now. Wrapped in tissue paper was the framed photograph of my mother. I wondered if she still looked as beautiful as she did in the photo. I wrapped it back up in the paper and tucked it back into the suitcase. Father's pocket watch was still there as well. I was glad to have it and I wound it up and sure enough, it still worked. At least I'd have something to help me know the time of day. I also made sure to pack my Webster's Dictionary.

"Pack a couple of extra pair of socks in there and some underwear. Here's a little bag with a razor and some soap for you. I figure you might need a towel and facecloth too. Here you go, pack them in there. You have a jacket in the cupboard too."

"Thanks Jerry."

"OK, kid. We have to make a quick stop in to the Superintendent's office on the way out. I'm driving you to

Regina. I don't mind though. It's an outing for the day and I like driving."

Mr. Anderson was on the phone when we arrived, but motioned us to come in and sit down. I looked around and noticed that the room looked the same as the day I arrived except now it somehow looked smaller than I remembered. Maybe that was because I was now a grown man. I had shoulders and muscles. My hair was thick and sandy blonde but my eyebrows and facial hair were dark. I had hair on my chest and my neck was too big to button my top button on my shirts. My hands were not calloused but they were large and strong. I had my father's watery blue eyes and his strong chiseled chin. My waist was trim and my legs were muscled. I stood 5 feet 10 inches tall. I came into this room a small boy but I was now leaving here a full grown man.

"Sorry to keep you waiting. I just need your signature on your file, Donald, before you leave. Ah, yes, here is your file. You can take a look and then I'd like you to sign down there where I've marked it with a red X. Just sign on that line there, please."

I looked at my file for the first time. I almost stopped breathing when I read the words: *Donald is a normal boy but he sometimes plays with dolls*. Below this was my mother's signature.

My God! There it was in black and white. The words used to keep me in this place for more than eight years! I had never played with dolls in my life but the day I held a doll in my sister's bedroom and Frank had stood glaring at me, with hatred in his beady little eyes, was the day that my fate had been sealed. He used that simple thing against a 9-year old

147

boy. I wanted to vomit all over that file. I wanted to rip that office apart but I put my shaking hand on that paper and signed on the line—Donald Johanson.

ഹൈ

My mind was still reeling over the words in my file as Jerry drove me to Regina. I sat dumbfounded and seething as the countryside seemed only a blur as we motored along.

"Ahem," Jerry clearing his throat brought me back from my thoughts.

"Uh, Don, you feeling worried?"

"Well, I guess I am a bit worried. I mostly just feel uncertain about getting the job. I know I have to get something right away."

"Yeah that's right but you know you have some skills, right? Like, don't forget that you're a good reader and that you know things about farming and animals; you've worked in the gardens so you learned about plants. Maybe you could work in a florist shop or a greenhouse. Oh, and you know how to build things from working with Pete in the wood shop, too."

"Yup, those things might come in handy, alright."

"You get yourself a newspaper and look in the Wanted Ads for work. You'll find something. The guys at the YMCA are nice and they'll help you out. You can ask them where to go and get directions from them."

"That's good, Jerry. Thanks and don't worry about me, I'll figure it out somehow. The one person I worry about is Martha. She relied on our friendship so much and I had to leave so suddenly. We can't even write to one another because I don't have an address yet and besides, I'm not sure

Martha will even want to write to me. And anything we'd write would be read by others since they read all the incoming and outgoing mail."

"Oh, I see what you mean. Well, if it gives you some peace of mind, I will check on her and watch out for her as much as possible and you know there are a lot of nice nurses like Nurse Beattie and Nurse Berk who like Martha. I'll tip them off to keep a close eye out for her too just to make sure she doesn't get down in the dumps too much."

"That does make me feel a little better, Jerry. It's not just the worry of her state of mind; although, I know she is pretty sad right now and maybe even a little pissed off at me. But, the big thing is watching out for the creeps that think they can hurt her or take advantage of her—you get my drift? That place has a dark side to it and I hope I never have to return."

The rest of the trip was passed by light conversation about the farms we passed and Jerry told me a few of his corny jokes to pass the time. Before I knew it, we were in Regina.

"Here we are, Don. I'll park over here and I'll come in with you to make sure we get you properly registered and settled into a room. Then, I'll go grab a bite somewhere and then head back to Weyburn."

Jerry was a good guy. We shook hands after we got me settled and I was a little sorry to see him go because I was now in a place where I knew no one and had no friends at all. I was alone in the world again, much like the first day in the Mental Hospital. But, I knew I had a mission to complete within the week and—by God, I was going to tackle it. As lonely as I might feel, I was determined not to

149

have to go back to the asylum. I had a fighting chance at a new life and I was going to give it my all.

Again, I remembered Nurse Beattie's good advice about keeping busy. I knew I'd be very busy and that would help me forget my loneliness. I also thought about what she had told me about how God is watching and how He has a plan for each of us. I thought maybe that night before I went to sleep, that I would try a prayer. I kept it very simple and to the point. I simply said, "Thank you God for giving me this chance at my freedom. Amen."

Chapter 21

Finding a job was a challenge. I circled anything in the Wanted Ads that I thought I might be able to handle and even some things that I had no idea whether I could handle or not. I wasn't keen on the one for a shoe salesman but I went to their store and filled out an application just the same. I knew if I got hired there that my first paycheck would have to be put toward some new clothes and a pair of new shoes from their store. I could tell that the people who worked there had to look sharp.

There was another one for a grocery assistant to work in shipping and receiving and to stock the shelves. I figured that one was decent but it didn't pay as much as the one for a dental clinic delivery man. I had to lie on the application for that one because they wanted someone with a grade 10 education and I only had grade 6. But, I felt they were overly particular on that score because I figured anybody who could read and knew numbers could handle being a delivery person. Besides, I was desperate. I'd been in Regina for three days already and hadn't landed anything yet. I knew it was cheating but I had to take the chance.

On the forth morning, I went to the main floor and the desk clerk told me there was a phone message for me from the dental clinic. I had to get the desk clerk to dial the clinic for me. This was the first time I'd ever used a telephone. I had the receiver upside down and the clerk reached over and corrected it for me. She shook her head. I think she thought I was playing around with her and trying to be funny. It was easier to let her think that than to tell her I had no idea how to use a telephone.

I got the job and was to start the next day. This was my ticket to my freedom and my independence! I celebrated by having a heaping helping of pancakes for breakfast.

ഈരു

The denture clinic was an easy walk from the YMCA. I got there 15 minutes early to show my ability to be prompt. I knew this was a good thing to do for starters. I remembered my mother telling me and my sisters that one should always be prompt and never late for an appointment. Funny how often thoughts of my parents popped into my head at times I least expected. It was almost as if I could hear their voices and words of advice. Things they were trying to teach me were still embedded. I liked this and it made me feel as if they were still with me in some way. I felt like they were giving me encouragement.

The receptionist was a pretty young woman who looked like she'd be close to my age. She had blonde hair tied up in a beautiful long curly ponytail. She had big blue eyes with dark eyebrows and long dark eyelashes. She wore a pale blue sweater set and a pink velvet cord with white furry rabbit tail pom-poms tied in a bow around her neck. The thought flashed through my mind that we already had something in common with my trusty rabbit foot and her rabbit pom-poms. I sure hoped that rabbit foot was going to bring Joe some good luck.

"Good morning. How may I help you this morning?"

"I'm Donald Johanson. I've just been hired to start as the delivery man for the clinic."

"Oh, pleased to meet you Donald. My name is Judy. Come back this way with me and I'll introduce you to Dr. Wagner. Would you like a cup of coffee before you start?"

"Oh, no thank you. I never drink it."

"Probably a smart thing—it just stains the teeth!" she chuckled. I smiled but didn't laugh. I was too nervous. I hoped she couldn't tell.

Dr. Wagner was a small Jewish man who had very little hair on top of his head other than around the base of his skull. He had a dark thick well-groomed beard and wore little round gold framed eyeglasses. He wore a shirt and tie under his clinical white jacket. He welcomed me with a strong hand shake.

"Welcome aboard, Donald."

"Thank you, sir. I see you certainly have a lot of certificates up on the wall." I tried to make some comment to disguise how nervous I was feeling.

"Yes, well, I was a dentist before I got into being a denturist. I was in a partnership and I decided I wanted something on my own and I found that I didn't really like working directly on the patients. So, here I am now. Follow me down the hall, please."

He took me to a small back room. There were wire baskets on shelves along the wall. Each one labeled with different dental clinics. On the counter top along one wall were stacks of labels, brown envelopes, string, pencils, stamps, a scale and several black binders standing beside a black telephone in the corner. There was a stool tucked under the counter and there were some cardboard boxes stacked to one side in the corner under the counter.

"This is where you can hang your jacket." He pointed to a coat tree in one corner and a boot tray beside it.

"If you get here early, as I expect you should, it would be nice if you would take turns with Judy to make the morning coffee. There is a coffee room just across the hall and Judy can show you where things are in there. There is an ice box so you can keep your lunch in there if you want."

"Thank you, sir. I'd be happy to help Judy with coffee in the mornings. I don't drink coffee myself so I'll have to get her to teach me how to make it."

"Well, I'm sure she will be glad to show you how to make the coffee. Now, when dental apparatuses and products are completed, they will be brought here to you and they will be placed into the baskets to go to the specified dentist offices. You will package them, and address the envelopes accordingly. The patient's name must be on a paper that goes inside the package. The particular dentist that requested the work done will need to be on the outside of that envelope. Some things won't fit properly in the envelopes so there are brown bags over there that will work. There are also little boxes there for some things that may be delicate and need to be protected from damage. The binders there have the different dental offices listed and their respective addresses and phone numbers. Judy is familiar with some of this and if you have questions, you can ask her or me. You'll get the hang of it all soon enough, I'm sure."

He continued to explain to me about the postage and the weighing of parcels and how to check the proper amount of postage in one of the black binders for the out of town dental offices. It all seemed rather straight forward and I knew there was a lot to remember all at once in the beginning but I felt like I would handle it just fine as long as I could deliver things within the city alright.

"Do you ride a bicycle?"

"Yes sir, I do."

"Well there is one out this back door with a basket and you are welcome to use it as I don't supply a delivery vehicle. You can ride it home at night and back to work in the morning. Look after it as if it were your own, please. You'll not only deliver finished products to the dentists in the city but you'll pick up the impressions they make and bring them here. Try to coordinate things with their offices so you aren't making more trips than necessary."

I was relieved to not have to drive a vehicle just yet but I did know how to drive a standard vehicle because I was driving my father's truck to the field when I was eight years old. I had to stand leaning against the seat, mind you, as my feet wouldn't reach the pedals if I sat on the seat. So, the thought was going through my mind already that one day I might even be able to buy myself a car now that I had a job. But, the first thing I needed was a place to live.

Chapter 22

For the first month, I continued staying at the YMCA but eventually I found a small furnished bachelor apartment just a couple of blocks from the clinic. I would ride the bicycle to parks on the weekends in summer and catch a ball game now and then. Weekends were a bit lonely at first but I walked and rode around to explore the city and that kept me occupied.

Judy was probably the closest I had to a friend in the beginning. She was bubbly and polite. She was helpful in my first week on the job. She explained which items needed to be boxed and which could be put in envelopes and she chatted about things going on around the area that were of interest.

"Have you seen the movie All the King's Men, Don?"

"No, I haven't been to any movies yet."

"It's up for lots of academy awards and should be a really good show. My boyfriend, Dave, and I are going and my roommate, Carol, would like to go. I was wondering if you'd like to join us for a double date Saturday night."

"Uh, well sure, I guess I could." I paused because I was apprehensive about any kind of date right now. I didn't go to the movies myself and wasn't sure I wanted to be on the hook to pay for a girl that I hadn't even met yet.

"Great! Oh, and you can just go Dutch. Carol won't expect you to pay for her. In fact, she'll insist on paying her own way in." I wondered if Judy could read my mind.

"Dave has a car so he'll pick us all up. I know you will like Carol. She's my best friend. She's pretty and she's smart and a really nice girl. You'll see."

"Sure, that's nice and thanks Judy."

ꙅꙩ

A date—my very first date ever! I wondered what in the heck I got myself into this time. But, Judy seemed positive about it all and I took comfort in the fact that we'd all be watching a movie so we wouldn't have to talk. I wondered what the heck do you tell a girl about yourself when you spent the last eight years in an insane asylum? God, I was going to have to think up some nice little lies if she asked too many questions. I could tell her I grew up on a farm and went to a country school. That was actually the truth for the first few years of my life so I wouldn't really be telling a complete lie.

It was unlikely that Carol grew up in Weyburn so it would be easy enough to keep that part of my life secret for now at least. Probably the less I said the better and if she asked too many questions, I'd just change the subject and maybe ask her a bunch of questions about herself. God, this was going to be a big expense for me. I had to get some new clothes. Well, I knew I needed some new shoes anyway for my new job and it was time to spruce up a bit.

I had no idea what was in style but I'd seen some men's clothes in the Eaton's catalog when I stayed at the YMCA. I picked out a light blue, short-sleeved shirt and a paisley necktie. I had to get the fellow in the store to make the knot in the tie for me. He showed me how to just loosen and slide the knot so I could put it over my head without untying it. I'd never had a tie before and wasn't sure I really needed one now but thought I should try to look more mature for my first date.

The young salesman was most helpful but he tried to get me to purchase an Argyle designed pullover. That seemed a bit too much all at once for my taste and besides it was the new autumn line and was way too expensive. I opted for a navy-blue cardigan sweater instead. I got a pair of black dress pants with the sharp crease ironed into them and pleating at the waist. I had never had a real pair of dress pants in my life. I'd only worn blue jeans up until now. Luckily, these items were on sale because I also needed to find a new pair of shoes. I chose a pair of black oxfords. The sales clerk tried to get me to purchase shoe polish and an extra pair of laces but I decided I'd already spent more than I wanted and I hadn't even paid for the movie yet. But, even if the date didn't go well, I needed the new clothes. So now I was set.

Carol Lipka took my breath away at first sight. As I opened the car door, Judy introduced me to Dave and Carol, I'm sure my eyes were bugging and my mouth might have been gaping. I had never seen anyone quite as beautiful. She had shoulder-length, black hair and with bangs across her forehead. Her dark eyebrows formed perfect arches above her big brown almond-shaped eyes. Her face was heart shaped; her lips were full and her perfectly straight teeth were white as snow against her tanned skin.

She wore a red-coloured, flared skirt with a short-sleeved, white tee-shirt. A red cinch belt accentuated her small waistline. Even her feet seemed pretty to me with white sandals that had straps around her tiny ankles. I noticed she had red toe polish.

"Hi, Don—pleased to meet you," she smiled as I slid in beside her.

I smiled at her, "Thanks and nice to meet you too."

"Hey, Don—I'm sure glad you could even things up for me so I wouldn't have to be alone with these two gorgeous gals!" Dave chuckled as he reached over the seat to shake my hand.

"Oh, stop it you tease!" Judy chastised him and he reached over to put his arm around her shoulder and she slid closer to him.

"I'm glad you could come too, Don. I've been telling Dave and Carol about you and how great it is to work with you."

"Thanks Judy. I'm really looking forward to the movie and it's nice to be out with people. Nice car, Dave. I envy you having your own car."

"Well, it gets us around. It's my Dad's old car. I bought it from him at a deal he'd never agree to for anyone else!"

The movie was really interesting even though it was about an American politician's life. It was the first time I'd seen such a serious film and Broderick Crawford played his part well. After the movie, we all went to a soda shop and I did offer to buy Carol a drink and she accepted. Conversation was pretty simple as we all chatted about the movie for the first while. But, it did eventually come around to what I'd feared the most.

"So, are you from Regina originally, Don?"

"No, I lived on a farm outside Weyburn. I just moved to Regina recently."

"Weyburn! That's where all the crazies live!"

"Dave! That's rude. Ignore him, Don. He thinks he's being funny." Judy gave Dave the evil eye.

"Oh, I'm used to hearing that. I'll just say one thing and that is that we don't have 'crazies' roaming our streets in Weyburn like you do here in Regina. We keep ours all locked up. You're probably a lot safer on the streets in Weyburn than you are here. And, probably if the truth were known, not everyone in there is crazy." That shut them up and I hoped I hadn't said too much already.

I turned to Carol and asked, "Where are you from, Carol?" I needed to reverse the line of questioning and get them off of questioning me.

"I was actually born in the Ukraine. My parents came here to get away just before the war."

"Yes, we met when we were in elementary school together. Carol had to learn English but she's so smart, she learned very quickly," Judy piped up. "We've been best friends ever since."

"Judy tells me you like ball games, Don. Maybe sometime you and I can take one in. Maybe the girls would come along; or, it could just be me and you." Dave was making an attempt at smoothing over his blunder about Weyburn and the comment about the "crazies".

The conversation turned to other things and the pressure was off. I wondered if Carol would want to see me again or if this blind date was as far as things would go. I hoped for another date but dates could cost money so I'd have to wait and save a little money up. I figured if Dave used his car for any further double dates, I'd have to kick in for a little gas money to be fair to him. I didn't mind that but I had to watch the money flow.

Chapter 23

I did get the courage to ask Judy if she thought Carol would like to see me again. The answer was "yes" and so we double dated with Dave and Judy for a ball game and we went on a picnic one afternoon in a park. Another time Dave drove us to a lake and we spent the afternoon on a beach. These dates took the worry of having to spend a lot of money that I just didn't have yet.

Carol was stunning to me in her bathing suit which was a red with white polka dots, two-piece suit. The bottom was a little flirty skirt that flipped when she walked. The top was like a halter that was revealing the shape of her bust. I tried not to stare but it was difficult and I darn sure did stare when she wasn't watching me.

Her hair was tied up in cluster curls with a silk scarf wrapped around and tied in a bow on top. With her hair up in massive curls, I could study her neck clearly for the first time. She had a long neck it seemed and it reminded me of the beauty and elegance of a swan. I knew I was really falling for this girl and it made me wonder about myself.

I couldn't help but wonder about my sweet little friend, Martha. I hadn't forgotten her entirely but I'd been so busy living my new life and trying to adjust to so many new experiences that I'd let myself forget the past. I sometimes really wanted to forget my past but I didn't want to forget Martha. I had never allowed myself to lay a hand on her in any way that might seem inappropriate. I had always felt we were really just good pals and yet, I think deep down, if I had been allowed to spend time with her in a normal life, we might have become sweethearts. But, I never felt living in that hell hole was the right time or place for me to have a romance.

೫೦೦ನ

Silver bells, silver bells, soon it will be Christmas Day . . . the music on the radio was playing Christmas carols. I was feeling particularly happy these days. Carol and I were officially sweethearts. We were going steady but I didn't own a ring to give her to wear like guys usually offered to girlfriends to make the relationship official. But, she said she didn't mind. She was too polite and sweet to care about that detail. However, I decided that I wanted to get her a ring for Christmas. Judy told me to go to The Bay department store and that I should consider a pearl ring because they were very popular.

It was Christmas Eve and Carol had invited me to come to her house to meet her parents and family. I was excited but nervous. I wondered what they would think of me and maybe even more importantly, what I would think of them. Carol came from a big family. She had three older brothers and two older sisters. She was the youngest. There were also a lot of aunts and uncles and cousins so when they got together for Christmas, it was hectic, noisy and crowded. The fact that I had spent so many years in a crowded asylum made it rather easy enough for me to feel some level of comfort in this situation.

Rose Lipka was a warm and welcoming woman. She had the same dark hair and dark eyebrows as her daughter but she was a little on the plump side. The way she cooked and fed the family was likely why she had earned some of those extra pounds. In the years to come, I never seemed to see her without her apron on or without a grandchild hanging on to that apron.

"Welcome to our home, Donald, and Merry Christmas." Rose threw her arms around me and her husband grabbed my hand and shook it while others in the living room looked up to view the new stranger in their midst. I could feel my face turn red. I wasn't used to hugs on first meetings. In fact, I didn't remember being hugged much at all in my life.

"Merry Christmas Mr. and Mrs. Lipka—it's nice to meet you." I handed them a box of chocolates that I had brought as a hostess gift. I'd read in a magazine that I'd picked up in a barber shop that this was the etiquette for a guest to follow. I think that other than the ring for Carol, this was the first gift I'd ever presented to someone.

"Call me Rose and you can call my husband Henry. We prefer that."

"Come with me." Carol grabbed me by the hand and took me around the living room to introduce me to all the brothers and sisters and aunts, uncles, cousins and grandchildren. I knew I'd never remember everyone's name. They all smiled and made an effort to make me feel welcome.

"What can I get you to drink? We have beer, wine, vodka . . ." asked one of the brothers, named Steve. He was a good-looking young guy with the build of a football player and the striking looks of a movie star with his black wavy hair and his handsome smile. He was studying law at the University of Regina. I thought he seemed a little cocky. Maybe I just wasn't used to someone his age having so much self-confidence. I tried to not judge him too quickly.

"Oh, I don't drink alcohol." I felt my face flush again as he stopped in his tracks and looked at me as though I was from Mars. It wasn't that I really disapproved of a drink but I had never had a drink and I figured I wasn't about to start that night with all Carol's family around to observe how I might act. I knew enough that it could affect one so I was choosing to be cautious. I wanted to be on my best behaviour.

"What? No beer or anything? How about a Coke then?"

"Yes, that would be good. Thank you."

Carol motioned me to follow her to the dining room. I had been so nervous that I had hardly taken notice of her until now. She was dressed up for this special evening in a red velvet dress with a black patent belt to match her shiny flat black patent shoes. She smelled pretty too. She always smelled good to me. Her hair was in a pony tail and she wore pearl earrings. I made a mental note of that and thought my gift for her was going to match her earrings very well. I had the pearl ring in my pant pocket but wanted to find a special moment to give it to her. That might be difficult with all these people around.

The dining room table was very long. It was, actually, two tables pushed together. It was covered with a red satin table cloth and set with rose-patterned china plates with matching cups and saucers. There was a centre piece of roses with tall slender candles on either side. I had never seen anything so beautiful and I had never yet eaten a meal by candlelight.

There was a Christmas tree in front of the living room window. It was decorated with bright coloured balls, icicles and twinkling coloured lights. This was a real home all decorated for Christmas with a huge family all chattering and laughing. I wondered what my own family was doing this Christmas. I wondered if anyone missed me or was wondering about me.

"Don, come sit over here. My sisters will sit over there with their kids so they can help feed the little ones."

"Oh, sure—this is so nice, Carol. Everything looks so festive. And you look festive and so pretty in that dress— and you smell good too," I whispered to her.

"Thank you. I think you look very handsome too." She winked at me. God, I thought she was so cute and no girl had ever winked at me before. I liked her spunky playful mood.

The food was amazing. I had never imagined having fish for supper on Christmas Eve. My family always ate turkey at Christmas dinner. Carol explained that the Ukrainian tradition was to have 12 meatless dishes due to the Nativity Fast or Advent to do with the proclamation of the birth of Jesus and his second coming. The 12 dishes represent the 12 apostles. The family does not eat until they see the first star appear in the night sky. Once we were all seated, Mr. Lipka (Henry) asked us to bow our heads and he said the Our Father.

I felt a strange, yet warm, emotion in my heart at that moment. Something resonated from my past when Father and my grandparents were still alive and we went to church on Sundays. I remembered how much I had always loved going to church during Christmas. I had not felt this for so many years and it touched my heart in that moment and it surprised me.

After the prayer, everyone made the sign of the cross on their foreheads with honey and Henry prayed, "In the name of the Father, the Son and the Holy Spirit: may you have sweetness and many good things in life and in the New Year."

There was pedeheh or pierogies—Carol said either name meant the same. There was sauerkraut, borscht, peas, mushrooms, doughnuts filled with jam, kutia (a poppy seed, honey and wheat dish), cabbage rolls with rice, salad with beets (I'd never seen beets in a salad before), bread, dumplings and stuffed fish.

I was overwhelmed by all this food but Rose was insisting I try everything and I didn't want to offend her so I did my best to taste a little of everything.

I had never eaten a pierogi before and on my first bite, I almost gagged. It was like eating raw dough. The way Carol's brothers wolfed these things down—I figured they must be something special. Over time, I became quite a fan of these when fried in butter and onions, served with sour cream and bacon; however, this first experience was not quite the best.

After this glorious feast, the women cleared the table and the men moved to the living room. The small children sat on the carpeted floor playing with toys and some of the older children went to the basement to play.

"So, Don, Carol tells me you moved to Regina from Weyburn." Henry pulled up a chair from the dining room as the sofa and living room chairs were all taken by the brothers and cousins.

"Yes sir—that's right." I thought, *here it comes . . . the question period.*

"Where do you work?" Now the brothers were watching me and I felt like there was a test coming my way.

"I work for Dr. Wagner at the Denture Clinic on Hamilton Street."

"I see. And what does your father do in Weyburn?"

"Uh, well my father was a farmer. He passed away some years ago. He was attacked by a bull and hemorrhaged to death."

The women began coming into the living room and the men jumped up to give up their seats and more chairs from the dining room were being brought into the room. One of Carol's sisters, named Ruth, went over to the piano and began playing Christmas carols. The children came flooding back into the room and everyone began singing and requesting favorites to be played next. I was glad for the musical interruption to Henry's questioning and the scrutinizing from the brothers. During one of the carols, I nudged Carol and whispered that I wanted to have a private moment with her.

We went through the kitchen and into a back porch area. There, I gave her my Christmas gift. I had wrapped it as best I could. I watched her face as she opened it and she lit up with a wide-eyed smile and I knew I had done the right thing.

"Oh Don—I've never had anything so beautiful! Thank you. Golly! It fits perfectly. You are the best boyfriend a girl could have!"

She kissed me and it was a long passionate kiss. This was a kiss I'd been waiting for. We had kissed before this but this was a kiss that told me something very special was on her mind and I knew we were heading for a deeper and more meaningful relationship.

"Wait here, I'll be right back." She ran upstairs and came back with a gift for me. I opened it. It was a smooth, black, leather wallet. I thanked her and used this as an opportunity for another long kiss.

"I figured you needed a wallet because I noticed you always just had your money rolled up and in your pockets. I hope you like it. It is genuine leather."

"Oh you bet I love it! I could tell it was real leather right away by the smell. Gosh, I've never owned a wallet before. Thank you so much!" I embraced her for one more kiss.

"Carol, Don—you kids out here? Come back and sing some carols. You are missing all the fun." Rose smiled at us as we came back into the kitchen. I knew my face was red. She had that knowing look on her face that told me she was onto me. But, at least she was smiling!

Chapter 24

I was grateful for my job and Dr. Wagner was always kind to me. However, it was a struggle at times during the winter months to get around the city on a bicycle. Sometimes, the streets were not cleared of the snow so I would ride on the sidewalks. But the sidewalks were not always shoveled off; so, I would be "zigging and zagging" from street to sidewalk. Ploughing through the snow drifts was tricky; sometimes, I took a spill and parcels flew out of the basket. I had saddle bags on the back end of the bike where I packed the smaller parcels. It was exhausting to peddle in even a few inches of snow; therefore, I couldn't always make good time. Many times I would have to walk the bike through the snow drifts.

Struggling with the snow was one thing but the bitter cold was the worst. There were days when it was so cold that it hurt to breathe in the air. I wrapped my face in a woolen scarf and it helped but it would get wet and icy around my mouth. There were times I had frost on my eyelashes. I found that wearing mitts was better than gloves for keeping my hands warm; but, even with mitts, I had numb fingers when I came indoors to the warmer air.

I wore a knitted toque on my head and pulled my hood up to break the wind. I found it too difficult to ride a bicycle wearing anything too long so my jacket had to be no longer than just below my waistline. Winter snow boots were far too awkward for pedaling the bike; so, I found a pair of second-hand Mukluks made by local natives. These were hand made from lightweight, soft leather which allowed for ease of peddling the bicycle. They were fur lined and came up to my knees so they worked when walking through deep snow. They kept my pant legs dry and they were very warm.

I soon learned that I also needed long underwear to wear under my jeans. Not only did they help to keep me warmer but, if I fell off the bicycle, they prevented me from getting soaked to my skin right away. Of course I had to learn the hard way and get wet a few times before I spent the extra money for the "long Johns", as they were called.

One afternoon, after coming back to the office looking like a snowman and with wet knees from falling in the snow several times, Dr. Wagner looked at me and said, "This is no good for you, Don. We will use taxi service for next couple of weeks until we get better weather and you will ride in a warm car. No more of this for you, Son; I am afraid you will get pneumonia."

He also suggested that I work at getting a driver's license and told me that next winter I would drive his car on days like this or I would take the taxi. I was not going to suffer the cold and icy conditions any longer. I was very thankful. I didn't want to complain but I was glad that the doctor had made this decision.

Getting through the rest of that winter was much easier. I didn't want to take advantage of Dr. Wagner's generosity so as soon as the weather broke and the streets were clear enough, I was back on the bicycle. Once the snow started to melt, and the streets became slushy, I had to resort to the taxi once more. My Mukluks were only good in snow; if they got wet, my feet would get wet as well. I had to purchase a pair of rubber boots for the wet conditions.

I studied the literature for the requirements to pass my driver's license. I knew I would have little difficulty doing the driving but learning all the driving rules that applied to driving in a city was a bit challenging for me. As a young boy on the farm, I had driven from the house to the field but that was a totally different thing than driving in busy city traffic. When I passed the test and achieved my license, I was as proud as if I'd just got a degree from a university.

Dr. Wagner trusted me with his car and I was always very careful driving it. I loved to drive but I was always fearful that something might happen while I was driving his car and I'd be held responsible. I never took his vehicle without his permission. I only used it when necessary. I promised myself that one day I would have my own vehicle.

I set myself a goal to begin saving money. I opened up my first bank account and put a small portion aside from each paycheck.

ଈଔ

"Don, are you ever going to introduce me to your family?" I had been dreading this question but knew it was coming. We had walked from Carol's house for an ice cream at the soda shop and then stopped at my place to be together for a while before I had to walk her back home.

"Well, yes, someday I hope to introduce you but you know I don't have a car yet. They don't live in Regina, you know so I'd need a car."

"I think that is a lame excuse, Don Johanson! There are buses, you know—or maybe they could come here. I am beginning to think you are worried that your family won't like me or they might not think I'm good enough for you. Maybe you think they wouldn't like me because I'm Ukrainian!"

"Oh, God, Carol—no—it's nothing like that at all. You are more than enough and you are too good to be true, in fact. Sweetheart, come here. Sit down. I have wanted to tell you something about myself that I haven't had the courage to share with you but I think it is only fair to you that I explain it now. When I'm done, you may change your mind about me but I hope that won't happen."

"What are you talking about Don? You are scaring me."

"Well, this is hard for me but I'll try to start at the beginning. I told you I grew up on a farm near Weyburn. Well, I did live on a farm; but, I was only there until age nine. See, I told you that my father was killed by the bull, right?" She nodded in agreement but looked like she was about to start crying.

"My mother took up with our hired hand on the farm and he proposed marriage to her but it was with conditions. He hated kids and so my three sisters were sent away to work for neighbours and one sister went to live with my grandmother. But, I was taken to the Mental Hospital in Weyburn and left there. They told me I was going to a summer camp on a farm with lots of boys my age to play with." God, I'd finally spit it out and told someone.

"Oh my God, Don! Are you kidding me?"

"No, I am dead serious. I'd never kid anyone about this."

"But how could they? I don't understand. Your mother actually agreed to that and left you there at that age? I'm sorry I just can't imagine a mother doing that!"

We sat for the longest time and I shared my story with her about Martha, Joe and the rapes I had endured. She began weeping. This was enough for her for now. I looked her in the eye. I was trying to read her and was afraid she would reject me after this.

"Do you still want me?"

"Oh Don—for sure, I do! More than ever I love you and I want us to spend the rest of our lives together." She put her arms around me and we both shed some tears. I had never felt so loved, respected and cared about as I did that night. We made love for the first time and it was so right. I was with the woman I loved and was going to marry.

Chapter 25

It was July of 1952. We had already been to Judy and Dave's wedding the year before. Judy was now expecting their first child. It was two years since I'd given Carol the pearl ring and I already had enough to buy her engagement ring. We knew we were going to get married but Carol insisted that I would have to ask her father for her hand in marriage. She refused to wear the engagement ring until I spoke to Henry. She explained that it was tradition and that her father would never fully respect me if I didn't follow proper tradition.

Henry was a robust, strong, proud Ukrainian who loved his family and worked hard. He and Rose had raised a big family and every child had great love and respect for both of them as parents. Henry could be stern but he was never unfair. I hoped he would grant his consent. I didn't know what the heck I'd do if he didn't.

One night after a delicious, filling supper cooked by Rose and Carol, I asked if I might speak to Henry in private. We went into the den and sat in the twin leather armchairs. Carol was his youngest child. She was his baby girl and I think he knew what was coming but he was darn well going to make me sweat it out and carry through.

"Henry, I hope you know how much Carol means to me. We've been dating for three years now, and—well, Henry, I'm in love with your daughter and am asking for your permission to marry her."

"I have seen how close you two have become. Rose and I have come to love you like a son. There's no reason why you two shouldn't get married as far as I'm concerned. But, before I consent, there is just one thing I must clarify. As much as I love and respect you, Don, if you ever hurt my little girl, you'll have me and my sons to face and it won't be good."

"I'd never hurt Carol, Henry. I have never struck a girl or woman in my life and I have no intentions of ever hurting her or any other person for that matter."

"That's good enough for me! Now, I think we should have a little something special to celebrate our bonding and your good news."

He walked over to his liquor cabinet and brought out a bottle of Vodka. He poured us each a small shooter and we toasted and knocked it back. I had my first and maybe last taste of straight liquor. I did my best to take it down like a man but I couldn't help coughing. He slapped me on the back and then opened the door to the den.

"Rose, Carol—come in here! We have some celebrating to do!"

෪෮

We were married the next month on August 17. Carol chose to only have one bridesmaid and she chose Judy so I asked

178

Dave to stand up for me. Of course we had the full mass wedding in a Ukrainian Catholic church. Henry and Rose wouldn't have it any other way. It was what Carol wanted too and I accepted whatever the family wanted. They all accepted me. It gave me a sense of worth to belong to such a wonderful large family.

Judy led the bridal procession wearing a turquoise, floor-length gown and carrying a cascading bouquet of pink flowers. She had given birth to a baby boy in May and already had her figure back in shape. As I watched Henry escorting Carol down the aisle, I felt a lump in my throat as my beautiful bride came to meet me. Henry stopped and stepped to the side and Carol joined me in front of the priest at the altar.

She wore a full-length, Chantilly lace gown that Rose had sewn for her. Her sisters had helped Rose to sew tiny round pearl buttons down the back of the dress and on the cuffs of the long sleeves. She wore the pearl ring which I had given to her on her right hand and I placed the gold wedding band on her left hand as we exchanged our vows.

If I thought this family celebrated Christmas in a big way, it was nothing compared to how they celebrated a wedding. There were more relatives than I had already met. They came from surrounding cities. Henry and Rose had both come from a large family. Most of their relatives lived in Canada and they all had families as well. We could nearly pack a hall with just family but there were many friends as well. People danced, gave speeches, ate and drank. The food kept coming. Rose just kept putting food out for the throngs of relatives that stopped by the house to party on even more after the wedding. People were happy and you could tell this family had enough love to go around the world. We were so blessed.

ଌ୰ଈ

"Don, can you step into my office for a minute?"

"Sure, Dr. Wagner." I hoped I wasn't in trouble on my job.

"Sit down, Don. I want you to know that I have been most impressed with your work here."

"Thank you doctor, I appreciate that very much."

"I know that you lost your father when you were very young and—well, you see, my wife and I lost a son when he was only five years old. He stepped in front of a car. My wife tried to grab him but he moved too fast and she just missed catching him by his hand. This was terrible for us but my wife has never quite forgiven herself. We never had any other children after we lost Sol."

"I'm so sorry to hear this sir. It must be very difficult for both of you even now."

"Yes, but we have learned to cope. But, why I'm telling you this, Don, is because you lost your father and I lost a son. I feel you are like the son that I could have had by now. If he were alive, I'd want to make him a partner in my business. My wife and I have talked it over and I am offering you a chance to apprentice under me to become a denturist. One day, you could take over this business when I retire. So, what do you think of my proposal?"

"Well, gosh, sir—I'm just surprised but I'm so honored that you would offer this to me."

"OK, so you accept then?"

"Yes, if you have confidence in me, I will do my very best not to let you down, sir."

"Good! Then we start tomorrow". He reached across the desk and we shook hands. "Lots to learn but we can take it slow and you will do fine. Oh, and I'll increase your wages from $30 per week to $45 per week to start. Now that you are a married man you will need an increase."

"Thank you so much doctor!"

"Oh, and you can stop with the 'doctor' and the 'sir' titles. Call me Ben. If we are to be partners, I think we can be on first name basis."

"OK, thanks, Ben."

I couldn't wait to get home to tell Carol the great news. She was still working at the bank but her hours were shorter than mine and she would be home before me.

I hurried through the City Park. The air was crisp and smelled of autumn leaves. They made a crunching noise under my feet as I hastened my pace even more. I was hurrying because I was cold but, also, I had exciting news for Carol. I put my hood up and stuffed my hands deep into my pockets to protect myself from the chill as the day was beginning to darken.

I ran up the stairs to our apartment. After our wedding, we had moved into the apartment shared by Judy and Carol when Judy married Dave. It was just easy for Carol to not have to move all her things somewhere else. I had nothing but my clothes to move so it seemed to make sense.

"Honey! I'm home!"

"Well, of course you are, silly. I can see you the minute you open the door. It's not like we have a foyer in this tiny place."

"I know, I'm just kidding with you and—man it smells good in here! Whacha got cook'n, good look'n?" I hung up my coat and took off my shoes. I blew into my hands to warm them up. I grabbed Carol and put my icy fingers on her warm cheeks to get a rise out of her.

"Oh Don! Your hands are like ice! Go run them under some warm water. We're having pot roast with vegetables, mashed potatoes and gravy. Oh, and I've got an apple crisp baking in the oven too."

I stepped into the bathroom quickly and washed my hands. I left the door open so I could talk to her from there.

"Well, I know neither of us drink very often but I have some good news for you tonight. I'm opening that bottle of red wine your parents brought over the other night." I went to the cupboard and brought out two wine glasses and started pouring.

"Ooh! That's exciting. Let's sit down at the table for a few minutes while the roast rests. You can carve it after you tell me your news."

"You aren't going to believe it but Dr. Wagner has offered me an opportunity to become his partner. He says he will train me as his apprentice and that he thinks of me as his son. Did you know they had a son who died at age five? He was run over by a car. His wife still blames herself for not being able to save him from stepping into the traffic. Poor woman. Anyway, I'm sorry I'm talking too fast. I need to sip some wine and slow down."

"That's terrible—I mean about their son. But that's wonderful about the partnership! Oh Don—here's to us! We have two things to celebrate tonight."

"Uh, two things?" I clinked her glass with mine and tilted my head to one side in a questioning pose.

"Yes, darling—you see, I have some good news of my own tonight. That is why I decided to cook us a special supper. I don't usually cook roast beef on a week night. I usually save that for the weekend . . ."

"Carol! You're rambling dear. Spit it out. What's your news?"

"I'm pregnant!"

Chapter 26

Old Man Winter hit hard on the prairies in 1952. A blizzard had people snowed in across the three Prairie Provinces. Children actually had to step over power lines to get to the school bus. People built tunnels through the snow to get to buildings. One newspaper reported a farmer having to cut a hole in the roof of his barn to get in to feed his cows. It was a winter like this that made me thankful that we lived in a city where city crews took care of snow removal, for the most part. I shoveled more snow that winter than I had ever before.

Carol's news of the baby coming sort of trumped my news of the partnership. I decided after that night that I should get a car so we could manage an emergency should one arise during the pregnancy. I also figured we were going to need a vehicle once the baby was born. I bought a 1945 red, four-door, Ford sedan from one of Carol's older brothers. He and his wife were upgrading to a station wagon for their family so we got their car for a very good price.

Carol worked until she could no longer hide the fact that she was pregnant. We needed the money. In those days, once a woman was visibly showing her pregnancy, she would be asked to leave her job—without pay. Luckily, she was small enough and with loose clothing, she was able to work up to her sixth month. With my increase in pay, we managed well enough. We were both quite frugal and knew how to save. We always had decent clothes to wear to work and church. Carol was a very good seamstress so she mended things and her mother would also help with making things for us. She helped Carol sew new curtains to brighten up our kitchen.

Once Carol started staying home, she and Rose got busy and sewed flannelette diapers, receiving blankets and baby clothes. Rose taught Carol to knit bonnets and sweater sets with matching booties. They were very productive and they enjoyed the time together.

With all Carol's family, we didn't have to buy a crib, baby carriage or toys. Everyone was so generous. We had all the baby furniture we would need and all the hand-me-down baby items from clothes to bottle warmers. It was all given freely and the women just shared everything. When someone in this family was in need, they didn't have to go outside the family for help. We were blessed.

ထာ

On June 8, 1953, at 3:28 am, our little Clara Rose Johanson, came screaming her head off into this world. Her middle name was in honor of Carol's mother, Rose, of course. The first name was my way of passing on something from my family using my sister Clara's name. I wondered where and what had become of my sisters.

I was proud of Carol. She did just fine. She took to motherhood very well and with all the other sisters and sisters-in-law and Rose, Carol had more help than she needed. I pitched in where possible and somehow we had managed to become pretty competent parents.

Having a child had opened up something in me that I had never thought possible. I had this instant feeling of unconditional love and devotion to this tiny baby. I had wondered if having a baby would hinder me in some way. I had some secret fears about the baby possibly coming between Carol and me. Would I be able to love someone else enough? Would Carol have less love or desires for me once she was a busy mother? I had some reservations but I always tried to be positive around Carol and the family. But once that little baby came, and I held her in my arms, I melted. I knew she was going to be the apple of my eye. There would never be anything in this lifetime that I would think was too much of an inconvenience when it came to her.

I also had a deep yearning for my own mother at this time. I now knew the love for a child of my own. How did my own mother deal, in her heart, with walking away from me? Did she wonder about her son? All these questions and feelings of abandonment came to the surface but I would suppress them once again. I knew, however, that I would never ever be abandoning my daughter or any child of mine. No one on earth could separate us.

Carol and I both loved Clara Rose so much that we repeated this whole scenario two more times! Doris Carol was born in 1955 and Jennifer Ethel was born in 1958. The names Doris, Carol and Ethel were passed on in honor of Carol and my other two sisters.

When Carol was pregnant with Doris Carol, our second child, we bought our first home. The apartment was no longer adequate for our growing family. This was a very happy time for us and we felt it was a great accomplishment to own a piece of property. It was a typical three-bedroom bungalow with a garage in the back yard. The yard offered room enough for a vegetable garden and a play area for the girls. I put up a swing set for them and built them a sandbox.

I loved gardening and was thankful that I had learned a few things about it while living in the hospital. I was meticulous about my garden tools just as I was about any of my other tools. Everything got washed after I had used it and each tool had a place in my little shed in the back yard. I hung things up and kept things in order. I remembered Pete's advice on this about how my tools would last me for years if I took good care of them. I smiled to myself when I remembered Pete and how much I had learned from him. It gave me pause to think back and to begin to see that I had several things to be appreciative about my time spent in the Mental. However, I was never appreciative to the point of wanting to return!

I loved the fact that Carol and I had our own home and we had worked hard for everything in our home. I liked having possessions. I had never had things of my own much while living in the hospital. Maybe that is why I appreciated everything and took such good care of things.

Carol loved puttering in our flower gardens. We put many new plantings in the front and back yards when we first moved into the house. Gladiolas were Carol's favourite flower and she would often cut a few and make a bouquet for indoors. She trimmed the stems every few days to make it last as long as possible. Having real flowers in the house always made it feel special. Carol's decorating and floral arrangements gave the house her special touch. We had a real home—and, of course, a real mortgage to go with it!

I often remembered Martha when I was digging in the earth or weeding gardens. I wondered how she was and where she was. I was bothered by thinking that she might be unhappy or that someone may have hurt her after I last saw her. This haunted me at times.

Carol was a "stay-at-home mom" now. Ben Wagner had retired and I was now the sole owner of the denture clinic. Judy no longer worked there. She was a busy mother like Carol. We still saw them and their family when possible. The women kept our friendship going and their children played with ours.

When Clara Rose was ready to start school, Carol was pregnant with our third baby. She asked if I could register Clara Rose for school. So, I agreed and took Friday afternoon off that week to meet my daughter's first teacher.

I removed my hat as I walked down the hallway to the classroom. The air smelled of floor wax, glue, paint and books. It was a smell that momentarily took me back to my own childhood in the old country school. Another parent had just stepped out and the teacher was sitting at her desk and was filing a paper so I didn't see her face until I'd got seated in front of her desk. She turned and I saw her face. My heart jumped up into my mouth. It was a good thing I was seated because I would have fainted if I'd been standing.

"Martha?"

"Oh my God, Don! Is it really you?"

I jumped up from my chair and reached across the desk and grabbed for her hand. She ignored my stretched out hand and came from behind the desk and put her arms around me and we just stood there hugging. When we released our embrace, Martha wiped her eyes with her lace trimmed handkerchief. She sat on a child's desk beside me rather than at her desk which would have put too much distance between us. She walked over and closed the door.

"You are the last parent I am seeing today so we can talk privately as long as we wish."

"Martha, I'm so happy to see you. What happened since I saw you last? How did you get out and how wonderful to see you as a teacher! I always knew you should be a teacher. Remember I told you that once?" I felt like I was gushing and thought I'd better slow down and let her speak. I was happy to see her but I was embarrassed and uncomfortable for the first few minutes. It had been so long.

"Yes—I remember everything. Well, to start my story, I escaped with Jerry McCarron. You remember him, the male nurse that was always good to us?"

"Yes for sure! Jerry was the one who drove me to Regina when they released me."

"Well, he not only took me away from that place but he married me. We have two children. A boy, Mark, and a girl, Lilly. I named her after Lulu from the hospital."

"What? Oh this is so unbelievable. So, you say you escaped? Do you mean you both just left there and Jerry left his job?"

"Well, it wasn't a dramatic escape like the day you and I ran away from there. We actually just walked out the door together and no one cared or asked any questions. As long as a patient was accompanied by a staff member, no one cared if you were leaving the building. As far as anyone might guess, we were just taking a walk. Jerry didn't like some of the things he saw going on and he became very protective towards me. He really questioned why children or young people of normal intelligence, like you and me, had to be kept year after year in that place.

So, we just walked out together one day and Jerry never went back for his last paycheck. We moved to Regina and he got a job in the Regina General Hospital. He didn't want to work in a mental hospital any more. He put me through teachers' college. He's been a wonderful, kind and loving husband and he's a great father to our kids."

"Oh Martha, I am so relieved and happy for you. You look wonderful. I often wondered about you and worried about how you were managing. I wanted to contact you but there was no way that I knew of to reach you. Visiting was not allowed and, frankly, I was afraid to try to phone you. I was so sorry about leaving you so abruptly and worried that you would hate me."

"Don, I could never hate you. I was very lonely after you first left—but Joe was still there and he missed you as much as I did. We valued our friendship even more after you were gone. With Joe's friendship, the kindness of Nurse Beattie and Jerry's love, I got through my darkest time."

I remembered asking Jerry to watch out for Martha but I didn't want to tell her that in case she felt that the only reason Jerry showed any interest in her was at my suggestion. I knew Jerry to be a good guy and I was just glad things had worked out so well for both of them.

"You know, I have thought about us over the years and I came to the conclusion that if we had been together in a different place in a different time, we might have . . ."

"I know, Don—I know. Things worked out the way they were meant to be. As they say, things happen for a reason. So, I've told you my story but what about you now?"

"Oh, yeah. Well, as you must have assumed, I did find a job in that first week. I went to work as a delivery guy for a denture clinic. The owner treated me like a son and eventually offered me a chance to become a partner in his business. I apprenticed under him and, after he retired, I became the sole owner."

"That's wonderful Don. I assume you are married and have a child since you are enrolling a child in my class. I have the name on my list here, Clara Rose, is it?"

"Yes, that's our oldest daughter. We have two little girls and another baby on the way. My wife's name is Carol. She's been so good to me—I don't know what I'd do without her."

I asked her if she knew what had happened to our buddy, Joe.

"Joe and Big Red both got placed into a Work Program. They worked at jobs, living outside the Mental. to see how they would cope in the world. People in the community rented rooms out to patients and gave them room and board at reasonable rates. Big Red got to go live on a dairy farm just outside Weyburn and Joe got to apprentice as a carpenter for a local contractor. He got his journeyman carpentry papers, got married and lives in Weyburn. He has just started his own business building houses. He called his business JJ's Construction. The JJ is for Joseph James."

It was the first time I learned what Joe's last name was. All the time we spent together over the years it had never occurred to me to ask his last name. It never seemed important at the time to me as a child.

"Gosh that is good news to my ears! Good old Joe. Good for him. And Big Red would be great working on a farm. He'd love that."

Something caught my eye in the corner of the room. "Martha, is that the pink teddy bear I won that day at the Circus for you? It can't be."

"Yes, it is. I just thought it might be fun for the kids in the class. It comes in handy on the first day of school when someone starts to miss his or her mommy. I just like having it here." She smiled.

We continued filling one another in on all that had happened. We promised we would share this news with our spouses and try to make a date to get together with our families. We both knew that finding one another didn't just happen. It was destiny. We were not going to let go of one another now. We were still friends and we cared about one another very much.

Chapter 27

With all the good things happening in our lives, you would think my life would be bliss. There were so many blessings for me and my family. I had a lot to be thankful for and I was thankful. However, there was something that bothered me and I think after I had a wife and children, it started to fester like a boil that was about to burst. Maybe meeting Martha again and hearing about Joe and Big Red had brought a lot of the old memories back. I don't know exactly but I had thoughts about what had gone on there and I felt like it was time I did something about it—but what and how?

Carol had noticed the change in me. I had a few nightmares that would make me talk or cry in my sleep and sometimes Carol had to shake me awake. Many times, although I wasn't trying to be sullen, Carol noticed my quiet moods. I was doing a lot of deep thinking and I guess I wasn't too good at hiding my thoughts.

"What is it Don? I know you and I can see that something is bothering you."

I shared my thoughts with her about my meeting with Martha and how all my old memories were beginning to haunt me. I was angry about being raped and abused and about Martha going through the same experiences and how no one had seemed to care. But I wondered why it was bothering me so much now, especially when I now knew that Martha, Joe and even Big Red were all doing fine. But the thoughts and old memories wouldn't leave me alone. I had trouble sleeping at nights.

"Don, I think there is even more to this than just your memories that are keeping you awake at nights. I'm not negating the terrible experience you suffered in the Mental Hospital but there is something that I believe goes even deeper with what is festering in you. I have wanted to bring this up to you before but didn't want to upset you or push you but I think you need to find your mother and your sisters."

I looked at her and just sat there. I had not thought this was something I'd ever pursue. I had thought that once I was part of Carol's loving family and we now had our own little family, that I would just bury mine. I felt they had thrown me away, so to speak, so I had figured I could just learn to forget about them too.

"Don, I think that you need to do two things for yourself that will be difficult, I know, but I think you must. I think you need to find your mother. You need to face her again. You need to find your sisters as well. Then there's another big thing that you need to think about as well. I think you should go back to that mental hospital and consider pressing charges against the people who may still work there that abused you. If they are still there, they are surely apt to be continuing their abuse to others."

"Oh my God, Carol. I don't know about that."

"Listen, Don. You know my brother Steve is a lawyer. We can talk to him. He'll know how you should handle this. But, you are going to have these feelings of abandonment from your mother and the feeling of being a victim of the abuse you suffered in the Mental unless you face these demons once and for all. You've done very well and we have a good life but I can see the change in you lately and I am worried. I'm willing to go with you if you want me to. I'm here for you, dear—you know that. We have to do something before you get sick. You aren't sleeping properly and you are getting run down."

I told her I'd think about it some more and we'd discuss it again. She had opened up to me and had shed light on the subject that I had not considered. I would think about it.

୫୦୯

I began to question myself about my true feelings toward my mother. If I was going to try to see her again, I had to be sure within myself how I wanted to behave. I pictured myself attacking her and screaming at her; maybe I could ram Frank up against the wall now that he was most likely a feeble old man, if he was even still alive. However, that didn't seem to be my style. I had managed to keep my cool and control my emotions while I spent eight years of my life in an insane asylum for no good reason so maybe I could continue to control my emotions now.

I had to stop and question myself about how I really felt about my mother. At the core of it all, I had nothing but love for her in my heart. That was the bottom line for me. She was still my mother and until Frank came into her life, she had been a wonderful mother to me and my sisters. Therefore, I decided that if I was to see her again, I would not attack her in any way. I would approach her in peace. I would abide by the Commandment, *Thou shalt honour your mother and father.*

The other issue of confronting the administration at the Mental Hospital was another thing. I had a lot of rage and disgust and fear about going back there. I thought about what Carol had suggested about talking to her brother who was a lawyer. That was a good suggestion and I would approach him first before making my final decision on this. For the first time in months, I slept well. I had come to some terms about how I would proceed. I said a little prayer and asked for "strength".

ഇൻരു

Steve came over one night and we discussed things. Carol and I had already disclosed my story about being held in the Mental Hospital to her family. We gave the information to Henry and Rose first and asked them to relay to the rest of the family. We both felt confident in the love of the family for us that we were sure we could safely share the story. They all reacted with understanding of my situation and they were all supportive and respectful toward me.

I had come to be very fond of Steve. He no longer seemed like the cocky, young university smart ass that I had first met. I really had not been fair in my first impression of him. He was just a fun-loving guy who had a lot of self confidence when I first met him and that did not mean he wasn't a good guy. He had worked hard to get his degree in law and he was the kind of man you could put your trust in and I felt very sure that if I had Steve representing me, I was in good hands.

He asked me questions and wanted the names of the perpetrators that had raped or assaulted me and Martha. Martha and Jerry were both willing to be witnesses. Martha had her own experiences and Jerry had knowledge of people who had abused patients. He had witnessed things and was willing to make a statement to that effect. So, Steve put together some documents and he offered to accompany me as my lawyer and was willing to speak on my behalf if I needed him. I said I would like him to come with me, for sure. He took care of booking an appointment for us.

It was a strange feeling driving up that long road to the front entrance of the hospital. Things were somewhat different now. It was 1968 and I was no longer a boy and I was no longer alone. No matter what the outcome of this might be, I was not alone. I had a great family behind me and I had a lot to live for and be thankful for. I focused on that. If I could accomplish something here today, that would be a bonus. If I failed, what could they do to me now? Send me to the snake pit? I don't think so. Not anymore! No one was going to touch me or harm me so I had nothing to lose by, at the very least, making my case known.

Other things looked different as we approached the building. There were no longer any flowers. There were no patients walking or working out in the flower beds. I saw no little huts in the trees and bushes as we drove under the trees that still formed that lovely shady arch along the road. I had heard that there was a new concept that work therapy for patients should no longer be used. Thank God I got out of there before that great wisdom was exercised. Fresh air and exercise and an honest day's work had done nothing harmful for most people. It gave them a sense of worth and purpose and helped them eat well because they'd worked up an appetite and they slept better as well without the need of medications.

We entered that same front foyer area and the smell of the antiseptic and floor wax was still there. It was a clean smell but a smell that made me queasy. It conjured up too many bad memories for me. We checked in with the receptionist and were escorted into the office of the Superintendent. It was not Mr. Anderson. He had retired years ago. It was a new chap by the name of Mr. Robert J. Wilson. He shook our hands as we introduced ourselves and we were all seated.

"How can I help you gentlemen today?"

Superintendent Wilson was dressed rather casual in khaki cotton drill pants and a summer shirt with no tie and soft suede Hush Puppy shoes rather than dress shoes. I supposed that things had changed here, too, and that people didn't dress up for positions like his as much anymore. His hair was a little on the long side and curled up around his ears and neckline. He wore large eyeglasses that looked like sunglasses to me.

"Mr. Wilson, my name is Steve Lipka and I'm Mr. Johanson's attorney. We've come today to speak to you about the matter regarding Mr. Johanson's confinement as a child in this facility. Mr. Johanson would like to explain things to you in his own words. I'm just here to represent him as my client so we can proceed with an understanding that he does have legal representation. Unfortunately, when he was brought here as a boy, he was not afforded any representation. Don, you can take it from here."

"Please go ahead Mr. Johanson," Mr. Wilson turned to me.

"Thank you. You can call me Don. I am more comfortable with that. Thank you for allowing us to speak with you today. I'll come right to the point." I paused just briefly and took a deep breath before beginning my story. No matter how many times I had told it, it was never easy.

"I was placed here by my mother and her boyfriend in 1940. I was 9 years old. I was brought here under false pretenses by these two people. They told me they were taking me to a summer camp where I would meet other boys my age. I was raped by a patient on my first night in this place and for years after that," I began. I was nervous and my voice sounded shaky. I cleared my throat to try to gain strength.

"Not only was I abused by patients but also, I was sexually and brutally harmed by some of the staff. I have named several people who I am prepared to bring formal charges against for sexual and physical abuse which I was subjected to while I was a minor confined here. Also, I would like my file today before I leave. I think you will see if you pull it out and read it that I was never mentally ill, emotionally disturbed, or mentally retarded in any way. There was no good reason for me to have been kept here. I am prepared to go public with my case, if necessary."

"I see. I've never read your file Mr. uh—excuse me, Don. Of course this all took place long before I was an administrator here. And you probably know that our hands were tied back then. If someone was deemed incompetent by a family member, we were obligated to keep them, regardless of their age."

"Yes, I'm aware of the standards, or should I say— lack of standards, this place operated under at the time; however, I am also aware that there was a strict rule about how patients were not to be manhandled or hurt by staff for any reason. Even if a patient was violent, the staff was never supposed to retaliate in a violent act toward the patient. Harming a patient was grounds for immediate dismissal. I'm here to tell you that rule was not enforced."

"Don, may I interrupt you for just one moment?" Steve interjected.

"Sure, Steve, go ahead."

"Mr. Wilson, you said if someone was 'deemed incompetent', the hospital was obligated to keep them. Is that correct?"

"Well, I think so. I would have to, uh . . ."

"Because, Mr. Wilson," Steve continued, "just as a point of reference here, a person is deemed to be incompetent when they no longer display the ability to make decisions that are in their best interests. I think you and I can safely agree that any 9-year old child is not yet considered competent to make any decisions of any great consequence in the matter of their own best interests at that tender age. If we base competency of a child on such a broad statement, we should probably put every child in a mental institution until they come of age. I think you can see how ludicrous this sounds."

"I see. Give me a moment and I'll have the file pulled so we can see what it says."

He called a secretary to find the file and she scurried away to the archives room. While she was gone, Steve went over some of the things he'd prepared in his document and letter which he left on the desk for the Superintendent.

Meantime, we discussed the individuals that I had named in the document. Mr. Wilson checked and verified that these people still worked in the hospital but that they were nearing their retirement. When the secretary returned with my file, I felt my heart speed up. I wanted these two men to read that file with me. I wanted someone to witness what Frank had been able to do to a mere child so easily without any attempt on this hospital's part to stop him.

Mr. Wilson opened the file and read. He sat silent and then passed the file over to let Steve read it. There it was again, that statement that took my childhood from me— *Donald is a normal boy but he sometimes plays with dolls.*

I told my story of how Frank had convinced my mother to leave me in this place at the age of nine and how I'd been left there for eight years of my life. I explained how I never played with dolls but had picked one of my sister's dolls up that day because I missed my sisters who had all been sent away according to Frank's instructions. I told them I knew now that the inference was that perhaps I was going to develop into a homosexual male because Frank had seen me holding a doll. This was, of course, ludicrous. And, as I pointed out, even if I had been a homosexual, that still would not have been any reason to withhold me as a child in such a place.

I asked Mr. Wilson if he was a father and if he would want his son or daughter left in a place like this to be manhandled by mentally disturbed male patients and abusive staff. Not only had I been traumatized and robbed of my childhood, but I had been robbed of any opportunity of an extended education. He listened and he shook his head in disbelief at what I described to him.

"Leave this with me for a few days, please. I am going to look into the matter. I'll make some enquiries and speak to these individuals. I will get back to you soon."

We thanked him, I picked up my file and we left. I felt relieved to have this much over. I'd have to wait to see what might come of it. Steve felt that Mr. Wilson was decent and that he would follow up with us as promised.

"Steve, you know I'm not really a drinking man but today, I'd like you to take me to a pub. I think I'd like a drink before we go home."

"Exactly what I was thinking! I could use a stiff one myself."

ॐॐ

About five or six days later, Steve received a call from Mr. Wilson. He told him that he'd talked to members of the faculty. Although none had witnessed any direct abuse regarding me, they believed what I was saying about these individuals. They told of other things they had witnessed and stated that it was common knowledge at the time that these individuals were abusing patients or, that in some cases, they allowed pedophiles who were mentally ill to abuse other defenseless patients such as in my case.

He also spoke to each person in question and explained to them that there was a strong possibility that charges may be brought forth against them. He informed them that he was putting them on immediate suspension until further notice.

After lengthy discussions with Steve and Carol, I decided that I wanted to proceed with legal action against the hospital as well as the individuals I was accusing. We decided that there was a serious case of negligence and abuse of a minor while in the time of confinement and that having my life disrupted against my will for 8 years was worth some compensation.

Steve brought another topic up for discussion as well. He told me that I should consider taking legal action against my mother and Frank for abandonment and deception which led to emotional distress and unnecessary confinement against my will. I said I would think about this.

Steve began working hard to build our case. He interviewed people and made a list of suitable witnesses. Martha, Joe and Jerry were all prepared to testify if necessary. Martha was prepared to add her own charges against the man who raped her and the inappropriate touching that Art had committed against her. Nurse Beattie was willing to testify that she had witnessed him touching her that day. Joe was also willing to press charges against Art for the beating he gave to Joe and me. The nurse who tended to having to stitch up Joe's chin that day was willing to testify that Big Red brought Joe to her in an unconscious state and that he told her what Art had done to Joe.

The doctor who had seen the bruises and abrasions on me was also contacted and he told Steve he had, in fact, filled out a report on the incident and that he had reprimanded and warned Art. There would be evidence of his report on file. Nurse Beattie, Nurse Berk and many others were on the list as witnesses to the fact that minor children were placed in the same sleeping quarters with known adult sexual predators. Also, they admitted to the fact that children (me in particular) were made to spend time in the Defective Ward, (Snake Pit). These witnesses would also attest to the fact that I was made to clean soiled beds and other disgusting tasks on many wards.

As the case mounted and files, reports, testimonies and other evidence were gathered, I began to feel as though I had the strength of an army behind me. It was quite empowering. I felt motivated and encouraged that something was going to come of all our efforts. The one thing still unsettled was whether I was going to lay charges against my mother and Frank.

CR୫ଠ

Our case never went to court. The employees, who were named, all chose to settle out of court. They were forced to resign, losing their pensions. I had the pleasure of sitting in a room with them and seeing their faces. I looked each one in the eye as they filed out past me. I wanted them to be sure to see me and to know they were defeated by me. They weren't dealing with a boy anymore and their dirty secrets were out in public now. They would suffer humiliation and the rumour mill would put them through the wringer. In a community the size of Weyburn, they might as well pack up and move away. Some of them did just that.

The government doesn't usually settle out of court but in this case they made an exception. They obviously considered the collateral damage that would cause a huge scandal and add to further the stigma against the mental hospital. Instead, by offering an acceptable monetary compensation and firing the guilty employees, they could preserve their image to some degree. They could almost look like the hero in the situation.

I felt I had accomplished something and I had been validated to an extent. Having my voice heard and believed meant a great deal after all these years. Knowing that these individuals had even a moment of shame and feeling of discomfort being brought up on the carpet gave me great satisfaction. Seeing them lose their jobs and respect in the community was justice to me—a "normal boy". The man I was now had managed to get justice for the boy I had been.

Bringing awareness to the new administration gave me hope for a better future for other children. I hoped no other child would ever be subjected to what I experienced. If it did happen, I hoped that someone might speak up if they witnessed something. The fact that other staff members had admitted they'd witnessed things was also enough to encourage me to believe times were, in fact, changing.

A load had been lifted. When it was over, I handed my file to Carol. She wept when she read it. I held her and thanked her for her support and her encouragement. I would likely never have done this without her insistence and her brother, Steve's, help.

Now, I had to think about seeking out my mother and sisters. I hoped I was up to the challenge and that I might find something positive in the end. I knew that Carol was right and that it was necessary to find them in order for me to go on. I needed to know if they were alive and if there was any hope of reconnecting as a family. If I didn't at least try, I would always be left wondering.

Chapter 28

"Dad, how long will it take to drive to Weyburn?" Jenny, the youngest was excited to be taking a vacation. We now had a 1960 Brookwood Chevrolet station wagon. Jenny had packed tiny suitcases for two of her favorite dollies. This was going to be a trip to accomplish the task of meeting my family. Carol and I had decided that after the stressful part of our mission was over, we would continue on to Carlyle Lake, Saskatchewan where we had rented a little cabin on Sandy Beach. We anticipated that our family would need some time to enjoy ourselves once we had dealt with meeting my family.

I had found my mother was still registered as living on the farm in the 1966 census records. She was still living with Frank. I had no way of knowing where my sisters were so I hoped to find my mother first and get information about them from my mother.

"It will take about an hour and a half to get to Weyburn. Does anyone need the washroom before we start out? I don't want you crying that you need a pee once I get driving."

"Dad! I don't think we need you to ask us about going pee! I'm 15 years old you know."

"I know, Clara Rose. But your sisters still need a little help. And mind your tone when you are speaking to me, young lady."

"Sorry Dad. Doris, move over. I don't want you touching me. You'll get my skirt wrinkled. Mom, make her move over!"

"OK, girls, we aren't even out of the driveway yet and you are already getting on my last nerve! Doris, give your big sister some room there, please."

Carol looked at me and we exchanged a look that we both knew to be saying, "God give us strength!" The girls were 15, 13 and 10. Need I say more?

ᔥᑎᘓ

The farm looked different to me. I always thought the house was so huge but now it looked smaller somehow. Perhaps that was because I was so small when I lived in it and now I was a 37-year old man. Although I was a man, was married and had three children, I felt like a child at that moment as we pulled up to the house. I was nervous and my palms began to sweat as I gripped the steering wheel extra hard. I knew I had to stay calm and not let my children see my fear. It was fear not only of what would happen but uncertainty about everything. What would we say? It had been 28 years since I'd seen her. What would she look like? Would she recognize me? Would she cry and tell me she loved me and be thrilled to meet my family?

As we pulled up to the front of the house, the door opened. I guess they had heard the vehicle approaching and before I came to a complete stop, there she was walking down the front steps to the driveway. Before I could open my car door, she came right up to the window. She was smiling. I rolled the window down. My heart was beating in my chest and I was sure everyone could hear it.

"Hello. Can I help you folks?" she was still smiling. She obviously did not recognize me. I had not dared to try to call her. I imagined that by this time she and Frank would have a telephone but I was too afraid she would not allow me to come to see her so I had taken the liberty of just forcing myself on her face to face. If I had warned her that I was coming, I was most sure that Frank would intercede and not allow her to speak to me.

"I guess it's been too long and you don't recognize me. It's me Mother—I'm Don."

Time had taken a toll to some degree but that was to be expected. It's just that even though I knew there would be signs of age, I was still somehow taken aback by it. There was no longer any shiny auburn hair and the soft curly lock that used to fall in front of her eye was no longer evident. Her hair was gray and cut short with a tight curly perm. Her once smooth and glowing skin had a worn and weathered look with deep crevices in her forehead and around her mouth. She wore glasses which seemed to slightly hide the deep-set eyes with dark rings and crepe-like skin beneath them. She wore a navy skirt and a pastel pink sweater set. She had a silver cross necklace around her neck. She still had that clean and tidy look about her. Her shoes were sensible black leather oxfords. She was still slim but she had a somewhat frail look to her as she approached.

She gasped and put her hand up to her mouth. Her body stiffened and she stepped back slightly from the car and the smile suddenly faded. Her eyes disclosed a look of shock and uncertainty. I felt a small feeling of satisfaction causing her to have this sudden look of fear. I couldn't help myself for that one quick moment. I felt no guilt. I think I was taking my cue from her reaction.

"Donald?"

"Yes, Mother, it's me alright. I figured it was about time I paid you a visit to introduce you to my family. This is my wife, Carol."

Carol reached her hand across my chest and leaned forward to manage to extend her hand to Mother. Mother hesitated and then responded with a limp, insipid, hand shake.

"It's so nice to meet you Mrs. Johanson."

"My last name is Schmidt."

"Of course, pardon me, Mrs. Schmidt."

I felt my muscles tense up with that. It annoyed me that she felt it necessary to correct Carol. I thought it rude, in fact.

"And these are our three daughters, Clara Rose who's 15, Doris who's 13 and Jenny back there who is 10." I smiled and hoped to see some warmth from my mother toward my girls.

Jenny rolled the back window down and put her tiny hand out and gave a little wave. Mother bent down and looked to see the smiling faces of her three granddaughters. She stood up straight again and folded her arms across her chest. No sign of warmth.

"Well, it's been a long time Donald. This is quite a surprise, I must say. I'm pleased to see you seem to be doing well and that you have a nice family. Where do you live?"

God! Who was this woman? I wasn't getting the reaction I'd hoped for.

"We live in Regina and I am a denturist now. We own our own home and Carol has a lot of family so we have a good life." I'm not sure why I felt compelled to blurt that out to her but I think I wanted to be sure to let her know that I had family and lots of it.

She managed a feeble smile but her lips were thin and tight. It was obvious we were not going to be invited to come inside her home—the home that should have still been home to me. The place I should have been coming to with my family for cookies and hugs and kisses from Grandma.

"I'm wondering if you can give me information about my sisters. Where are they and are they well? We're on a little vacation and we thought we'd see if it is possible to connect with them. I imagine they might be married by now and I have no idea what names they go by."

"Oh, well, Ethel married a fellow who works for the CP Railroad. They live in Estevan and have one child who had polio and now lives in a hospital in Moose Jaw, I believe. Clara married a business man who owns a furniture moving company in Brandon, Manitoba. I think she has four children but I'm not sure any more. Doris is also in Brandon and has three children. I get a Christmas card from her every year and she is married to a man who works in the Mental Hospital there."

She dropped her eyes as she mentioned the words Mental Hospital. I could almost see the gears in her brain turning and the guilty expression said it all. I again felt a little stronger and less nervous as I saw her squirming. She was obviously very uncomfortable. It was becoming clear to me that she had become distant with my sisters as she knew little about their lives; or, she was just not going to share much with me. Regardless, she was coming across as distant.

"Could you give me their addresses, please? Carol, do you have something to write on in your purse?"

"Well, I'll have to go inside to get my address book. Please wait here, I'll be back right away." Obviously, there was still no invitation to come into her house.

No one spoke a word in the car. We waited. Mother returned with her address book in hand and wrote the addresses on a piece of paper I handed to her. My fingers touched her hand ever so lightly. I now knew who this woman was. She was Mrs. Schmidt—not the mother I remembered. I lost my mother 28 years ago. I thanked her and smiled and said good-bye. She made no invitation to come back at another time. She was caught off guard— granted; however, she could easily have told us to come back at a later time if she had any desire to see us and get to know us. I backed up and we left. I vowed I'd never see her again.

As we drove, everyone was quiet. Then Clara Rose reached from behind me and put her arms around my neck and leaned her forehead against the back of my head. Carol looked at me and put her hand on my knee.

"Dad, was that your Mom? Was that our Grandma?" Jenny broke the silence.

"Yes, dear. That was my mother and your grandmother but she has not been part of our life and our family so she doesn't know how to react to us."

"Well, she should have invited us in so we could get to know her better. I wanted to see inside her house. I liked the look of her house and all the flowers she had on her front step and I wanted her to like me too." Trust Jenny to say exactly what she was thinking.

"Be quiet Jenny," Clara Rose spoke now. "Dad doesn't want to talk about it."

"Why? What's wrong?" Jenny asked.

"It's OK girls. I can talk about it. Let's pull into the park here. This is Nickle Lake just ahead and it used to be called the Seven-Mile Dam when I was a little boy. Mommy packed us a picnic lunch so we'll find a good spot with a picnic table and I'll tell you all about my Mother and me."

ഇൽ

Carol and I explained to our girls how I had been taken to the Mental Hospital under false pretenses and left there by my mother and Frank at age nine. We deliberately left out the part about being sexually and physically abused. We just left it at something like, "Some people were quite mean." They all listened with big eyes and gaping mouths in astonishment that triggered a deep sense of remorse in me. I hurt to the core telling this story to my children. I saw the sadness and love for me in their eyes. I hated to see that they had to feel pity for their father.

"Daddy, do you hate your mom now? You didn't say anything bad to her today but you should have!" blurted out Doris.

"Well, I admit to you that I've been hurt by what happened today. I had wished for a much different outcome. But, no—I don't hate my mother at all. I can say I don't like things that she's done but I don't want to hate anyone. Maybe I should have tried to phone her first. I probably handled this all wrong. We caught her by surprise and some people don't like surprises. I can't really blame her for that. I hoped that we would have been accepted and welcomed with open arms. I had hoped for a nice hug from my Mother. But, girls, I want you to try to understand that my mother was somewhat a victim herself."

"Oh no way, Dad! She's a bitch for doing what she did to you and your sisters."

"Clara Rose! You don't use words like that to describe anyone. I expect you to set a better example for your little sisters than that," Carol admonished.

"But Mom—I agree with Clara Rose. I hate that lady and I will never call her my Grandma!" Doris came over and put her arms around my shoulders and Clara Rose patted my hand.

"Girls, when I say that my mother was a victim I mean that she was a frightened woman when my father was suddenly killed. She had four children and no fixed income to live on. She had a lot of bills and expenses to keep the farm running. She was not the farmer. My father was the farmer and now she was left with heavy responsibilities. When Frank offered her support and companionship, she took it. She reached for a life line that he was throwing out to her and, the way she saw it, her daughters were almost ready to leave the home anyway. It was only me that she may have struggled with but she ultimately came to believe I would be taken care of where she left me."

"But didn't she ever go see you to find out how you were doing? Didn't she want to know how things were in that place?"

"No, Clara Rose. No one came to visit that place in the early years. It was not allowed. Letters and phone calls were monitored and controlled. People were kept from loved ones and friends and it is only by the grace of God that some of us got out."

"What does the grace of God mean?" Doris asked.

"I had a very nice nurse who explained that to me years ago. It means that God was watching over me and He must have taken pity on my situation and made things happen so I could eventually be released from there."

"Daddy, are we going to go back to that farm again? I still want to see inside that house and I still think that Grandma would like me if she would let me come in and talk to her."

"Jenny, you are an eternal optimist! And Mommy and Daddy love you, sweetheart. I won't say "never" but for now we have other things to do. We still have to go meet my sisters and then we are going to enjoy time on Sandy Beach at the cabin. Won't that be fun?"

"Yes Daddy. Can we go get some ice cream now?"

"You bet, Jenny. Let's walk over there now and then we'll pack up the car again and head to Estevan."

"Yay! Ice cream!" Jenny squealed as she ran ahead. Carol took my hand and again I felt such love for my wife and daughters. I had people that loved me and I loved them so much. I was a lucky man even though I still felt a hole in my heart over how my mother had reacted. I forced myself to push that thought aside and to try to be thankful for my blessings.

While the girls ate their ice cream, Carol and I took a walk down to the beach. I had come to a decision about something and wanted to talk privately with her.

"I've decided I don't want to sue my mother and Frank."

"I see. I have to admit that I'm a bit confused about this in light of how things went today with your mother."

"I just don't want to fight any more. This other thing with the hospital and the individual abusers is enough for me. I haven't the stomach for more fighting with an elderly couple."

"Well, what about just going after Frank then?"

"No—I've thought of that but I can't go after him without hurting Mother as well. Like it or not, they are as one. When I saw how feeble she seems to be, it makes me wonder if she's ever been happy. I noticed how her shoulders sag and she's becoming a bit bent in her walk. She's old and I feel like maybe she's suffered enough already. I suspect that her life with Frank has been so controlled. It makes me think that she's suffered enough. I don't think I could feel good about myself if I added to her suffering."

"OK, if you are sure."

"Yes, I am sure and I'm going to call Steve tonight when we get to a phone."

Chapter 29

Estevan was about the same size as Weyburn with a population of just over 10,000. It originated when the Canadian Pacific Railway emerged in the area. The major industry at this time was mainly the coal mines. Although the city was similar in size to Weyburn, it was not quite as pretty, to me, as Weyburn. There were fewer trees and many of the houses were very small. The people were a more transient population with people moving in and out as work on the railway moved employees about. I did find the main street to be most impressive compared to Weyburn, however, as it was a lovely wide street with decent shops and buildings on either side.

As we parked the car in front of my sister, Ethel's house, I was struck by how neat it looked. It was a small yellow house with a steep-pitched roof, dark green shingles and matching green shutters flanked the windows on the main level. It was a story-and-a-half home with an arched dormer window in the upper portion. There were window boxes under each window and they were full of colourful, cascading flowers and green ivy. I felt like we were walking into a storybook picture of an English country cottage as we opened the front white picket-fence gate.

"Oh, this is such a pretty house, Mommy! Look at the flowers and there's a butterfly. I want to catch it!"

"Jenny! Come here." Carol reached for Jenny's hand. "Let your Dad go first, girls. No running. Just let Dad knock on the door and he'll do the talking. Jenny, keep your tongue quiet for a change, please."

"OK, OK—jeepers!"

Once more, I had that nervous feeling in my stomach and all the same questions were on my mind. Would Ethel recognize me? Would she welcome us? Would I like her husband? Would he like me? So many feelings all balled up into this precise moment.

I knocked on the door. We waited and then I heard movement and someone shuffling to the door. The door opened and there was a very skinny man with a thick mop of slightly graying, wavy hair. He had a narrow face, protruding chin and one of the largest noses I'd ever seen. He wore a plaid shirt and suspenders on his trousers. I assumed that was necessary since there was nothing much to him to keep his trousers up! He smiled with a questioning look as he didn't know who we were.

"Good afternoon, my name is Donald Johanson. I'm Ethel's younger brother. Is she home?"

"Well, for gosh sakes—yes! Come on in. She's just out in the back yard picking some peas from her garden. Come right through here with me." He opened the door wide and patted me on the back and extended his hand in a friendly and firm handshake.

"I'm Jim, Don. Jim Hoy, Ethel's husband. I'm so pleased to finally meet you. Come on through. I'll get Ethel."

I smiled and removed my hat as we walked through the tiny but sparkling clean kitchen. There were cookies cooling on the counter and the smell of the morning's bacon for breakfast still lingered. There was a large window over the kitchen sink with white ruffled curtains all starched and looking crisp. The round table had a linen tablecloth edged with a striped border of primary red, yellow and green. A bowl of pears sat in the middle of the table looking very appetizing. It felt like a very cheerful kitchen.

"Ethel, honey—you have a special guest!" Jim called as he opened the back door and motioned us to go out into the yard.

A rather pleasantly plump woman stood up from her task of picking peas and turned to face us and looked up from under the wide brim of her straw hat. Thick massive red copper curls framed her still freckled face. She wore what looked like an old blue denim shirt of her husband's with the sleeves rolled up. It hung open exposing a light cream yellow tee-shirt and a full Mexican print skirt. She removed her gardening gloves and began walking closer to see if she could recognize us. She was obviously not able to recognize me at first glance.

"Hello Ethel. You probably don't recognize me, I'm . . ."

"Donnie? Is that you? Oh my God—it is you! I could tell as soon as you opened your mouth to speak. Oh God, come here and give me a hug."

I didn't have to be asked twice. I almost jumped over Jenny to get to Ethel and we embraced in the warmest and biggest hug I had ever experienced. She held me and I held her and we rocked back and forth almost dancing as we savored the moment. As we finally let ourselves relax, we stepped apart an arm's length, yet were still holding hands. We studied one another's faces. I could still see Ethel and her happy sparkling blue eyes that were now filling with pools of tears. Carol and Clara Rose were wiping their eyes. I hadn't realized it but now felt warm tears running down my own cheeks. I quickly wiped my tears and smiled. For the first time in a long time, I was crying tears of joy. We all were. This was the warmth I had craved and was seeking. I was welcome here. This was the sister who helped bring me into the world.

We were quickly invited in for tea and cookies and Ethel was insistent that we would stay for supper and overnight when we explained we were on a vacation. Although their home was tiny, she had a guest room and the sofa in the living room made up into a bed. She said she'd make a tiny bed for Jenny on the floor with the sofa cushions and the two older girls could share the sofa bed in the living room. She assured us that it would be no trouble and that we must stay.

"We need time to talk and try to catch up with things, Donnie. Please stay. Carol, I want to get to know you too. I'm so happy to see you all and look at your beautiful daughters. What are their names?" Ethel was chatting, asking questions and putting the kettle on to boil all at the same time. She still had that shrill and high-pitched, loud voice but it was like music to my ears. This was my big sister. I found her!

"Well, if Don wants to stay the night, I'm fine with that and thank you Ethel. I'd like time to get to know you too."

"Yes, that sounds great Ethel as long as you want us to stay, I'd love to spend some time catching up with you and getting to know Jim too."

"Dad," Jenny tugged at my arm. "She asked you our names".

"Oh, yes, sorry. These are our daughters, Clara Rose. She's 15 going on 18," I chuckled.

"Dad—really!" Clara Rose was at that age where she seemed embarrassed by her parents' comments quite often.

"And this is Doris Carol but we just call her Doris. Clara Rose is the only one who goes by both her names. And this little jelly bean is Jennifer Ethel. I guess you can see that we have passed on the family names of you and the other sisters. It was important to me to carry the names forward. I hope you approve."

"Oh, I'm so honored! That is very special and the other girls will be thrilled. You might be surprised to learn that Jim and I named our son, James Donald. So, it was important to me also to carry your name forward.

I don't know if you know or not but our Jimmy is not with us here. We had to place him in a home in Moose Jaw where he could get the care he needed. He contracted polio and is quite disabled. He was too much for me to continue lifting in and out of the wheelchair and with Jim Sr. being gone a lot on the rail, well—he's just better off where he is and we go see him whenever possible. Jim gets free passes on the railway so we go fairly often. He seems to be adjusted very well and is treated very well."

"Mother did tell me about your son having polio. She thought that he was living in Moose Jaw but she wasn't entirely sure and she didn't mention his name to me."

"Oh, so you've talked to Mother? How did that go?"

"Well, let's just say that it was a meeting but it was rather stiff and we weren't invited inside. I suspected that may have been because Frank was inside and she was fearful of us meeting. And to be fair, we did arrive unannounced just like we have done today to you and Jim."

"Yes, if Frank was there, that would likely be why she didn't invite you inside. You know, we tried in the beginning. When I was forced out of the home, along with the rest of the family, I did want to stay in contact with Mother. I was working on a farm not far away and I ran into her in Weyburn at times in the Co-Op grocery store. When I met Jim and we were planning our wedding, I invited Mother and Frank to come. They didn't come and I was really hurt. Jim was just plain mad."

"You've got that right! That was the last straw for me as far as they were concerned right there." Jim was lighting a pipe and the sweet smell of his tobacco wafted into the room.

"Yes, well anyway, it just never got better from there on. When I had Jimmy, I thought for sure she'd want to spend time with her first grandchild. She did send me a gift for him and a card. Once she saw him in his wheelchair after he got polio, she was visibly uncomfortable and that made me very angry. Up until then, I would have kept trying to have a mother-daughter relationship but that was it for me. No more. So, that's why she doesn't know much about our family anymore."

"I'm sorry to hear about Jimmy. But it sounds like you've done the best thing you possibly can for him and I'm glad you get to see him quite often. Mother told me that Clara and Doris are both in Brandon and that Doris does send a Christmas card every year."

"Yes, that is the only way she hears anything about any of us. Doris does seem to think it is important to have some connection. Perhaps she's right, I don't know."

"Mother said that Clara married a man who owns a furniture moving business—is that correct?"

"Yes, Cev married Milt Clark and they have four children; three boys and one girl. When Cev married Milt and settled in Brandon, Doris was not far behind. She lived with Cev and Milt for a couple of years until she met her husband Sam Hoy who just happens to be my husband's brother. Jim and I go spend most of our vacation time with the sisters. It is nice for Jim and Sam to have time together and we are all very close. Thank God for my sisters and brothers-in-law because after our experience at home after Father died, there was nothing much left of family for us."

"I'm glad at least you sisters have been able to stay connected. I had no connections with anyone." I didn't want to sound sharp with my remark but I couldn't help mentioning this fact to her. She seemed to feel uncomfortable.

Ethel got up to pour more tea and turned to the girls who were sitting pretty still listening to all this adult conversation.

"Would you girls like a Popsicle and you could take it out into the back garden. There are lawn chairs on the grass out there and you can watch the birds at the bird feeder.

There are lots of American Gold Finches out there most of the time. They are such a beautiful bright yellow bird. Here you go, there are two flavours—orange and strawberry. Pick your flavour."

The girls happily accepted and went outside. I was sure she had wanted the girls out of earshot for our conversation which was becoming more serious. Ethel sat down and blew on her hot tea before taking a careful sip.

"Don I know you were the one who was alone. You were the youngest and needed us and we weren't there for you. I'm so, so sorry. We did try once to go see you but they wouldn't allow any visitors at that time. Then we were so busy with having our babies and with Jimmy being disabled and Jim away, I was taxed to my limit here. You were never forgotten and we would cry every time we got together and talked about you. We did know that Grandpa was determined to take some legal actions to have you released. We went to see him when he was dying and he wanted us to promise we'd pursue it with his lawyer if you were not released before his death. His lawyer sent us notification of your release just days before Grandpa died. Right after that, Grandpa went into a coma and passed away.

By the time we were able to communicate between the lawyer and the hospital and learn that you had been staying at the YMCA in Regina, you were gone. They had no forwarding address for you so we hit a dead end. There was a Donald Johanson in the Regina telephone directory so I called but it wasn't you. There was no other listing."

"I'm glad to hear this. Thanks for explaining it to me and I was sorry to learn about Grandpa's dying as well. I had no choice but to head directly into Regina. In fact, I was told that was where I had to go. I was told by the Superintendent that I had to get a job within that first week or I'd be taken back to the hospital. So, I had no time to go look up Grandpa on his death bed, nor any means to travel back to Weyburn."

"I understand. Do you want to talk to us about how things were for you while you were away?" Ethel rubbed her hands together as she broached this topic.

It struck me rather funny that my chatty sister, who was never lost for words, seemed to be unable to use the words "Mental Hospital". How could I begin to describe my life for those eight years to someone who couldn't even bare to speak the words and give it a name? But, none of this was her fault. I had to keep that in mind.

With Carol's help, we both relayed the story one more time. Carol had heard it enough times by now that she could tell it as well as I could. Ethel put her hands up to her face and ran her fingers through her hair as she rested her elbows on the table. She held her head down, cradled in her hands, looking into that cup of tea while I described my first night in that asylum being raped by a pedophile at age nine. She pushed her teacup away as the tears began to fall. She reached in her apron pocket and took out a hanky and wiped at her eyes.

I told them about Martha and Joe and all the things that had happened to all of us and how Martha and I had tried to escape only to be caught and hauled back to the asylum. I told them about the Snake Pit and the Defectives and the shit and urine that I had been forced to clean up. I described the violence and abuse and I spared them nothing. Once I got into it, I wanted them to fully understand what I'd been put through while they were dating, getting married and having babies. I knew none of this was their fault but I was not stopping until I got it all out. Jim kept relighting his pipe and drawing on it and shaking his head in disbelief.

Carol explained about her brother, Steve, helping me to accomplish getting the individuals fired and the compensation from the mental hospital. Then she changed the subject to my career as a denturist. This eased the conversation to a level of tolerance for everyone. Ethel and Jim were able to smile again and gave their congratulations to me on my success and again complimenting us both on our beautiful family. Carol talked about getting our first home and some of the funny antics of parenthood. Carol always knew just what to say and how to handle a situation in the best way possible.

Our evening was pleasant. Ethel chatted about Cev and Doris and she telephoned them both so we could have a chat. However, at the cost of long-distance calling, we made it short and to the point. I let them know we had plans to come to see them and would be on our way the next day to Brandon. They were most receptive to the idea.

When we finally tucked into bed that night, Carol cuddled up to me and whispered, "This was a good day wasn't it darling?"

"Yes, dear, it was a good day."

Chapter 30

Heading east to Manitoba was really when I began to feel that I was actually on a holiday with my family. Up until now, I had tension and anxiety with the meeting of my mother and the meeting with Ethel. But, now, after the warm welcome from Ethel and Jim and the anticipation of another happy experience waiting for us in Brandon with my other two sisters, I felt light heartened for the first time since we'd left home. Also, it was rather exciting because I had never been out of the province until now. When I was a small boy on the farm, family vacations were unheard of during the Dirty Thirties. People were just working shoulder to the harness every day to put food on the table for the family. But these were better times and Carol and I had worked hard and this was something we had both dreamed of doing for a long time.

For the past several years I had been training another one of Carol's brothers to work with me during the summer. This was Robert who was just a year older than Carol. Robert was in university and was helping his parents to pay his tuition by working for me. He was studying law like his older brother, Steve. Robert was so quiet compared to Steve that I sometimes wondered if he would ever make it as a lawyer but he was not as interested in criminal law as he was in corporate law. He certainly had the brains to do whatever he wanted. Although he had that Lipka family resemblance, he was more slender than most of the other brothers. He had the same dark hair as the rest of them but he wasn't quite the dashing good looking hunk as was Steve. Robert was a more serious person.

He had a girlfriend that he'd been going with for about six years. Her name was Bella and everyone in the family loved her. She was the perfect match for Robert because she was so outgoing and so personable. Where he was quiet and almost awkward at conversation, Bella was chatty and at ease with most people. We all expected a diamond ring any day but he seemed bent on finishing his law degree and landing a job before he made that move. He fit in well in our office and had no problem learning what we needed him to do.

With the help of the other two women I had working for me, Robert was a great asset. I had one young woman who was the front desk receptionist and another who assisted me with the denturist work. Business had grown since Dr. Wagner had retired. Having competent staff allowed me a little freedom to finally have a family vacation.

I found the drive most enjoyable and I was deep in thought about the business. My thoughts turned from thinking about the business to soaking in the beauty of the prairies. The vast open space gave me such a feeling of freedom. There were fields of bright yellow sunflowers. It was amazing to see how every flower head on every stock was facing toward the sun. The flowers will follow the sun.

Amazing! There were crops of blue flax next to yellow mustard and the wind was just breezy enough to make the blue flax look like waves in water. Jenny wanted to get out and go to that lake. We had to explain to her that it wasn't water but a crop of plants with little blue flowers. She'd never seen blue flowers before.

There were cows in pastures standing up to their bellies in the cool water of the sloughs. Calves were feeding and other cattle were lying in the cool long grasses while red-winged blackbirds flew up from the ditches to scare us away from their nests as we drove past. We saw many beautiful horses running freely with their manes and tails flying in the wind. I was admiring all the country scenes and day dreaming of my childhood days on the farm when I could run through the corn and wheat fields, climb trees at whim, ride my bike and explore all areas of our land. I was brought back to the moment with the frequent splat on the windshield as grasshoppers and wheat midge butterflies made a mess as they were squished on the windshield. Good thing I had that bug screen on the front grill. It stopped a lot from coming inside.

"So, Daddy, um, like are Ethel and Cev and Doris all your sisters?"

My lovely moment of peaceful bliss was interrupted by Jenny once more. Carol was dozing and having her own moment of peace and quiet.

"Yes, Jenny, they are all my sisters. They are all older than me. Ethel is the oldest, then Clara and then Doris."

"So are they my aunties then?"

"Yes, that is right. And their children are all your cousins."

"Oh, like my cousins back home who are on Mommy's side of the family?"

"Yes, dear—that's right. You've got it."

"So how come you call your sister Clara, Cev? That's weird."

"Well, that is just her nickname. I think when Ethel was a toddler, she couldn't say Clara very well and it came out Ceva and that got shortened to just Cev. It is kind of the same as we call you Jenny instead of Jennifer."

"So, is Jenny my nickname too then?"

"Oh—for Heaven's sake Jenny! Stop asking Dad so many stupid questions while he's driving."

"Shut up Doris! Who made you the boss of me and what I say?"

And the war was on and the girls began hitting one another and Clara Rose tried smacking them both and that made matters worse. Carol woke up with a start. No kidding! And she went right into her Mother Mode and reached over the seat and pulled them apart and threatened them with further action unless they sat still and behaved.

"Stop it you two or I'll get Dad to stop this car and I'll bash your heads together. Now sit down and behave!"

Ah yes! Life was great on our first family vacation.

ഇരു

Brandon was a larger sized city and it was, for the main part, considered an agricultural community. It was known as the Wheat City of Manitoba. It was built along the Assiniboine River and this was key in the early history of the City's fur trade. It was located just about 75 miles east of the Saskatchewan border. I noticed the colour of the soil was a very dark, almost black compared to our Saskatchewan soil which was more brown. I thought this must be a very rich soil and great for growing crops and vegetable gardens.

We had no trouble finding Doris and Sam's house up on the north hill. Ethel had given me very good directions. Doris's house was rather similar to Ethel's place. It was a white two-story but instead of green roof and trim, this house had red shingles and red trim. The front walk was a curved, cement sidewalk that lead from the driveway up to the front porch. Like Ethel's place, there was a white picket fence around the manicured lawn. There was a large spare lot on the north side which was all garden. It looked well cared for with very little sign of weeds. There was an old 1951 sage green coloured Chevrolet Stylemaster sedan parked in the driveway.

I took a deep breath and rapped on the front door. Jenny was bouncing around having a difficult time as she had to go to the bathroom. She had gone not long ago when we stopped for gas but she had a very small bladder it seemed. Everyone else lined up on the steps behind me as the front porch wasn't quite big enough for us to all stand at the door.

The door opened and Doris clasped her face in her hands and her eyes and mouth opened into a beaming smile and her eyes began to tear up immediately.

"Oh here you are! Welcome Donnie and family. I'm so happy to see you."

She flew into my arms and we did the same little hug and dance thing that Ethel and I had done. She quickly wiped her tears away and wiped her hands on her apron and extended her arm to greet Carol.

Just then, a huge burly man stepped into the frame of the front door and he pretty much filled the doorway. He had thick wavy white hair and black eyebrows. He had handsome, chiseled facial features. He wore a blue sweater vest over a blue and white gingham shirt. He extended his hand to me.

"Hi there—I'm Sam. Pleased to meet you all. Come on in everyone."

"Yes, please come in and have a seat," added Doris.

"I hate to seem impolite, Doris, but we have a young gal here who is in bad need of your washroom, if you don't mind. This is Jenny and these two over here are Clara Rose and Doris Carol."

"Oh certainly, come with me, Jenny. I'll show you the way. By the way, Don, I like the names you've given your girls!"

"I hoped you would like that, Doris!" I replied.

"We've got a lunch ready to serve you folks but I'd better wait until Doris is back because she's the boss," chuckled Sam.

I knew Sam was a brother to Jim Hoy, Ethel's husband. But, they were quite different other than for the fact that they each had a great head of hair.

"This is my wife, Carol, Sam. She's my better half for sure."

"It's great to meet you Carol and I think Don was a lucky guy to find such a pretty wife. Your girls are all so cute too."

"You're too kind, Sam, but thank you," Carol blushed a little.

Jenny came bouncing back into the living room with Doris right behind her.

"Mom, Dad! You should see the bathroom. They have a powder-blue bathtub, sink and toilet! It's real pretty in there."

Trust Jenny to blurt out her opinion on the bathroom décor! What next?

"Have a seat everyone. We'll help you bring your luggage in after we eat lunch. I hope you all like cucumber sandwiches. I remembered that Donnie liked them when he was little."

"Oh yes, thank you so much. We all love cucumber sandwiches. I hope you haven't fussed too much for us. We're pretty simple folks you know," Carol rose from the armchair she had sunken deeply into.

Conversation flowed and lunch was followed by a pleasant afternoon of giving us a tour of their home and garden. Doris and Sam were very proud of their garden and you could tell they'd toiled in it to produce the healthiest and most prolific bounty of vegetables. Doris explained how she enjoyed canning and pickling and preserving a stock of vegetables to enjoy over fall and winter months. I could tell that these were hard working and frugal people. Much like Carol and myself, actually.

Doris explained that she had met Sam at a dance in 1945 just as the Second World War was ending. They married in September that same year. Funny to me when I thought about it—the world was at war while I was trying to survive my own world war in an asylum. It had felt like it was me against madness.

They had three children. Don, aged 23 (who Doris told us she had named after me), Robert, aged 21, named after a brother of Sam's and Margaret, aged 19, who was named after a sister of Sam's. Don was married with one child. He and his wife, Marie, a French girl from Quebec, lived in Winnipeg and Don was a successful car salesman there.

Robert was in the Canadian Air Force and was stationed at Rivers, Manitoba. He was still single and had promised Doris that he'd do his best to get home to meet me and my family while we were in Brandon. Margaret was in the university in Brandon but still lived at home. She arrived in the later afternoon.

Margaret was tall and slender and had Doris's big blue eyes and dark lashes. She had the same sprinkle of freckles across her nose and cheeks. She seemed quiet and a bit shy when she was first introduced to us. I felt like I was seeing Doris all over again the way she was when we had last been living as brother and sister in the same home. Margaret was polite and smiled but excused herself to get ready for supper. We had all been invited over to Clara and Milt's home for a family gathering.

"We'll have to take two vehicles. Sam I hope you've got gas in your car. Honestly, Don, Sam hates driving and he's had that old car since we first got married and it sits there most of the time so I never know for sure if we've got gas in it or not!"

"Well, that isn't your concern, Doris. I look after it and because I don't drive it often, why would I be out of gas?" Sam piped up.

ৎ০০৪

Clara's home was distinctly different from the other two sisters' homes. Her house was a tall, narrow, stone two-story house with architecture that seemed very European and old world in style to me. The front yard was very close to the sidewalk and was fenced with a low wire and wooden fence. This allowed passers-by to notice the colourful array of the mixed plantings of a very English garden. There were hollyhocks in deep reds, pinks and yellow. Roses unfurled their pink petals and pushed their way through the wire fence to soak up the sun. There were purple and blue hits of foxglove, lavender and delphiniums and an added punch of yellow morning glory vines that wound and twisted their way around the wire fence.

Even the front door seemed stately and aristocratic with a leaded glass window and a big brass door knocker. Doris rapped the door knocker and then opened the door and hollered in, "Yoo-hoo! Anybody home in this place? You've got company!"

"Oh, coming right away!" answered Clara and I heard footsteps on the stairs in front of us inside the entry hallway. Down the stairs came Clara, just like the "Queenie" she had always been—still elegant and beautifully dressed and coiffed. Her hair still blonde and shiny was now perfectly twisted into a French roll up the back of her head. She still had her figure and it was shown off splendidly in the fitted, pink Fortrel dress with the high Empire waistline. At her neck she wore a single simple strand of pearls and her shoes were clear slip-on heels that looked like Cinderella's glass slippers. Of course her nails were painted bright pink to match her toe polish. She was like something out of a fashion magazine. She smiled from ear to ear and when she got to the bottom of the stairs, she dashed toward us. She grabbed me in her arms and I lifted her off the floor and those "glass slippers" fell off her feet!

"Donnie, you're finally here. Oh my little brother! It's so good to see you. I've missed you for so long. Let me look at you!"

I set her down and just then, Milt poked his head into the entry hallway and made his way toward me to extend his hand. He was a big, strong brute of a man. He had a strong square jaw line and a thick neck like a wrestler. He wore khaki coloured denim pants and crisply ironed matching shirt. The sleeves were rolled up and it was obvious the top button at the neckline had to be left open to allow him to breathe. He had straight, dark chestnut coloured hair and one stubborn piece kept falling over his forehead. He was extremely rugged and handsome and a strong contrast beside my tiny, curvy sister.

"Welcome," he squeezed my hand in a strong handshake that nearly crushed my hand.

"Come on in everyone so we can all get properly introduced. It's a bit tight here in the hallway." Cev led us all through into the living room. We made the introductions and I could see Carol and the girls looking around the room in awe of the exquisite room décor. The ceilings were ten-foot height which gave the place an instant sense of grandeur.

There was a cream-white sofa placed under a very large picture window. The window was beautifully draped in rich gold brocade draperies and nearly reached the ceiling. In front of the fireplace, were two matching white Queen Anne chairs on either side of a small pedestal side table. A hard cover book lay on this table as though one of them had just been reading there. The coffee table in front of the sofa was glass. There was a brass cigarette lighter and ashtray on the coffee table along with a couple of decorator magazines. The area rug under foot was soft and also in a light creamy white colour. It almost touched wall-to-wall.

Adjoining the living room was a front parlor with a dark cherry-wood dining table and matching china cabinet. The table had been extended and had a white linen cloth on it with beautiful bone china place settings for all the adults. The front parlor had a large bay window and Chintz floral curtains that draped from ceiling to floor. A crystal chandelier hung over the table and sparkled like diamonds. Everything was sparkling for that matter. The house was spotless.

The kitchen was opposite the dining and living rooms on the back side of the house. It was spacious and welcoming with built-in cabinetry and lots of counter top prep space. There was a butler's pantry room where steps led to the basement. Everything was perfectly placed. Things in the kitchen were tidy even though Cev had been busy preparing the meal for us.

The square kitchen table with floral tablecloth sat in the middle of the room. This table had been set for the children with brightly coloured Fiesta dinnerware. There was a little blue vase with sweet pea flowers picked from her garden. Their sweet scent was mixed with the smell of a roast turkey. A smell of a home!

ৡৄৎ

Cev and Milt had met during the war. After a year of working as a domestic for farmers in our neighbourhood, Cev had moved to Brandon with a girlfriend and they were roommates in a boarding home owned by Milt's parents. Cev had taken jobs in the neighbourhood cleaning houses. She impressed Milt's mother and she also caught Milt's eye. They were married in 1943. Milt had not been able to serve in the war due to having a glass eye. He had an accident while moving a piece of furniture and a leg from a table had poked his eye out. He had worked for his father in the furniture moving business and had taken the business over when his father began to suffer from arthritis and was forced to retire. Milt and Clara spent the first year of their marriage living with his parents but once they were about to have their first child, Clara insisted they get their own place.

Clara and Milt's oldest child was Jack, aged 24. He was married with one daughter and worked as a liquor salesman for Seagram's in Vancouver, British Columbia. Carl, aged 22, owned a hair salon in Vancouver. He had followed his older brother Jack to BC. He was still single. Anna was 18 and had just got married to Ben Chalmers and they had moved to Victoria, BC. Ben was an accountant and had been invited to join an accounting firm in Victoria.

Clara lamented over how much she missed having her daughter around. She was heartbroken but was trying to adjust and get over being an "empty nester". She had named Anna after our mother. She explained this was her way of paying tribute to the mother she had loved and wanted to remember. She preferred to remember the first part of that mother-daughter relationship rather than the latter part.

"Now that I have you back in my life, Don, I have something happy to think about and you are not so very far away that we can't manage to see one another once a year, I hope."

"I hope so too, Cev. I can't tell you and Doris and everyone how happy this has made me to be back with my sisters and to meet my new brothers-in-law and hear about your families."

"I'll toast to that," piped up Milt and we all clinked our glasses.

Just as we were clinking glasses, the door bell rang. It was Robert, Doris and Sam's son. He had managed to get a 24-hour pass from the military base at Rivers and had caught a ride to Brandon just in time for supper. He was a tall lanky lad with big ears and large hands that looked too large for his thin frame. It gave him a bit of an Ichabod Crane look from the story of Sleepy Hollow. His shaven head made his face seem even longer than it was. But, his smile and his uniform made him seem quite handsome. He greeted us with a big handshake and then a hug. He was jovial and obviously the apple of his mother's eye. Doris beamed from ear to ear while he entertained us with a few of his latest air force jokes. He stayed for supper and then hurried off when his buddies came to the door for him. They were taking off to the movies to meet some girls. I was happy he had made the effort to meet us.

After a delicious supper we sat around chatting about our children, our jobs, and our plans to continue building our family unit. We were invited to stay the night with Clara and Milt as they had empty bedrooms for us all and much more room than Doris had at her place. Carol excused herself to go upstairs and unpack and get the girls bathed and ready for bed. Our conversation and mood turned more somber at this point.

"Don, I want you to know that we never forgot about you and we were sickened that Mother and Frank had placed you in that Mental Hospital in Weyburn. We all knew that was not a place for a child and that you certainly didn't belong in an asylum. But, honestly, Don, we just didn't know how to get you out. We were told that once someone was committed, only the people responsible for placing them could have them released. We were all single and none of us had jobs that would sustain anyone else but ourselves until we met and married our husbands. But with Doris and me moving to Brandon, not having a car, and then beginning our families . . ."

"Oh, I know, Sis. I've heard it from Ethel and Doris. I know how you girls were struggling and just trying to survive and live your own lives. I think for the first couple of years there, I managed to cope just believing that Mother would show up at some point and scoop me up in her arms and take me back home. I think I couldn't allow myself to accept the reality that she was never going to come get me. When I did finally feel forced to accept that, I was depressed to some extent. I found school to be a good diversion for me and there were other kids there that I made friends with so that helped immensely. We were in the same boat and we kept one another afloat, so to speak."

"I didn't know you could go to school in there. Doris did you know that?" Cev turned to Doris.

"No, I didn't realize it but I'm glad to hear it. So, how much education did you get in there, Don?" Doris was the one who had got the most education in our family and I remembered how important it was to her when Mother had wanted to pull her out in high school after Father died.

"Well, there was nothing formal after Grade 6. So, one of my biggest regrets is that I was not only robbed of my childhood but, also, of the opportunity to further my education properly."

"But you've done very well with becoming a denturist." Cev seemed to want to point out the positive side of my experience for me.

"Yes, that is true but most people get to decide what they want to do for themselves. I was desperate to find any job. If I didn't find a job within the first week of my release, I was going to be taken back to the Mental."

"But, I guess you can be thankful that you landed into such a good job. Maybe the Lord was directing you and you seem to be successful and happy with your career now, don't you?"

"Sure, Cev, I am thankful. And, you're right about me being happy. I am happy with my wife, my kids, my work, my home, and what future I have now with you girls back in my life. I didn't mean to sound like sour grapes. I was just trying to point out that sometimes I do feel a little bitter when I get talking about it. I go back in my mind to the things I saw and experienced that no kid should have to see or live through. I guess once I had my own kids, that really hit me even harder; knowing how I could never, ever want my kids or anyone else's kids to suffer through that."

"What kind of things, Don?" Cev seemed to want to hear it all.

"Well, being raped the first night I was there for starters. I was raped by a patient who was a pedophile. For the first few years, I was groped and manhandled by male patients and physically and sexually abused by some members of the staff. I was punished by a teacher for climbing a tree. She sent me to the "Snake Pit" as it was referred to. It was the bowels of hell where naked men slither around on their bellies in their own feces and piss and the place stinks of their foulness. These creatures were called, Defectives or Little Boys."

"God, Donnie! I am so sorry. I've never been in a place like that. Sam, is it like that in our Mental Hospital here in Brandon?" Clara turned to Sam with a pleading look that begged to be told it wasn't so.

"There's human disparity in all asylums, Clara. People are not always at their best. I don't mean to negate anything you are telling us, Don. Please don't think I don't understand or believe what you're telling us. I'm just going to point out that sometimes we have high school students working in our wards during the summers who have no special training. They are usually young and immature and if a patient hits them or throws their feces at them, they will sometimes retaliate in a violent way. It's not good but it does happen."

He went on, "And, there are people who are adults that do have the training but they're tired and they work long shifts and may lose their patience. They may not be able to focus on the fact that the people in their care are not responsible for their actions. Am I saying this is alright or excusing it? No, certainly not but when you put thousands of people under one roof, you'll get sin and secrets. Humanity is not always good to their fellow man."

"I was their fellow child," I corrected him. "However, I'm not a child anymore and I took legal action recently against all of them. Carol's brother is a lawyer; he helped me and we were able to settle out of court."

Carol returned to the living room and we all shifted in our seats. Clara jumped up and offered tea and cookies before bed. We all lightened our mood and enjoyed the rest of the evening before saying our good nights to Doris and Sam.

I knew Sam was right about making the point in some small defense for the shortcomings of mental health workers. He was right—they are only human, after all. There were many great nurses and orderlies and other staff members who were wonderful and caring most of the time. I knew Sam had a point about defending workers. However, Sam was not a nine-year old boy who had to learn to survive in the Snake Pit and fighting for his life every day in the halls of a mad house. No one was groping and touching him against his will. He got to go home at the end of his day. I did not.

Chapter 31

Now that we were back on the road, heading to Carlyle Lake for our winding down last week of our vacation, I felt a real sense of satisfaction. I had not only found my sisters but also all the new members of the family that I was anxious to get to know better. The sisters and I had talked about having a family reunion in the next year. We all promised to stay in touch and to make a plan for the next summer, if possible. Again, I felt that it was my darling wife, Carol, who I owed my gratitude to for pushing me to make the effort to contact my family. Although the part about Mother had not been what I had hoped for, I had so much more on the positive side to think about.

"Penny for your thoughts." Carol sat with the road map on her lap and the girls had all fallen asleep in the back seats of the station wagon.

"Oh, actually, I was just thinking how I think I should treat my lovely wife to a steak supper tonight when we get to the cabin. Maybe we can stop in Carlyle and pick some groceries up before we head to the lake."

"Oh, that sounds lovely. Maybe a bottle of red wine too?"

"Why the heck not? I'm in. Seriously, though Carol, I want to tell you how much I appreciate you for your insight into my issues around my life in the Mental and my mother and my sisters. You made me see the light and I'm ever so grateful. I'm happy with meeting up with my sisters and their families. I have a new sense of a belonging again. Your family has been so wonderful to me and I really thought they were all I needed. But, being with my sisters again has connected all the dots again for me."

"I'm glad, dear. You had to do the soul searching though and you had to make it happen. I'm glad it has been so worthwhile for you. I think we have all benefited from the experience. I like your sisters and their husbands. I'm looking forward to meeting all their children if we can manage the family reunion next summer."

"Me too."

"Me three!" shouted a little voice from the far back. Up popped two more sleepy-eyed heads with hair all messed up yawning and stretching after their naps."

"Are we there yet Dad?" Jenny was already climbing over the back seat to the middle seat to squeeze in between her older sisters.

"Yes, we are almost there. We're stopping in the town of Carlyle for some groceries and then we'll be there. It's a nice sunny day so maybe we'll have time for a little dip in the lake before I make supper for all my girls."

"Yay Daddy!

ഇ‍൫

Our cabin at the lake was quaint and perfect for a summer retreat close to the beach. The girls jumped into their swimsuits while Carol and I unpacked some things and put groceries away. Jenny was the first one ready even though she had her rubber [9]thongs on the wrong feet. Carol grabbed a brush and began brushing Jenny's hair up into a pony tail to keep it out of her eyes in the water.

"Mommy! Ouch! That hurts."

"I'm almost finished, Jenny. Hold still, please. Clara Rose, will you help Doris put her hair up before we head down to the beach, please?"

"Yes Mom. Where's my beach towel?"

"Oh, Don, honey, can you go get that big beach bag out of the car for me. I must have left it in there. It has all our towels in it."

"I will right after I finish blowing up this air mattress. Girls! Make sure you all go pee before we leave for the beach, please."

"Oh Dad—there you go again! Gosh, we don't have to be told to go pee all the time. What's with you?"

"Clara Rose, I've told you before. Your sisters still need little reminders. OK, I'll get the towels. Why don't you all just come outside when you are ready? I'll wait out on the deck for you. It's a bit crazy in here right now with all the commotion."

The beach was an exciting new experience for us as a family. The feel of the hot sand under our feet had us dancing and running to the water. The water was clear and cold but once we were in, we were frolicking in it. The girls

---

[9] Thongs – Word commonly used before 1970 to describe rubber footwear known today as flip-flops.

climbed up onto my shoulders and jumped into the water coming up giggling and sometimes choking a little on water they'd swallowed. Carol moved away from us to keep from getting splashed. She put her hands together in a diving motion and gently sunk forward into the water doing a graceful breast stroke. I thought she was so swan like in her gentle gliding through the water. I remembered back to the first time I went to the beach with her and that red and white polka dot, two-piece swimsuit.

"Carol! Where's your red and white polka dot swim suit?" I teased her.

She splashed water at me and swam away. I tried to catch her foot but she splashed me again.

ഇൻരു

Our time at the lake was spent doing things that one never seems to do in the City. We walked into the bush on hiking trails, went horseback riding, and picked wild Saskatoon berries and wild raspberries. I even bought myself a fishing rod and tried my luck at fishing. I managed to catch a few perch and we fried them in butter and had fresh corn on the cob that we'd purchased at the farmers' market. Carol made Saskatoon pies which we thoroughly enjoyed as well as raspberry jam to take home with us.

One rainy afternoon the girls were playing board games and Carol was reading a book. I had never known how relaxing and satisfying a day could be. I sat and looked out the window and watched the blue jays and chickadees fluttering around the bird feeder in the rain. Squirrels scurried up the trees and disappeared into hiding to cuddle up with their furry tails to keep dry. I was almost hypnotized by the sound of the rain falling on the roof.

Carol put her book down and stood up.

"Do you want a cup of tea or hot chocolate, Don?"

"Tea would be great, please."

Carol brought a snack of cookies in for the girls and brought tea and cookies over to me. She sat down and looked at me.

"What have you been daydreaming about all afternoon while I have been reading?" she asked.

"Well, you know—I've been thinking a lot about how wonderful this place is and how it has brought us together with the girls. Back at home, we are busy with jobs, school and social events. It is all good; but, I feel this place takes me back to the feeling I had as a boy on the farm. I don't see me ever being able to live on a farm again. I love the nature and wildlife around us. I love seeing a deer walk right through the yard. Taking the girls to the beach and doing all the things we've done have made me realize how important family vacations really are. I didn't experience anything like this when I was a boy because Father and Mother had work to do on the farm all spring, summer and fall."

"I know it has been great for me too. I am more relaxed with the girls and it is such a break to have less work to do."

"I'm thinking maybe we should look at buying a cabin. What do you think?"

"Oh, I don't know Don. Its one thing to come to a cabin for a vacation but it is a whole other thing to take on owning a property and having all the upkeep to worry about.

And you aren't retired so we can't stay at the lake all summer, you know."

"I know. I've thought of that—but, you and the girls could stay here all summer, or as much as you wanted. I can take a couple of weeks' vacation. After that, I'd drive back to the City and work all week and then drive to the lake on weekends. I could leave on Thursday after work and stay until Monday morning."

"I'm not sure I'd like being out here with the kids all week and you back at work though."

"Well, I'm sure one of your sisters or your parents would love to join you and the girls to keep you company. It isn't just a place for our family. It can be shared with friends and relatives as well." I tried making a strong case.

It took some convincing on my part but I coaxed Carol into at least having a look at a couple of places. We found a waterfront cottage with the name, Bobolink. It had been built in 1930 by Americans. They named it Bobolink after the bobolink bird that was almost extinct. The bird was known as the longest migrating bird and it flew from the United States into Canada. So, the American family that built the cottage decided the bobolink bird was much like themselves—living in both countries part time.

The cottage had a lot of charm. It had two small bedrooms on the main floor and one in the loft above. There were shutters on the windows and flower boxes under the windows. It was in need of a new coat of paint and it smelled rather musty when the realtor opened the doors but Carol and the girls fell in love with it instantly. Everything had been left behind by previous owners. There were beds, furniture, refrigerator, stove, dishes, cookware and even some beautiful old handmade quilts.

We took a vote and it was unanimous. We bought the cottage and got possession before we had to head back to Regina. I knew this was going to be a great thing and my mind was already planning that family reunion with my sisters. We now would have an ideal place to meet. I phoned all three sisters when we got home to share the good news. It was the first time I had someone from my own side of the family to make a phone call to. What a great feeling!

Chapter 32

The phone was ringing. Carol was busy making Christmas cookies and the girls were all helping her. It was the week before Christmas, 1969. The house smelled of pine needles and cookies baking. Carol and her mother and the girls had been busy for the past few weeks with all the joys of writing Christmas letters and cards, baking, cleaning, decorating and shopping. There were gifts already wrapped under the tree for all members of the family. Carol and her mother were all about Christmas and their excitement had certainly passed on to our girls.

"Don, can you please answer the phone! We've all got flour on our hands in here."

"Hello."

"Hi Don—Doris here."

"Doris! How nice. How are you?"

"We're fine here, but it's about Mother—she called me this afternoon just after lunch. It's bad news, Don. Mother was almost hysterical. I had to get her to calm down so I could understand her."

"What's wrong Doris?"

"It's Frank. Apparently, for some time now, he has been rather violent toward Mother. She has been too ashamed to tell anyone until now. I think she's been putting up with this for a long time but I am not too sure. She said that he has been losing his memory and that he started getting a bit rough lately. He has grabbed her by her arm or pushed her at times. She said he's left bruises on her, and I suspect it has happened more often than she's willing to admit. She thinks that at times he doesn't really know her and he thinks she is someone else. He gets angry very easily. When she tries to convince him of who she is, he gets even angrier."

"Oh God, Doris, I'm sorry to hear this. I would never wish this on her in a million years."

"I know we all feel the same way. Apparently, this morning was a bad scene. She made breakfast and he thought she was a stranger who was trying to poison him. He jumped up and upset the whole kitchen table and broke dishes. Mother was terrified and ran upstairs. He chased her and she managed to get to a bedroom and pushed a dresser of drawers in front of the door to barricade herself in the room. She called the police and also a neighbour. The police came and put him in cuffs and took him into Weyburn to the police station. He is being assessed but it sounds like they will take him to the Mental later today."

"What?! I'm sorry to hear this. What will Mother do now? Is she alone out there now?"

"No, the neighbour is with her for now. Here's the thing; I've phoned Clara and Ethel but since Ethel lives the closest, it makes sense for her to go there first. She's already driving in to Weyburn from Estevan. Can you make a trip from Regina to meet with Ethel for some moral support? She's going to get a hotel room and she said she'd get an adjoining room for you if you can make the trip. She doesn't feel comfortable expecting to stay at the farm.

She's going to call me once she gets there. I told her I'd call you and let her know what you decide. I know it is asking a lot of you but it would help Ethel. I'm willing to make my way there too but I'd like you and Ethel to talk to Mother first and then phone me to let me know the situation. I'll keep Clara in the loop and she might come with me later. Maybe Milt and Sam will accompany us but for now I'll wait to see what you can tell me. Maybe from there we could all go back to Ethel's rather than spend too much time in the hotel in Weyburn. I'm just trying to figure out how to handle the immediate thing for now."

"Okay, I'll make some arrangements at my office and I'll head to Weyburn before supper. What hotel is Ethel heading to?"

"The El Rancho—do you know where it is?"

"Yes. I'll meet Ethel there. Tell her I'm coming."

"Oh, thank you so much Don." Her voice broke and I knew she was to the point of tears with some relief that I was cooperating. Poor Doris and poor Ethel; neither of them were on greatest of terms with Mother and they certainly had no love for Frank but as strange as it seemed, none of us siblings wanted this to be happening to our mother. It was strange indeed. I had a shock that ran through my veins and it went from my toes to my head. I felt almost sick. I was shaken to my core. My mother was suffering and I was terrified for her. This was such a turn-around in my mind from the day I'd last seen her and vowed to never see her again.

I made arrangements with work and Carol helped me throw a suitcase together and I was on the road within the hour. The drive gave me a little time to gather my thoughts and get my head around the crisis that I felt we were heading into. Part of me was unsure about meeting up with Mother but the other part of me was very sure that I wanted to be there to support Ethel.

ଡୀୠ

Ethel was on the phone talking to her husband, Jim, when I opened the door to my side of our adjoining rooms. She had already opened the connecting door between the rooms for my arrival. I entered her room just as she was saying her good-bye to Jim. I was touched by how, although she was much older than I, right at this moment she looked like a little girl. I could tell she had been crying and I could see the vulnerability in her expression. I knew Jim had been giving her words of comfort.

"Alright, yes I will. Don just walked in the door, Jim, so I'll say good-bye, dear, for now. Yes, I'm feeling better. Bye-bye." She hung up the phone and looked up at me with a smile.

"Thank you Don for coming—it's so good to see you again. I was just chatting with Jim to let him know I was here alright and that you were coming to join me."

"Well, Merry Christmas Sis! What the heck kind of Christmas predicament is this we're in?" I tried to sound at least a little on the jovial side to lighten the moment as we hugged one another.

"I know, isn't it crazy? I haven't had anything to do with Mother in years now—other than our annual Christmas card exchange. Suddenly, I'm upset and worried sick for her welfare. I fell to pieces when I got Doris's call. I don't understand myself at all right now."

"I brought a little bottle of rye with me. I don't drink much—but, at times like this, I feel it would be acceptable for us to have one to steady our nerves before we head out to the farm. A little Christmas cheer can't hurt. We are going out to the farm, aren't we?"

"Yes and yes! Let's have that wee drink first and then we'll go to the farm. I think it is just the thing I need right at this moment. I'm so grateful to have your support. I feel so much better already just having you here with me."

I poured our drinks, adding Coke to the rye. "Yes, I'm feeling exactly the same as you. But, all I can say is that we are still her children. She is always going to be our Mother— even if she's been absent in our lives and has not been a good mother. There is still some bond there that we can't deny." I offered my thoughts to her.

We discussed the difficulty in understanding how adult children are suddenly more "child" than "adult". It seems there is always that little child within us and especially when the child has been rejected or abandoned by a parent at some point. Even if the parent has had—what they would consider—a good and valid reason for taking the action that separated them from their child, the child will always have that feeling of uncertainty about the parent's love for them. There will be a feeling of abandonment no matter how the parent justifies his or her actions. The child in us may always be reaching for and striving for that parent's love and

259

approval. We have an innate need to know we are good enough to be loved by our parent. And that doesn't change just because you reach adulthood.

A child that is abused and beaten by a parent will keep trying to be good enough to be loved and accepted. There's an intrinsic need for that bond to be there. The child may not consciously understand this or have any intent to manipulate the parent but it is naturally in us to want acceptance. The first experience in our life, of love and acceptance, is with our parents. It is through being nurtured that we learn to nurture and care for others. A mother is the foremost person a child will bond with. If we miss out on this, it can become a problem in future relationships with others.

For my sisters and me, we did experience that for part of our early life. We did get the nurturing, love and support of two responsible parents. But the shock of having that ripped away from us, left us very vulnerable, scarred and lacking the tools to deal with the situation that was now upon us.

How were we supposed to react to a parent that had abandoned us and—for all intents and purposes—pushed us out of her life? If our family life had not been so abruptly interrupted, we would likely be able to cope with this better. It would just be a normal thing to rush to Mother's side and hold her hand through her ordeal with Frank. But in our case, our mother was almost a stranger.

I think, perhaps we were able to allow our mother some grace because of Frank. We knew her circumstances after Father's death had left her with great fears of how she would survive on the farm raising us kids and then ultimately living alone out there as we all would eventually leave home. However, this comes back to knowing her reasons but not understanding her ability to abandon her children for Frank's sake. She had put her needs and his wants ahead of her own children.

Although we had been disconnected and banished by our mother, here we were—all four siblings, gathering our combined strength to try to do the decent thing and come to Mother in her time of need. In spite of all the lost years, was it possible that the bond we had with her in our early childhood was still a deep and lasting emotion? Had we just buried our needs and emotions all these years, thinking we were adjusted and moving on only now to discover that these emotions had all resurfaced to make us come face to face with them now? Did she deserve our help? Perhaps not—but, here we were just the same. Maybe we were still all deeply yearning for that connection and bonding with her before it was ultimately too late in life.

ഇരു

When we got to the farm, we were met at the door by the neighbour, Ed Jefferson. His wife, Mildred, was sitting with Mother in the living room. They had been drinking coffee and I was really glad they were there. It softened the harshness of the moment of setting eyes on Mother in the home that I hadn't set foot in since I was nine years old.

Walking through the kitchen to the living room, I had noticed the kitchen had been renovated with new kitchen cabinetry and new cushioned vinyl flooring. There was a dishwasher now, a modern convenience that would have been nice to have had when we were a family of six. It seemed to me a bit of a waste now that there were only two of them living here. Of course there was no such thing back then and my father would have been the first to veto anything so frivolous when there were four children to do the dishes.

The living room had not changed much other than there was a new sofa and a big Lazy-boy recliner which I assumed to be Frank's chair. The dining room was exactly as I had remembered it. The smell of lemon furniture oil still lightly scented the room.

Mother looked old and extremely tired. She was now 78 years old and I couldn't imagine that a life with Frank had brought her an abundance of joy. Certainly, what she had been living with recently must have taken its toll on her. She was very thin and her skin looked like crepe paper; there were noticeable bruises on her wrists. Her face was no longer pretty and there were dark circles under her eyes; her forehead had deep furrows and her expression showed the worry and fear that she was obviously feeling.

Typical of Mother's style, she was wearing a floral house dress and a thin beige cardigan sweater. I don't think I had ever seen my mother in anything other than a skirt or dress. I'd never seen her in a pair of pants. Father used to compliment her on her shapely legs but now I saw varicose veins and heavier ankles. She looked up at us as we entered the room and managed a feeble half smile with one side of her mouth—a sheepish attempt at a welcome?

We shook hands with Ed and Mildred and they told us they remembered us as children. We remembered them as well but it had been such a long time. The weird thing about that was we felt almost as strange with our own mother as we did with Ed and Mildred.

"Thank you Ethel and Don for coming out today. I didn't know what else to do. We just got a call before you arrived from the admissions doctor at the Mental. They had to put Frank in a straight jacket and they've sedated him so he will sleep. He was so agitated and it isn't good for his heart to be so riled up. He didn't understand what was going on or where he was being taken so he got very violent."

"I'm so sorry, Mother. Has this been going on for a long time?" Ethel asked.

"Yes, it's been about two years of this but it has been getting increasingly worse and lately, the manhandling was most terrifying for me. I know he doesn't mean to hurt me but he thinks I'm someone else. He thinks I'm a stranger or intruder that is out to harm him. He attacks me trying to throw me out of the house."

Mildred kindly poured coffee for all of us. She had brought over some homemade muffins and cheese. We all ate but Mother said she just wasn't up to eating.

"So, Mother, have you had time to think about what you would like to do in the short term? Do you want to move into town or stay with someone temporarily?"

"Well, I don't like being alone, of course, but I don't know anyone that I'd feel comfortable enough with to ask them to let me stay with them. Frank was not a sociable person so we didn't see people in town other than at the church on Sundays."

"You are welcome to come and stay with us Anna, if you'd like," offered Mildred.

"Thank you, Mildred, but I think I'd sleep better in my own bed."

"I understand. Ed and I will gladly check on Anna every day," Mildred turned to us. "We can phone her daily to check in with her and Ed will clear the snow from the main road to her house when necessary. We can help her get through winter here at least, can't we Ed?"

"Sure. We'll pick her up and take her to town with us for groceries and to church. We go right past her place on our way in anyway." Ed smiled and patted Mother's hand.

"The doctor told me not to bother to come to see Frank for at least the first two weeks. They want him to settle into his new surroundings and they said it is worse if I show up every day to confuse him. He'll just want me to take him home," she explained.

"Well, then I guess you have a good support here, for the time being, and it sounds like the doctor has a plan for Frank for now as well. Maybe we'll head back home to our families and Don has his work to go back to as well. We'll stay in touch and you know you can call us anytime. You have my number." Ethel was doing most of the talking and I was content to leave it at that.

"Are you driving home tonight? It's so dark out now." Mother actually seemed concerned for us.

"No, we got a hotel room and will leave after breakfast tomorrow morning."

"Mother," I finally found my voice. "Would you like me to pick you up in the morning and take you out to breakfast with us? I'd be happy to do that and then we'd drive you back here on our way home."

"Well, I suppose I could do that. What time will you come for me?"

"How about 9 o'clock?"

"Yes, I'll be ready. Thank you."

With that we thanked Ed and Mildred for their support and gave them our numbers in case of emergency in future. As I lay in my bed that night in the hotel, I had difficulty getting to sleep. I never was good at sleeping in hotels and I had a lot to think about. I couldn't help but think to myself that it was sweet justice to learn of Frank's fate. Here he was now, alone, frightened and fragile—just as I had been many years ago as a little boy. He was now going to dwell in the house of horrors that I had come from. The place he had placed me as a child. He would now live out the rest of his life in the same asylum. The difference was that he deserved and needed to be there—I had not.

As for Mother—well, one might say she was also getting what she gave. Her biggest fear when Father died was living alone one day after us kids grew up. She feared living on that farm alone and now, at the age of 78, that was exactly what she was doomed to be doing. If I had wanted to be vengeful, I could not have come up with a more fitting outcome for both of them. However, the quotation from the Bible kept running through my mind that night, *Vengeance is mine, saith the Lord.* (Romans 12:19).

Well if God was involved, He was taking action on his own. I had not dreamed such a thing could happen and I had not ever willed it to happen. Had I experienced anger toward them both? If I was honest with myself, the answer was certainly "yes"; however, I had not ever asked God to punish them. But, now that it was happening, I couldn't help but think that what goes around comes around, as they say!

The next morning Ethel and I picked Mother up and took her for breakfast at the Town and Country restaurant. I wanted to have a conversation with her without Ed and Mildred so this seemed like the best opportunity; we all had to have breakfast anyway. I was exhausted from my sleepless night and probably looked a bit disheveled. I know I had bags under my eyes.

"Mother, I know you have the help of Ed and Mildred to get you through the winter on the farm; but, I don't think you can expect them to continue that sort of vigilance on a continued basis." I got right to the point.

She stopped cutting her bacon as I spit that out and just looked at me.

"Yes, Mother, Don and I think you should consider the idea of getting a little place in town come spring. You might really love that and you'd be able to get your own groceries and get to church. You could take a cab to get around in town." Ethel tried to sound encouraging.

"I don't think Frank would be happy about that idea and if he comes home one day, he'd hate to live anywhere else but the farm."

"Oh Mother, I'm sorry—but, you have to face the fact that Frank is never coming home. He is suffering senility. I'm sure of that. It is impossible for you to try to have him back at the farm. You are too vulnerable out there. What if the neighbours are not home and can't come to your side on short notice?"

"Ethel's right Mother. Frank is where he needs to be and you need to think about doing what is best for you from now on. And besides, if Frank was able to come back home, he is getting way too old to do the work out there. I know you don't have cattle or livestock any more but he can't even be responsible for cutting the grass in the yard any more. It is too much for him and certainly for you."

"I suppose. I'll think about it. I guess I can make that decision over winter."

We assured her that we would be around to check on her and that she could certainly call us. We would be willing to help her find a new place come spring. That was the agreement for the time being. Ethel and I would return home and report all this to Doris and Clara.

As civil as this all had been, there was still something very void in our conversations with Mother. I don't know what I expected from her and whatever it was, it was clearly not happening. I wasn't getting any sign of affection from her and neither were my sisters. No words of apology were spoken for pushing us out of her life to please Frank. I guess my stubborn pride was also not going to allow me to ask her for anything. In my heart I felt she would either give it freely—or not. It would be up to her.

Chapter 33

Christmas was always a joyous time with Carol's family. This year the family gathered at Steve's home as it was much larger than Rose and Henry's place. Their family was growing and we all agreed that if it kept going like this, we'd soon have to consider renting a hall to get together. Rose still insisted on cooking some of her traditional Ukrainian dishes. She didn't trust Steve's wife to do as good a job at it as she could. Carol and the other sisters-in-law all helped as well.

The family was growing and there were some changes to the dynamics of the family as well. Carol's brother, Robert, had finished his law degree and had gone into partnership with his brother, Steve. Robert did not get engaged to Bella as the family had anticipated. Much to the disappointment of the family Robert had suddenly brought a new girl to meet the family and announced their engagement just a few weeks before Christmas.

The new girl, Gina, was in and Bella was out. Bella was heart-broken and the family was shocked. Robert, apparently, had been seeing Gina and Bella at the same time unbeknownst to Bella. We learned later that Gina did know about the relationship between Robert and Bella but she had decided to go after Robert anyway in spite of this long-term relationship with Bella.

This Christmas gathering was our first large family affair that included Gina. She was a very beautiful woman of Italian heritage. She had the smoothest olive complexion and shiny black hair that fell softly to her shoulders. Her eyes were like big brown saucers with long dark lashes. Her teeth were white and her lips were full and usually very red with a shiny lip-gloss. I thought she wore a little too much makeup but she was still a strikingly, sexy looking woman. It was easy to see how Robert had been attracted to her.

Gina was not just a pretty face; she had the brains to go with it. She was a lawyer and that is likely how Robert had met her and been able to keep it from Bella for some time. Although her beauty was stunning, she would have a lot to prove to this family to take Bella's place. She knew it as much as we did and she started on day one with a determination to win us all over.

Rose was a loving mother but she made her comments now and then to Robert and it was clear to everyone where she stood. However, Gina was wearing an engagement ring that Christmas and we knew we had to make a concerted effort for Robert's sake or we would lose him. No one wanted that.

Steve's wife, Cynthia, was the perfect hostess. Cynthia and Steve now had two children, Leandra and Liam. Cynthia was a tall and slender blonde. She was a no-nonsense type of woman who wore very little make-up and kept her long hair in a simple pony tail most of the time. Today, she did look a little more festive and had a bit of lipstick on and a red velvet bow holding her pony tail. She welcomed Robert and Gina in and Steve took their coats.

"Welcome, Gina. It's lovely to meet you. I'm Cynthia and this is Steve."

"Thank you, Cynthia, it's nice to meet you too. I have met Steve before once at the courthouse. So, it's nice to see you again Steve," she smiled and her eyes seemed to sparkle as she extended her hand to Steve.

"Oh, yes- –that's right. Nice to see you again, too, Gina, and welcome to our home. Come on in and we'll get you both a drink," Steve led the way over to the bar in the family room. "The usual for you, brother?" he looked over at Robert. He reached for the bottle of rye. He started pouring.

"Sounds good. Easy on the Coke and a lot of ice, please."

"And, what can I get for you Gina?" Steve asked as he stirred Robert's drink and threw in a couple of lemon wedges.

"Oh, I'm not drinking these days, thank you anyway." She turned to everyone in the room as she said this as though she wanted to let us all know that she wasn't drinking. "I might have a glass of Ginger-ale though, if you have some." Gina made a tight-lipped smile and looked out the corner of her eyes at Robert in as if to say, *we have a secret.* Her expression was a smug little all-knowing grin.

"Here you go then," Steve handed Gina her drink. She took the drink and then gently tugged at Robert's elbow and looked up at him with that same sly smile and said, "Don't you think this is a good time to share our good news Babe?"

Babe? Calling my brother-in-law Babe just made me want to laugh out loud. I almost choked on my drink. I thought to myself, *this girl is so different than any of the women in this family*. I could see trouble coming. I looked at Carol and I could see her eyes growing wider. I knew what she was thinking. In fact, I could see it in the faces of everyone in the room. Mind you, I figured the men were not as disapproving as the women. It was hard not to stare at Gina.

Robert seemed a little uncomfortable but you could tell he didn't dare put Gina off. He cleared his throat and held up his glass.

"Gina and I have more good news to share with everyone. We are happy to announce we are having a baby," he smiled and looked down at Gina and she stood on her tip-toes to give him a kiss. Everyone tried to sound jubilant, offering congratulations and making little jokes like, "Welcome to the club of sleepless nights" and that sort of comment.

Rose had been standing in the doorway to the kitchen with oven mitts on. With hands on her hips, she rolled her eyes and turned and opened the oven door. "Most people wait until after the wedding to make that announcement," she muttered as she basted the meat. Several of the woman scurried off to the kitchen to help with dinner preparations. You could tell they didn't want to add any further annoyance to Rose!

ℬℭ

Rose never did seem to accept Gina from that day forward; although, she loved their baby daughter, Maria Jeanette, as much as any of her other grandchildren. Gina was a strong personality. Maybe that is why she and Rose never did hit it off too well. I suspect they were too much alike and even if Rose had not loved Bella so much and even if Bella had never been in the picture, I don't think it would have mattered. They were like oil and water.

Rose was the matriarch of the family and she liked her position. Her family was everything to her and she was the one who taught the women to cook and sew and how to run a household properly—by her standards, that is. She liked all the glory and accolades regarding her fine Ukrainian culinary skills.

If you ate at Rose's table, you ate Ukrainian food and you got a lesson in the tradition around a particular dish and the explanation of how she had made it and you would be expected to believe that her way was the best way in all these wonderful dishes. No one argued. We all loved Rose and her cooking.

If Gina brought a dish to anyone's home, rest assured it would be a traditional Italian dish. She would expect equal time with Rose to explain her dish and the history behind it and how she laboured over it to make it just right—the way her grandmother or mother had taught her. She would go on about using fresh basil or grating her own Parmesan cheese or how she'd used a special Italian red wine to make her own salad dressing. The great thing about this sort of back and forth silent war between these two women was that the rest of us ate very well at every family gathering and we loved both women's cooking.

One time as Gina arrived carrying her casserole dish of beef braciole, Rose looked at the dish and said, "We're having cabbage rolls tonight and we didn't really need another meat dish. Italian doesn't mix with Ukrainian."

"That's alright, Rose," Gina responded with a smile. "It's a favourite of Robert's. He actually prefers it to cabbage rolls. And, anyway, it will give people the option of eating both or choosing one or the other. You know what they say Rose—variety is the spice of life!"

You could cut the air with a knife and you could see Rose ready to blow. For Gina to tell her that her own son would prefer his wife's dish to his mother's delicious cabbage rolls was a low blow. Gina kept smiling and you just knew that she felt pleased with herself for scoring a point on that one with Rose.

Gina was not a bad person. She was just a woman who knew what she wanted and she knew how to get it. Robert was her man and she was determined to have her rightful place as his wife and she wasn't about to cow-tow to anyone in the family—not even Rose. She was always respectful when she spoke to Rose. She was careful of that. But, it was in a rather condescending manner. Rose was rather cold and indifferent. Gina was not stupid. She knew Rose didn't love her or gush over her the way she did with the other daughters-in-law. However, Gina was not going to give Rose the satisfaction of hurting her. Gina just smiled and chatted and made the best of it all. I had to kind of admire her for that. I knew I wouldn't ever want to be on the wrong side of my mother-in-law!

Chapter 34

Carol had made the suggestion that we invite Ethel and Jim to stay with us for New Year's Eve and spend New Year's Day with us as well. We had come to enjoy a quiet way of bringing in the New Year rather than attending a public dance or house party. Ethel and Jim were happy to come to visit us. It gave Ethel something pleasant to think about since Christmas without her one and only child was never a very happy time for her. They would visit Jimmy over Christmas at his care home in Moose Jaw.

Carol had come to really enjoy being with Ethel. In a way, Ethel was almost like a mother to me. She had helped Mother to bring me into the world and she had always been very good to me as a child. All my sisters had been good to me. Perhaps it was because I was the youngest and the only boy, I was never picked on by any of them. Maybe if I'd had three older brothers, it would have been a different story. I think Ethel felt more like a mother-in-law at times to Carol than a sister-in-law. She seemed like a grandmother to our girls and they all loved her very much. She had never had any daughters and with Jimmy being in the care facility in

Moose Jaw, Ethel missed the interaction with family and with children, in particular. I felt that Ethel did fill the void of my mother in a way that was most comforting to all of us.

Ethel came bearing lots of goodies. She not only came with wine and baking, she had puzzles and games for the girls. They adored her. She didn't want their visit to be a burden on Carol. She needn't have worried. Carol always had a freezer full of cabbage rolls, pierogies, homemade buns or pies. She had learned well from Rose to always have things prepared and on hand.

We were rebuilding our family relationship. I felt it was a great idea that Carol had suggested we have Ethel and Jim come alone at this special holiday. It seemed appropriate to begin a new year and a new phase of our lives with the first person other than my parents who had special meaning in my life.

ഇരു

That spring in early April of 1970, Clara, Milt, Doris and Sam all came to spend a few days with us in Regina. They were all retired now and had the time to travel. Clara and Milt loved to play the card game of Hand and Foot Canasta so they taught us the game. We played the men against the women and it was always a robust and jovial time of competition between the two sexes. We had Carol's parents over to meet my family one night. My sisters were impressed with our home and with Carol's great cooking skills. Of course, Carol had to be sure to let them know she learned everything from Rose. Rose smiled and nodded.

The women all chatted about recipes and got on very well together. My brothers-in-law both liked their booze a lot more than I did but they behaved and the only thing that was bad about their drinking was that they both snored all night and kept the rest of us awake. Carol managed to find some earplugs which saved us.

It was nice to be surrounded by family on both sides. I sometimes felt that the sisters had an advantage of having been able to spend more time together as a family while I was in the Mental but I tried not to let that overshadow our good times together now. I just had to remind myself how fortunate I was to have reconnected with them and I was determined to make up for lost time whenever possible. There was another purpose for their visit and that was to help me to start looking at suitable places to move Mother to from the farm.

We had planned that we would all drive into Weyburn to visit Mother. I thought we should take our daughters but Clara Rose wanted nothing to do with that idea. Doris and Jennifer were willing to go but Clara Rose was downright stubborn on the issue.

"I am not going to go see that woman. She is not a grandmother to us in any way and never has been. She did a terrible thing to my dad and I'll never forgive her for that. She deserves everything she gets and she deserves to die a lonely old woman!"

"Shush, Clara Rose! We have company in the house. Please keep your voice down."

"Mom, I'm sorry," she quieted down and continued in a low but determined voice, "but I just don't understand why you and Dad think we should go see her at all—any of us. I hate her."

"Clara Rose, there's a saying that hatred only hurts the vessel in which it is contained. Hating someone will only hurt you in the end. You mustn't use that word and you don't really know her. You can't possibly understand at your age what that woman had to deal with. We haven't lived her life and walked in her shoes. So, it isn't fair to judge her."

"But Mom, Dad was just a 9-year old kid and he was all alone in a place that was unfit for most humans let alone a little boy. He was a normal kid who had his life robbed from him. His mother didn't love him. She's a witch as far as I'm concerned."

"Sometimes mothers will do things out of love that are hard. Some women give a baby up for adoption even though they love the child and want to keep it. They give it up and never see it again but it is because they want the child to have a life that they cannot offer. They give their own flesh and blood away in hopes that the child will have an opportunity at a better life," Carol explained.

"Yeah, but Mom, do you believe that his mother actually thought he'd have a better life in there? I don't think so!"

"Well, maybe. I don't think Anna had any idea what it was like in that place. Most people had no idea really. After all, there weren't even visits allowed so most people never saw anything in there unless they worked there or were a resident. I understand how you can feel so strongly in defense of your dad, dear. But your dad is not choosing to hold hatred against his mother so we don't need to either."

Carol went on, "He has struggled with his feelings toward her but he certainly doesn't hate her. If you hate her and refuse to try to reach out and be decent, then you are not allowing your dad to open his heart to her. You will make him feel that you are ashamed of him if he chooses to love her in spite of her weakness as a mother. She is his mother no matter what kind of mother she was. From what I've heard from him, his mother was a very good mother for those first nine years of his life. She is the only mother he'll ever have and if he has any chance at reconciling with her, you should not stand in judgment over either of them. This is not our fight or our relationship. This is between them. So, you will come along with us and you will hold your tongue and you will be supportive of your dad if he wants you there. Do you understand?"

"Yes, Mom—but I still don't like her."

"You don't have to like her but you will show respect and behave like the young lady we've raised. Now, let's have a hug and then let's make a New Year's resolution tonight to work at forgiveness."

"Oh Mom! You're really pushing it now. I can only handle obeying you but I'm not sure I can go as far as forgiveness toward her yet."

"Well, you can at least think about it and work on that idea. This will help to build character. It is not always about being right. Sometimes you have to learn to bend and also to bite your tongue. Being right does not always make you the winner. If you shame your father for loving his own mother, you will not come out on the winning side. You'll only hurt him which will, in turn, hurt you."

Clara Rose groaned and rolled her eyes, turned on her heel and retreated to her room. The lecture was over and she'd have to think hard on all this. Carol shook her head and whispered to the ceiling, "And this is why mothers go gray! Lord, give me strength!"

While this had been taking place, I was in the kitchen with Clara and Doris helping to clean up the kitchen after our brunch. The phone rang so I picked up.

"Hello?"

"Hello, is this Don?"

"Yes, speaking."

"Don, Ed Jefferson here. I'm sorry to tell you that your Mom has had a fall. We went to pick her up to take her to church and found her on her front steps. She slipped on some ice. The snow has been melting and then refreezing overnight. I think she went down pretty hard."

"Where is she now? Is she at home?"

"No, I'm calling you from the hospital in Weyburn. They are trying to assess her now but all I know is it isn't good. Can you let your sisters know?"

"Yes, they are actually here now with us and we had planned to go out to see Mother so we'll head to the hospital. Thanks Ed for letting me know and for being there for her."

I called Ethel to let her know and she said she and Jim would head out to Weyburn right away. In light of the situation, I told Carol that she and our girls could stay home if they wanted. I told them Mother would not be in any shape to visit so many people. This way if they stayed home, I could take the others in my station wagon. Clara Rose put her arms around me and gave me a big hug and looked up and said, "Dad, I'm sorry this happened to your Mom. I know she's old and kind of helpless. This is sad for her and for you. I'm so sorry Dad. I'm sorry for saying nasty things about her. I really don't want to see her suffer."

"Thank you sweetheart—you've got a good heart and I'm so proud of you. Stay home with Mommy and I'll call you all later to let you know how things are going."

It seemed that Carol's lecture had an effect on Clara Rose's attitude after all.

ଛଡ଼

Ed and Mildred were still sitting with Mother when we arrived. Ed stood up right away and offered his chair to Ethel. Mildred also stood and offered her chair to Doris.

"Glad you folks got here alright. They've taken ex-rays of your mother and there is a hairline fracture of her pelvis bone, apparently. She has been sleeping some of the time and I'm not sure if it is the drugs or what but she seems to be seeing things that aren't here at times. But, anyway, now that you are all here, Mildred and I will head for home. It's been a long day already for us."

"Of course—thank you both so much for everything. We're so grateful and it was lucky that you arrived to find her when you did." I shook Ed's hand and quickly introduced him and Mildred to my family. They all shook hands and added their praises and thanks to the couple. We explained that we had all been gathering to come to Weyburn to see Mother and we had hoped to start hunting for an apartment for her. Ed just shook his head and said he was very sorry but wished us luck with our plans for her.

Mother had been sleeping but with all our chatter, she had now opened her eyes. The girls quickly stood and leaned over her and spoke softly to her and Doris gently stroked Mother's cheek. She had a bump on her forehead and a terrible bruise on one wrist. I moved in closer and stood on the opposite side of the bed. Mother turned her head slightly and looked at me with a shocked expression.

"Charlie? Is that you? Where have you been all this time?"

She had mistaken me for my father. Perhaps Ed was right. Maybe it was the effect of the drugs they had given her.

"It's me Mother, Don, your son."

"Don? oh . . . Oh yes, I'm sorry. Frank was here a while ago but I don't know where he's gone to now."

Frank had not been there and would not be coming so we all knew this was just another hallucination and that Mother was not herself at all.

Ethel offered Mother a sip of water. Her lips seemed very dry and her forehead felt rather warm. Perhaps she had a slight fever. Jim and Sam excused themselves and told us they'd wait down the hallway where there was a waiting room for family members. I slipped out with them to see if I could find a nurse to talk to about Mother's condition.

I went to the nurses' station and made an enquiry. I was told that there had been a hairline fracture just as Ed had said and that they had given Mother a sedative for pain. She said the doctor would not be around again today but that if we came back in the morning we could speak with him.

I reported this back to the family and we decided we should stay the night in Weyburn and try to speak to the doctor the next day. We booked in at the El Rancho and I called home to update Carol and the girls.

The next day, Mother seemed a little more coherent and more herself. She was eating a bit of breakfast when we arrived. It was still too painful for her to sit up so she was slightly elevated and a nurse had been assisting her. She indicated to the nurse that she couldn't eat any more so the nurse left us to visit alone.

"Were you all here last night? I thought I remembered seeing all of you already but I'm not sure. I seemed to be dreaming a lot."

"Yes Mother, we were all here. Milt and I and Doris and Sam were all in Regina at Don and Carol's place when your neighbour, Ed, called to tell us about your fall." Clara was the first to sit down beside the bed and start the chat.

"Well, I had a bad fall. I went out on the front step to get the cat inside before the Jeffersons arrived to take me to church. The cat was there but she just stared at me and wouldn't come in so I stepped out to pick her up and down I went."

Just then the doctor stepped into the room. He read Mother's chart and listened to her heart and took her pulse.

"Well, Anna, I don't think you should plan to go out dancing for the next little while yet," he teased her.

"Oh doctor! Ha! As if!" she retorted, almost blushing.

I followed him out to the hallway and introduced myself. Doris slipped out along with me. I asked him what he thought we should know.

"Well, she didn't break a hip so that part is good. However, she does have a hairline fracture of the pelvis bone and, at her age, this can still be very serious. I'd like to keep her here for a few days before I release her. We'll just monitor her. I know she lives alone so I would like to be sure she's able to walk and get around here in the hospital first before she goes back home."

We thanked him and went back to the others.

"It looks as though Mother will be here for a few days yet. So, I guess we'd better decide if we all want to stay on and book our hotel rooms again for another couple of nights," I told them.

"That's silly. Why don't you all go out to the farm and stay there. The beds are all made up and besides, I'd like someone there to see to my cat. I know Ed will go over to check on the house and the cat but if you are there, you'll save him the trouble. I also think if you are there, I might get you to bring me some of my personal things that I'd like to have here."

We all looked at one another, stunned and in disbelief. Our mother was actually offering us a bed in her home. I couldn't help but think this wasn't so much about helping us as it was about getting something for herself. I immediately felt the need to resist the invitation.

"Well, I don't know about the others, but I'm not as far from home so I think I may head home in the later afternoon. I can always come back in another day or so. I have a few places lined up that I hope we might go look at today. We need to get looking for a place suitable for you to move into now that winter is over. You shouldn't be going back out to the farm after this experience. You'd be far safer in town where there are people around you. You were very lucky to have Ed and Mildred find you when they did but you can't rely on that happening again."

Just then a nurse came into the room with medications so we told Mother we'd be back later and that we'd think about her offer of staying at the house. Ethel offered that someone could slip out to the house to pick up whatever Mother might need.

"I'd like my own bathrobe and slippers that are in my closet in my bedroom. Oh, and also my own hairbrush and comb that are in the drawer in the vanity in the bathroom upstairs. There's a book beside my bed that I wouldn't mind having to read as well. Could you please feed Muggins some cat food while you are there? I left a little dish in the refrigerator for her. Oh, and give her some fresh water as well. Here's the key to the house. I've got it in my purse."

Once we were out of earshot, we discussed what our plan was for the day and for that night's accommodation.

"I think I'd like to stay at the farm tonight. I haven't been inside the house in years and, truthfully, I'd rather be there when Mother is not there for the first time I set foot in the door." Clara made the first comment. She was curious to see what changes in décor Mother might have made over time. Typical Clara, more interested in the decorating than in anything else. But, I understood her curiosity. It was a natural thing.

"Well, I think we could stay another night as well and I want to help Don to look at these places he's lined up for us. I don't want the drive back to Brandon after house hunting all afternoon. What do you think, Sam?"

"I think it is whatever you want Doris. I am interested in seeing the farm as well. The only time I've ever been there was the day we paid them a visit to tell them we were getting married. I didn't feel very welcome by Frank so I didn't care if I ever went back but it might be nice for us to see it one more time and for you to have an evening there with your family."

"I'd like to go home to Estevan because Jim says his back is bothering him and he'd like to get a good night's sleep in our own bed, but that would leave everyone here without a vehicle since you plan to go back to Regina, Don. That is—if you have really decided that you don't want to stay out at the farm for the night."

"No, I am willing to stay at the farm if you and Jim need to go home, Ethel. I was just having a first negative reaction to Mother's slightly selfish invitation. I guess it stuck in my craw that after all these years, the only reason I was invited to her home was so we could feed the cat and bring her things she wanted. I just had a sudden surge of resentment. I feel we're doing enough as it is to try to find her a place to live. I know she isn't asking a huge favor for us to bring her a few things, I just sometimes get these vibes that burn my ass a little."

"Can't say as I blame you," Sam piped in. Everyone nodded in agreement.

"I'll get over it. I always seem to have these sudden reactions and then I calm down. Let's agree then that I'll stay so we'll have my vehicle and you and Jim go back to Estevan in the afternoon sometime, if you like Ethel. We'll look at some of the places and then we'll maybe have a coffee in the afternoon and discuss things."

With that plan in place, we all piled into my station wagon and began the house hunting.

After seeing several places, we stopped for coffee and had come to the agreement that the best place of all was an assisted-living, ground-floor, one-bedroom apartment right beside the public library. It was located right downtown and was within walking distance to the Co-Op grocery store and the church Mother attended. There was a large common room on the main floor where residents could have a home cooked meal served to them once a week. Each unit had its own tiny kitchen so meals could be prepared if desired. Residents were checked on every morning to make sure they were well. Laundry service was available if needed, but each unit had a small laundry room as well.

After having a coffee break together, we drove out to the farm to get Mother's things. Ethel ran upstairs to fetch Mother's robe and slippers, and Doris fed and watered the cat. Muggins was at the door wanting out as soon as we went in but we managed to stop her. God help us if we let her escape. Again, it seemed to me that Muggins was mother's baby and rated better than I did.

I looked down at Muggins and she rubbed up against my leg. "Mother loves you more than me, Muggins," I told her resentfully.

Clara wandered around on the main floor and then went upstairs to snoop some more. The men and I remained downstairs. Doris decided to do a quick cleaning out of Mother's refrigerator. She threw a few things out and I carried the garbage out. Then we made our way to the hospital.

Mother already had her supper tray in front of her when we arrived. She still was not able to sit up straight but was elevated slightly and a nurse had been helping her with her meal. She still wasn't eating enough to keep a bird alive but at least she was taking some nourishment. She gave us a smile as we came in.

"Mother," Ethel took the lead. "We've found a perfect place for you. It's right downtown next to the library and less than a block from the Co-Op grocery store and another block from your church. There is a unit available on the first of May on the ground floor. There's one bedroom, a nice living room with a large picture window that looks out on a small grassy area and there's even a tree right in front of that window. Not all units have that so this one is a lovely one."

"Yes, and it's an assisted living place so if you need them to do your laundry or if you want them to provide transportation, it is all available to you. They even have a lovely large common area where residents can sit and visit or play board games and once a week they provide you with a home cooked meal with other residents if you want it," Doris added excitedly.

"It sounds very nice but I'm not in any shape to handle a move by the first of May, I'm afraid."

"Of course, we've talked about that," Clara sounded reassuring. "We'd all take turns coming to help with the move. You won't have to lift a finger. We can move whatever pieces of furniture you want and leave the rest at the farm until you are up to making decisions about things."

Mother turned away from us and looked toward the window. Without looking at us she took a deep breath and spoke quietly, "Well, I guess I have no choice do I? I haven't lived in the city ever before in my life. But, I know the house and yard at the farm are too much for me."

She turned now and looked at us. "And I do like the idea of being able to walk to get my groceries or go next door to the library. I love to read. And I could even walk to church and I'd be able to attend Bible study classes on Tuesday night. I've never been able to do that before because Frank wouldn't drive me into town for it."

She managed a smile now so we said good night and left her to have her own thoughts. Ethel and Jim left for Estevan and the rest of us headed to the farm.

Chapter 35

While the women were all over the house, looking in cupboards, closets and chatting away about Mother's china, ornaments, lace table cloths and old photographs, Milt cracked open a bottle of rye and poured himself a drink. He offered Sam and me one too and I accepted. Sam declined but said he'd have a cold beer and went out to the car to get a six-pack that he'd picked up earlier. It had been another tiring day and I wasn't so interested in the snooping around the house as were the girls. I was ready to sit and relax. It was the first time I'd had an opportunity to just chat with the brothers-in-law without the women around.

Milt and Sam were both big raw-boned men. I was nearly as tall as they were but much slimmer. I was built like my father. I sensed with both of them that still waters run deep. Although neither was real talkative, I could tell they had deep thoughts and opinions. I wondered what they thought of our "family dynamics".

"So, Milt, how the heck do you feel about our mother and has she affected life for you and Clara in any way in particular?"

"I'll tell you this much. I have very little regard for any woman who does what your Mother did to you. As far as our relationship goes, I think Clara and I have handled our life together pretty good. Clara had a lot of years with a mother that she loved—more years than you got, obviously. She's always had a good relationship with her sisters so I think that always gave her the sense that she still had a family. We raised the kids and I was so busy with the business that I don't think I gave your sister's family life much thought. I guess Clara didn't bring it up very often and when she did, she didn't seem too critical of her mother other than she never liked that you had been sent away. We had my parents nearby and the kids kept Clara busy so maybe thoughts and conversations we should have had about your mother were pushed aside. It seemed easier that way, I suppose."

"I see. That makes sense. Sometimes maybe when things or people are out of sight, they are out of mind as well. To be honest, I would have to say that my thoughts were often preoccupied by other things and other people while I was away from my family as well. Sam, how about you and Doris?" I pushed.

"I try to stay humble and let people think what they will," Sam sipped on his beer and seemed uncomfortable with this type of frank conversation. I had the distinct impression that Sam, being a man of few words, would rather just be a listener rather than a contributor to this topic.

"Doris is a pretty strong woman," he continued. "She has managed to stay in touch with her mother over the years so I'd say she never totally detached herself like Ethel or Clara seemed to do. I know it wasn't what you'd call a close or loving mother-daughter relationship but Doris always sent a card for birthdays or Christmas and kept in touch that way. My own relationship with my father was rather strained so I certainly understood how these things can happen in a family. Families can be complicated. I think it is a bugger that you got sent away though. I am truly sorry, Don, for what you endured. Working in the mental hospital in Brandon is enough for me to be able to imagine some of what you may have experienced."

I knew Sam meant this from his heart and I respected both these men for being good and strong husbands to my sisters. I felt they were as close to me in this moment as they could have been if they were my own brothers.

"Thanks guys for being there for my sisters. I'm glad they have someone strong to lean on and speaking of that, I should call my wife. I'm sure she's wondering what we discovered today as far as the house hunting and she'll wonder how Mother is doing."

"Sure, Don, go ahead. Sam, you want another beer? I'm pouring another rye. It's going down good tonight."

"Why not, I'm not driving anywhere!" Sam chuckled.

ॐ

My attic bedroom was pretty much just as I remembered it. My baseball cap collection was still hanging on the wall and my bat and ball glove were still in the corner beside my dresser drawers. The single brass bed looked rather tiny now. The bedspread with cowboy hats and cowboy boots motif still covered the bed. The patchwork quilt made by my grandmother was still neatly folded at the foot of the bed. About the only thing different was that Mother had moved her sewing machine into my room. She likely didn't use it much and wanted it out of her way. Everything was still very clean and neat. Even though Mother was getting on in age, she was good at keeping things in order. I climbed into bed and looked out the window at the stars and remembered how cozy and safe and loved I had always felt in that bed.

ༀ

After breakfast, we headed back to the hospital. The sun was shining and the snow was completely melted away. Crocuses were peeking out of the earth and the robins were back. I was feeling a little light hearted and thought maybe I'd suggest the girls take a break after lunch and go to a movie or shop while us men might take a drive so I could show them around the area a bit.

Mother was snoozing when we arrived so the men went out to the hall and the girls followed. For some reason, I seemed unable to leave the room. I thought we should just go back to the nurses' station and tell them that we would all come back later. But, I couldn't move. I just stood there. Finally, I went over and sat in the chair beside Mother and just looked at her. Again, I questioned myself as to why I was doing this. It seemed silly to watch someone sleep but I was not in control of my own actions. I seemed under a spell in a way.

Mother looked so peaceful and I studied her face and found that I could still see some of that pretty woman that I loved still in her face. Again, I couldn't seem to make myself leave but I didn't fight against it. I only wondered why.

Mother opened her eyes.

"Oh hi Don, I must have dozed off for a bit. Where are the others?"

"They're just down the hall. I can go get them. We had a good night at your house last night and just wanted to check in on you this morning."

"No, don't get them yet please, I want to talk to you alone. Can you please close the door?"

"Sure."

I came back and sat down again.

"The doctor was around early this morning and said he wants the nurses to get me up because he is concerned that I might get pneumonia if I keep lying here like this. He said he detected a bit of fluid in my lungs already. So, if they are going to discharge me, I'll have to go back to the farm and they brought me in here by ambulance so I need some clothes and a coat to go home in. I know you brought my bathrobe and a few undergarments earlier but now I'll need to be dressed properly and have my coat. I wonder if you could get me those things and then come back."

"Sure, but you said you needed to speak to me alone. What's on your mind?"

"Son, I want to ask for your forgiveness. I know what we did to you was wrong. I didn't want to leave you there— honestly, I didn't. I was so frightened of life alone on the farm and Frank was the only option for me at the time. At least that was how I felt. He was a very strong- minded man who knew so much about farming. I was used to a strong man like your father, but I know they were totally different men. They were both very strong willed and knowledgeable so I felt I needed that strength in a man. I couldn't survive without it. I tried to convince him to just send the girls away as they were almost grown up and ready to leave anyway but I wanted to keep you at home. But . . ."

"I know Mother. I know you felt that way but I guess I don't understand how you could have left me in that place and never have found the strength to stand up to Frank and come and get me. I was a little boy, Mother. I was a defenseless child all alone and for eight years. I was raped the very first night and that wasn't the last time. I was also beaten when I was a teen."

"Oh God, Don—I had no idea. I always tried to picture you in there and I envisioned you playing with other children and being treated well by the caregivers."

I ignored her comment and went on, "I suffered deep loneliness and despair without a single visit or a card or letter from you. And don't tell me about the fact that there was no visiting allowed. I know that already. But, I'm a parent now myself and I know I would never be able, or think, to do what you did to me. I know you want to blame Frank but I was your own flesh and blood Mother. Didn't I count more to you than him? How could you do that to me?"

I felt my voice breaking and without realizing it, I now was aware that tears were streaming down my face. But I felt I was this far into it and I was going to finish. The years of hurt and abandonment were all right there in my throat. I was no longer able to choke them back down to the pit of my stomach where I could usually suppress things. This was the time and she was going to hear it whether she was old and frail and lying in a hospital bed or not.

"I tried to come to you with an open and an un-accusing heart that day that I brought my wife and children to meet you. You were like the ice queen, standing there in your driveway not even asking us to come in. God damn you Mother! I brought my babies, your grandchildren to meet you that day. You stood there and had nothing for me. Nothing!"

"Son, I'm so, so sorry. I know I seemed terribly rude. I wanted desperately to invite you all in that day. I didn't know how to handle the situation. Frank was inside and I knew he'd be totally rude and I was afraid you might turn violent toward him. I didn't know what to expect from you as a grown man and I had no forewarning that you were coming. I was taken by complete surprise and was so shocked, I could hardly think."

By now she was sobbing and she held her arms up to me with a pleading look in her eyes. I fell to the bed and let her embrace me. I cried like a child and I wanted my mother's love and needed to be held. I was angry, heart-broken and yet wanting to be able to accept her apology. I needed to be able to hear her words and she had finally spoken them to me. We wept together and she kissed the top of my head like she had so many times as a little boy. I raised my head up and looked into her eyes. She cradled my face in her hands and smiled at me through her tears.

"Son, let's turn this around today from this point forward. I want us to be able to put it in the past and I want to be a better person. I know I love you and your sisters. I know I've been wrong. I can't change it now but I can tell you I love you and I want to spend time together for the time I have left. Frank is no longer a threat and he is not in the picture. No one need be exposed to him any further. I want to meet your children again. I want them to come into my house. Please Don, please, please say you'll forgive me."

"I want that too. I've always wanted that. I have never stopped loving you and wanting a mother-son relationship with you. It's funny how I can love you but still hate what you did to me. I thought so many times that I would not hold you responsible and that I would forgive you and just blame Frank. I've thought I had already forgiven. I even resent my own sisters at times. I struggle with my feelings nearly every day of my life. I've wanted to hear this from you for so long and I'm glad you finally have said these things. I do want to forgive you and I want to tell you that I totally forgive you. But, I'm afraid that it doesn't just go away like that. I'm willing to work on it though. I do want to build trust and love between us again. I want to bring my girls to you. I want them to have a Grandma to love. They love Carol's mother but I want them to be able to love you too. All I can say is we can work on this."

"Fair enough, Son. I'm relieved to hear you can still love me. I don't want to go to my grave thinking you hate me."

"I never, ever have felt hatred for you. Only love. Hatred—no; hurt—yes. Incredible hurt. The wound is very deep but for some reason, I've always had a desire to be a survivor and maybe you and Father gave that much to me in my first nine years of life. I'm stronger than you are, I think. Maybe I get that from Father. Who knows, but I'm thankful for it. There were some decent people along the way—even in that terrible place. They offered me some sort of level of caring, love and respect and I guess you grow from the love that you receive from others. I grew and am still growing with the love of my wife and children. I do hope we can share that love going forward."

"Me too, Son—me too. Can you hand me that glass of water, please? I feel quite dry and I'd like to have my face washed before anyone comes in and sees I've been crying."

I hadn't heard her call me "Son" for so many years. It somehow seemed odd to me now but I was happy that she wanted to use that word.

"Good idea, I'll get a cold cloth and we can both wash our tears away before anyone comes along."

I washed her face for her and then wiped my own face. We smiled at one another and I touched her cheek. It was a bittersweet tender moment that I'll never forget. The air had been cleared, finally after all these years. We weren't home free yet but we were on our way to happier days. I knew we had love in our hearts for one another and that was a very good feeling. It could surely be a place to start to rebuild.

There was a rap at the door. A nurse poked her head in.

"Time to get you washed up and dressed Anna. The doctor says you can go home today."

"OK Mother, we'll dash out to the farm to get your clothes. I'll be back as soon as I can with them. Nurse, you'll have to let her wait until we can get her some clothes. We can't have her going home like that!" I winked at her.

I gave her a quick kiss and then hurried out the door.

I explained my required errand to return to the farm to the others. Clara said she'd come with me to pick out something suitable for Mother while the others stayed behind to keep Mother company until we returned. We got to the farm and while Clara gathered clothing for Mother, I fed Muggins again. That cat was fat and could likely live off her fat for a month but I knew I'd better be able to report to Mother that Muggins had been properly looked after.

As we were driving back into town, we were talking about what to do next. Mother couldn't move into Weyburn until May 1; so, she would need some care and help in the meantime.

"I think when we get back to the hospital we should go talk to the staff about getting her some in-home care until her apartment is ready," I suggested to Clara.

"Well, we'll have to get a recommendation from her doctor for that first. We can't just order Home Care for her. Maybe we can rely on Ed and Mildred for this month. They seem so willing."

"I know but I just think she's so weak right now that I think she is going to need someone to stay in the house with her for a few days until we see how well she can manage on her own."

"I think you're right, Don. Maybe Ethel and Jim would consider coming back and staying with her for a few days until we can get some extra Home Care in place. They might help for a temporary time until we can move her to Weyburn."

I didn't tell Clara about the conversation with Mother earlier. I am not sure why I didn't feel like telling her. I suppose it might be because my feelings had been so raw and because I was even a little ashamed of the way I had broken down and sobbed like a child. Maybe it was because I still wasn't truly comfortable in my, somewhat new, role as the little brother to these sisters. Part of me still held back something from them all.

We were back to the hospital. We'd only been gone about 45 minutes. As we stepped off the elevator, we were met by Milt.

"Oh God, Don and Clara—thank goodness you are back. I've been waiting and watching for you to come. Your mom's taken a turn for the worse. The nurses tried getting her up on her feet and she took a spell. It's not good. Hurry up and get in there!"

We rushed to her room and when we entered, Doris, Sam and four nurses were all around Mother's bed. She was moaning and her eyes were closed. The head nurse was listening to her heart with the stethoscope. She came over to me.

"Don, she's having multiple little heart attacks. If there's anything you all want to say to her or if there is anyone else you want to call, now is the time. She's on her way out, I'm afraid."

Well, we have another sister to call but she's in Estevan. The nurse shook her head. Apparently, there wasn't going to be time for Ethel to get there. I mentioned the Minister of her church, Reverend Parker. One of the nurses piped up, "He's actually here right now. He's just down the hall visiting another patient. I'll get him."

I walked over to Mother and joined my sisters and we all touched her. Milt and Sam were close but stayed behind their wives. When we touched her, she stopped moaning.

"Mother, we're all here with you." I tried to be of some comfort to her but she kept her eyes shut.

The nurse returned with Reverend Parker. I asked him to say the Lord's Prayer with us. He quickly moved to the opposite side of the bed to get close to her.

"Mother, Reverend Parker is here and we're going to say the Lord's Prayer for you."

We said the prayer together and when we finished, Doris, kissed Mother on the cheek, followed by Clara and then me.

"Mother, if you can see the light, go toward the light. There will be someone there to meet you and we promise we'll join you on the other side one day. And, Mother, you are forgiven. You are loved and you are forever in our hearts. Go in peace. You are free to go with our love."

I hoped and wanted to believe she heard my words because they were straight from my heart to hers and I meant every word. In that instant, she stopped breathing. The nurse listened to her heart again and then touched each of us and said she was very sorry. Mother was gone.

Chapter 36

We buried Mother beside our father. We all agreed that none of us ever wanted to visit our mother's grave one day beside Frank. It made sense to us to bring our parents together in one place. Instead of moving her into the new apartment, we were burying her. At least she was at peace and she never wanted to live alone so she really managed to escape that great fear of hers for the most part.

I don't remember feeling a great sense of loss by Mother's death. That is not to say that I didn't care about her passing but I felt that I had suffered the "loss" of my mother as a young boy. I grieved the loss of her when I realized she wasn't coming to get me from the mental institution. I suffered another loss, so to speak, when she didn't welcome me back the day I took my family to meet her.

Now, I was at peace knowing that we had made amends with one another. I had been able to give her my total assurance of my forgiveness as she was dying. I no longer had to wonder if I could someday forgive her. I forgave her with all my heart in that moment. I felt we had given one another a great gift. She could go to Heaven with the peace of knowing her children all loved her and that I had forgiven all the hurt.

I could now move forward knowing that she had made an attempt to ask for my forgiveness. She wasn't perfect—but, she was not evil. She was as much a victim of her circumstances as I was of mine. I could let all the bitterness go now. I felt my life was always in that thrust of moving forward, even when at times I might have chosen to give up or just throw in the towel on things. I never did. Something in me always said, "Buck up Son". . . Father's words came to mind.

80CR

After Frank had been placed into permanent care at the Mental Hospital, Mother had changed her will. She made provisions to allow Frank to be cared for as long as he lived but upon his death, anything left from that provision would go back into the estate and go to her children to be divided equally. So, as long as he lived, his expenses would be covered but the land and home on the farm went directly to us children. I was made executor of her will.

For the immediate time after Mother's death, we held up an agreement she had previously made with Ed Jefferson to rent the land to him to plant crops. That way there would be some income and we could take the time to deal with closing up the house and dealing with the final steps necessary. During the summer, we got together and had an auction to sell off the machinery and some of the larger household effects.

Doris wanted the dining room table furniture which was fine with everyone else. Ethel took Mother's rocking chair, some silverware, and a couple of handmade quilts and linens that had been embroidered by Mother. Clara took some of the crystal goblets and a few bone china tea cups but wanted nothing much. No one wanted all the bone china dinnerware that had come from the old country so the sisters offered it to Carol. Carol was overjoyed to receive this as she had never had such beautiful dishes to set her table with for those many special family gatherings. The sisters were very kind and generous in this and they pointed out that we had three lovely daughters who could share in the inheritance of it one day. Anything else from the house was donated to the Baptist Church that Mother had always attended. The church had garage sales to raise funds for charities so they were happy to receive what we didn't want.

I roamed through the house helping to box things up and made trips up and down the stairs carrying things out. At one point, for some reason, I took a look inside my old closet and there on the floor in a dark corner were my father's leather work boots that I had placed there just after his death. All of a sudden I remembered that I had wanted those boots and that I was not going to leave them anywhere where Frank might decide to wear them. I had a little chuckle to myself as I picked them up. I remembered how I had tried them on as a little boy and how they were way too large for me.

Now I was curious so I slipped off my shoes and stepped into them. Well, by gosh! They fit perfectly. I was the same size as my father. It felt good. I decided I would take these old boots home and place them in my workshop space in my garage. The sisters and Carol had the things that they wanted and now I had something that I wanted too. This was a real treasure for me.

"Dad! Are you upstairs?"

"Yes, Jenny. I'm up here but I'm coming down now."

"Are we leaving for the lake now? I want to go for a swim."

"Jenny, your dad is doing his best to get things finished up here. Don't bug him to hurry," Carol smiled at me as I came down the stairs.

"It's alright girls. I think we are about ready to head out and I think we'll make it in plenty of time for you to have a swim. It's only about an hour's drive from the farm."

We were heading to our cottage at the lake and my sisters and their husbands and all their family members were coming out to join us on the weekend. Some had camper trailers and some of the younger ones had tents. Ethel and Jim had a special lift put onto their large motor home which allowed for lifting their son's motorized wheelchair into their unit. I don't know who was the happier one—Ethel or Jimmy Jr. Ethel was over the moon to be able to take Jimmy to the lake and to have him be part of our first family reunion. Jimmy smiled from ear to ear and everyone helped him wherever possible.

I wanted to spend some special time with Jimmy because I felt there was something we had in common. He was a boy trapped in his own body. I had been a boy trapped in an asylum. He had no choice in what had happened to him physically. I also had no choice in what happened to me both mentally and physically at times. I'm sure he had lots of struggles with his feelings just as I had gone through my struggles. He was amazingly cheerful and I admired him for his strength and resilience. I realized that of the two of us, I was the luckier one by far. I had a chance at a whole other new life and I had so much to be thankful for. Seeing him trapped and knowing that he knew he would never be completely free of his disability and yet seeing how loving and happy he seemed to be, was a real eye opener for me and for anyone who would spend a little time with this precious boy. I felt I was learning a lesson and it was an honor to be in his presence. *There but for the grace of God, go I ,* came to mind once again.

Clara and Milt had a large motor home as well and had accommodations for some of their family. Others pitched tents. Doris and Sam stayed in our cottage in our guest room. The campgrounds were within walking distance of our place so we congregated at the campgrounds some of the time and other times we all sat around the camp fire in our back yard. We had a wonderful time over the long weekend in August. People swam, hiked, golfed, fished and sometimes it was the men off doing one thing while the women enjoyed some peace and quiet just having a coffee or relaxing in the sun together. Everyone agreed that this was something we would make an annual summer event.

After everyone had headed home, Carol and I and the girls stayed another few days to enjoy the quiet time before going home to get the girls ready to go back to school. The girls were out on the back deck making beaded bracelets and drinking lemonade. Carol poured two glasses of lemonade and brought one to me. I had just been sitting in my armchair doing a crossword puzzle. I put it down and thanked her for the lemonade.

"Just what I was thinking I needed—thank you dear. That's so refreshing on a hot day. Sounds like the girls are having a good time with the jewelry-making kit Ethel gave them."

"Yes, it's good for them to have a project so I can sit for a little bit and enjoy my lemonade with you in peace and quiet. I'm exhausted after such a busy weekend."

"You deserve a break. You and the sisters did a lot of cooking over the weekend. Everyone loved your Saskatoon pie. It was a hit!"

"I know. Next year they want to help me pick the berries and take some home with them to make pies and muffins. Honestly, did you see how much some of those boys could eat? It makes me glad we're raising girls who are always watching their waistlines!" Carol laughed.

"Well, it was a busy weekend but I know everyone had a great time. We were lucky to have perfect weather. I feel like we have become a real family again. Your family is so great but I think mine is pretty darn good too, don't you?"

"Oh, of course they are! I love your sisters. They are all so kind to me and make me feel like I'm one of them. Everyone is so nice to our girls too. Did you notice how our girls were having so much fun with Anna. They seem to really look up to her and everything she wears or how she styles her hair is of great interest to them—especially to Clara Rose."

"Yes, and it was nice that Anna and her husband, Ben, made it all the way out here from Victoria. That's a heck of a long trip for them. Now that she's expecting, I am not so sure they'll make it out here next year," I sipped on my lemonade.

"You know, Don, I've been thinking. . . "

"Uh-oh, do I see dollar signs in your eyeballs?" I teased.

"No, but I do have an idea about something. Actually, it is not totally my idea. Your sisters and I were all talking the other day and someone mentioned that they thought maybe you should write a book about your life and . . ."

"Oh are you kidding?" I almost choked on my lemonade.

"Well, just wait a minute. Just think about this for a moment. You have lived through something that most people could not ever imagine could happen to a child. There's been so much secrecy about what went on in mental institutions at the time that you were a boy. People didn't even know there were children being kept in that place."

"Well, obviously, some people had to know. But, I think you are right that most people had no idea that a normal child could end up in there, and certainly those who were aware were not doing anything about it," I added.

Once again, Carol had planted a seed in my brain and I now had something else to think about. That woman was always coming up with something for me it seemed. But, as usual, I had to agree with her. This was something I should at least put into my memoirs. So, over the next year, I did write. I relived every memory and it wasn't an easy process. I wept at times because every emotion and every experience was so vivid and painful. Also, if this was to ever be published, I was feeling vulnerable and ashamed of the rapes and the abuse. I had to decide how much I could bare my soul.

During the process, I called upon Martha. I talked to her about wanting to write my story and asked her if I could include the part about her and also Jerry. I told her I would change the names for their privacy. I explained that I would also be including the part about the charges we filed against the hospital and the abusers. She and Jerry were both on board with it and gave me their blessings.

It was so good to see them both again and to see Martha was happy. We would always be special friends and she, more than anyone else in my world, understood completely what I had lived through because she had shared the same life. Even Jerry, as wonderful and kind as he was, did not fully understand what we had lived through or how we felt. I know he saw a lot of things first hand but he hadn't lived our life as children in that place.

My adoring wife was so supportive all these years; but, even she could not really feel what Martha and I had felt. No one who hadn't lived it could understand it.

Chapter 37

My close feeling of friendship and affection for Martha did pose a problem at one brief time. When I had called her about my book, we had decided to have a coffee one day and discuss things. It wasn't a secret from Carol or Jerry but something happened that day that was rather significant. We got into a discussion about her father.

"I have some news about my dad to share with you. We found him a couple of months ago."

"That's great—or is it?" I asked. I remembered that Martha's father had been a serious alcoholic and that he never did come to retrieve her from the Mental. She, like I, had suffered the feeling of abandonment by a parent.

"Well, I'm glad I did find him but he was still drinking. Jerry decided we needed to seek him out and see if he was still alive or what."

"Where did you find him?"

"Jerry and I started volunteering some time ago at the Salvation Army and Jerry made some enquiries in small circles in town. The word got out and it turned out that the Salvation Army was quite aware of him but they talked to him first, privately, to see if he wanted to be contacted by me. Luckily, he was very much in favour of meeting me."

"So have you met him yet, then?"

"Yes, we did meet last month. I could hardly recognize him though. I hadn't seen him for so many years and he looked so old to me."

"How did it go? Was Jerry with you?"

"Yes, I wanted Jerry to be with me. It went OK but I had hoped that he would have been completely over his drinking."

"Ah, I see. I'm sorry to hear. So, what do you think will happen? Do you want to see him again?"

"Yeah, I do—and actually, we've seen him several times over the last couple of months. Jerry kind of let him know that if he wanted an ongoing relationship with us, he'd have to quit drinking. Jerry made it clear he didn't want him around our kids when he was drinking."

"So, did he agree?"

"No, not that day, but, just last week he told us he had taken his first step and had gone to an AA meeting. He's got a sponsor and he says he wants help now to learn how to stay sober. But, I just don't know yet how this is going to all turn out. I feel like we're starting all over and I feel like we are two different people from when I was his little girl and he was my daddy. Do you know what I mean?"

"I know what you mean. It was like that for me and my mother. We've both had parents that have let us down in a way and it is very difficult to forgive sometimes."

"Jerry says that we can only hope that Dad will be able to achieve sobriety. If he can't then we have to decide if we can accept him on some level in spite of his shortcomings.

312

But, he is trying and I'm thankful for that. I guess we have to just take things one day at a time." She had tears in her eyes now. I certainly did know how she felt.

I had reached for Martha's hand as we were sharing her story and for a moment, she grasped my hand as well and we sat—our gaze suspended—our eyes locked on one another and we both knew there was something happening.

When I walked her to her car, we walked arm in arm and when we got to her vehicle, I kissed her on the cheek and she responded with a kiss on my lips. I grabbed her and held her and kissed her hard and long. The kiss was a real kiss—a kiss that had deep meaning and passion. She quickly broke from my embrace but not so quick that she was being indignant with me. She jumped in her car and didn't look back at me as she drove away as quickly as she could. I knew we both wanted one another in that instant but we knew this was a forbidden desire and I'm sure she wrestled with her feelings that day as much as I did.

All the way home, I swore at myself, "What the hell are you doing man? God, you are an idiot! Why, why did you have to go and do something stupid like that? Shit, shit, shit!"

I had trouble looking at my wife that day and when we went to bed, I just gave her a peck on the cheek and rolled over to face away from her. I hardly slept a wink that night. I tossed and turned and felt sick to my stomach. What would Martha be thinking and feeling tonight. I worried that I had upset her.

I waited for a few days and then called Martha again. I had to apologize to her for my advance. I couldn't allow her to feel ashamed or that I had disrespected her and Jerry. I asked if we could meet again to talk. She was reluctant but

313

finally agreed. She suggested we meet in the park rather than in a coffee shop.

I told Carol I was meeting Martha again.

"Again? Haven't you managed to get all the things you need to discuss about the book taken care of yet?" Carol quizzed me as she folded laundry at the kitchen table. Carol was no dummy. I almost felt she could read my mind at times. It was most unnerving.

"Not quite everything," I lied, "but this chat will be the last one I need to have with her on this. We got a bit side-tracked the other day talking mostly about her father. So this time, I want to discuss some details pertaining to my book."

"It just seems to me that you could talk on the telephone," she looked at me with a questioning and rather suspicious look. Then she resumed folding the laundry. I felt so guilty and I hoped she didn't see anything telling in my eyes.

I waited in the park for Martha but she never showed. God, I worried about what the reason for this could be. I hoped she was alright.

At work the next day, she called me.

"Don, I'm sorry I didn't show up yesterday. Well, no, I'm not sorry. Actually, I was relieved to not see you in person. I was afraid to see you."

"God, Martha, I'm so sorry. I was out of line and I just wanted to apologize to you in person. I'm sorry you feel afraid of me."

"No, I'm not afraid of you—I'm afraid of me. I knew if I met you again in the park that I would likely do something to lead you on. I couldn't trust my own feelings or actions." She sounded near tears. "There's just way too

314

much at stake here for both of us, Don. There's always been an attraction on my part toward you. I know I was just a girl when we were together and I was happy to just hold hands. But, I'm a woman now and the attraction is still there. I need to back off."

"I get it Martha. It was always that way for me too. I promise you that I'll never do anything to jeopardize our friendship again. I am ashamed of myself and feel guilty for what I've done and especially for my betrayal to Carol and Jerry."

"You haven't betrayed them. Emotionally and mentally you feel that you have but you are no more guilty of a betrayal than I am. If there's any betrayal, we're both guilty. We both love our partners and we are not going to betray anyone. We just need to have a strict understanding from here forward. No more meetings without our spouses, agreed?"

"Agreed—I hope you will still want to see us as couples though. I hope I haven't ruined that for everyone." I begged.

"Of course—we will get together but not for a while. Now, let's cheer up and be thankful for our families and for our friendship. We will always be special friends to one another. But, we do have to keep things in check." She said her good-bye and I thanked her for being so understanding.

We did see Martha and Jerry again in the years that followed this incident and, although we never spoke of it again, I never forgot it and I'm sure she never did either.

Chapter 38

Writing the book made me take a hard look into my past. I wanted to remember every detail and, although many memories were unpleasant, not all of my past was terrible. I could take comfort in the happy memories of my life on the farm with two great parents, three sisters, and wonderful grandparents. I had a normal life doing all the fun things that boys do like catching bugs, frogs and snakes, swimming in a dugout or at Nickle Lake, riding my bike, climbing trees, playing in the haystack, hunting for gophers, helping Father to fix a machine or at least thinking I was helping. All the things that I loved were there in my past.

I don't know what the path would have been for me if Father had lived. That bull was really the one that was to blame! In that one blasted moment of terror, that bull changed the course of my life. I had to kind of laugh about that, even though the tragedy of my father's death was no laughing matter at all.

Delving into my life in the mental institution was complicated. It was almost as if I had lived the life of three separate people. The first life was the little boy who was happy living on the farm—it was easy to reflect on happy times on the farm. The second life was the little boy all alone in a frightening world trying to grow into manhood. And finally, the third life was my struggles, joys and accomplishments as a man living my life to the present day. On the surface, my first gut reaction to my memories in the asylum was painful. I needed to look beyond this. I came to the realization that there were some positive things in that time.

I had acknowledged this in the past but it was easy to forget the good things that were there. I started to make the mental list of events like the picnics outdoors with lots of nice food prepared by the kitchen staff, music and dances where staff took time to get people up to dance and to help them to enjoy themselves for even a moment, kindness shown to me and others by nurses like Nurse Beattie, Nurse Susan and Jerry, the gentle souls that touched my life like Big Red, Miriam, Arnold and my special friends Joe and Martha.

It was good to reaffirm this in my mind and by writing it down, it seemed to help embed it and make it stand truer. I was finding that with every positive thing I remembered, I smiled and was lifted. I began to appreciate and understand that maybe God had a purpose after all for me in all this seeming madness. There was good in my past. The sad and evil things that had happened were not enough to consume my life. I had survived and I had flourished. Each good memory helped cancel a negative one or at least significantly lessen its hold on me.

And so I wrote, and wrote . . .

ೞೞ

The hospital called one day in June 1971 to inform us that Frank had passed away. It was just a little more than a year since Mother had died. Because there was no family or a single friend to take care of Frank's remains—that was left to us. We decided to have him cremated and to scatter his ashes on the farm. The thought ran through my mind to scatter his remains over the old pig pen but I didn't think that was something that would meet with God's or Mother's approval.

It had been mentioned by someone that we could spread his ashes over Mother's grave but that idea didn't sit well with me. I felt that Frank had intruded into our lives and he had taken our mother from us and he had her to himself for all those years. This decision gave me a sense of power and control over Frank, finally. It was too great to ignore. I thought, *No, you can't rest beside my mother ever again.* I wouldn't allow him that last privilege.

So, on a warm breezy day, we let old Frank free out in a deep blue field of flax. Jenny, who was now 12, had captured a few yellow butterflies in a jar and she wanted to let them go into the air along with Frank's ashes. This was just too sweet for the last farewell to this bitter man who hated children so much. But, to please Jenny, I told her it was a great idea.

Ethel and Jim came that day but it was more out of respect for me and my family than it was for Frank. Clara and Doris decided they wouldn't attend. I understood as they had a longer drive and I knew they would have come if I had insisted but it really wasn't that important. None of us could begin to pretend that Frank was important to us. However, I

319

felt that even though this man had nothing but contempt for us, the respectable thing to do was to at least put him to a final resting place. Nothing seemed more appropriate than allowing him to rest on the land he had taken care of for so long. He had worked hard to look after it as though it were his very own. That much was indisputable.

I suppose that it was because this was the end of Frank that I was now able to think about this man. While he was alive there was an odd element of fear that kept me from venturing near him or asking any questions about him. As a child, I felt a fear of him but as a man, I feared of what I might do to him physically if we were to ever butt heads. It seemed safer to keep my distance as much as possible.

Now, we would never know what had been his story. Everyone has a story of some sort. We are products of our environment. The people who raised us, the experiences in life that we live through are all bound to shape us and make us who we are today. What or who did something to Frank to make him hate children? Did he have a terrible childhood? I suspected that he must have grown up without much love and tenderness because he seemed incapable of giving it to others. You cannot live what you've never seen. If he had never had a role model such as a father who loved him, an older brother to look up to, or a mother to teach him to be kind to others, then perhaps some of his callous and uncaring nature could be explained.

Thinking about him and the mystery of how he had developed made me feel all the more thankful for the first nine years of my life. I had two loving and nurturing parents in that time. I also had three older sisters who were loving and protective towards me. Up until the fracture of my father's death that caused my life to crack and splinter into pieces, I had at least received the basics of what a human being should learn in order to have the capacity to love and to be kind to children. Frank had missed that somehow it would seem.

I wondered if he loved my mother. Was a man such as he even capable of loving a woman? I assumed there had been a sexual attraction on both parts in the beginning. I remembered how they acted around one another after Father died. But having a sexual desire didn't necessarily mean there was deep and lasting love between them. There must have been some tender moments shared, of course.

He wasn't brutal to her until he started losing his mind. But, did he love her? Did she love him? Or was it just a marriage of convenience for both. I suppose that was part of it. She needed a strong man to manage the farm. He needed a home and a woman to cook and clean and run a household. He had set boundaries and had given her an ultimatum and she had agreed to it. None of my questions could be answered now. Perhaps if Mother had lived a little longer, we would have had some conversations about Frank. Maybe she knew something about his childhood or his young adult background. But now we would never know.

"Dad, when can I let the butterflies out of the jar?" Jenny was asking as we walked into the field.

"I want to read a poem first," Doris said. "I figured since we aren't in a church and we don't even have a minister here with us, that somebody should at least say something."

"That is a very nice idea, Doris. Thank you for being so thoughtful." Carol patted Doris on the back and smiled up at me as if to acknowledge how blessed we were as parents.

Moments like this do touch the heart of a parent when the child seems to be more thoughtful than the parent. It catches you by surprise to realize how suddenly this child has become an independent thinker, with morals and compassion for others. Did we teach her? Or did she just have this in her naturally? Did Frank learn his behaviour? Or was it in him naturally?

Doris was now 15 and she loved poetry and had written a short poem which she read and then I opened the urn and flung Frank's ashes into the wind as Jenny released her butterflies.

৪৩৫৪

August was hot and the crops were in great shape. I had offered to help Ed Jefferson with harvest on weekends. Carol and Mildred met at Mother's house and shared the cooking to bring out to the field. Doris and Sam came one weekend to lend a hand.

"Thanks for bringing extra hands on board this weekend, Don," Ed jumped down from the combine to stop in the field for our lunch. Mildred had set the food out by dropping the tailgate on the back of her truck. We gathered around on folding lawn chairs and took our break.

"Well, they volunteered to come so it was pretty easy to enlist them."

"We're happy to help out. We just wish we lived closer so we could do more." Doris poured glasses of lemonade for us and she and Carol passed them around. "It brings back some happy memories of the busy times during harvest on the farm when we were young."

"I often wish I could have brought our children here to visit and see this farm and to let them learn about farm life by experience." Doris sipped her lemonade and got up to pass around the Tupperware container full of homemade sandwiches.

"Well, you know you can certainly bring your children down here any time to show them around and tell them things that you want them to know about the life we were once living here," I offered.

"Thanks, we just might bring Margaret down with us one weekend. She has fallen in love with a young farm boy who she met in the university in Brandon. He just finished his degree in agriculture."

"Do you think they are getting serious?" Carol asked.

"It seems she's pretty serious about him," Sam piped in. "I hope they don't rush things. She's only been seeing him for a few months."

"Well, we'd love to meet him so bring them down here any time. We'd better get back to work. Ed's already back in his seat on the combine. Thanks ladies for the lunch!"

I climbed back up into the other combine. Sam and Doris drove the grain trucks and Ed and I operated the combines. I thought to myself that Father would have loved to see the machines we were using today compared to when he first started out. How often I thought of him and especially when I was on this land. I felt his presence and could hear his voice in my head even after all these years. It felt good to be on his land, our land . . . working together as a family.

Chapter 39

Doris and Sam did bring Margaret and her now fiancé, Derrick Thompson, to the farm one weekend in September. I noted that Sam was not getting his wish as far as the young couple not "rushing things". They seemed to have moved their relationship along quite quickly.

Margaret had achieved her degree in education majoring in music. She was a beautiful young woman and she and Derrick made a striking couple. They were both tall and slender, both had dark hair but her body was like a willow tree and his was like an oak tree. He was muscular and had striking good looks with a great smile. He was very friendly and he brought out the best in Margaret it seemed. She seemed so relaxed and at ease with him at her side. She smiled more and chatted more. Of course, she was a little older now and had been around us enough to get somewhat over her shyness. It was nice to see this change in her. She seemed to be blossoming with her new love.

As it turned out, Derrick was very interested in our farm and he was looking to purchase a place of his own to get started in farming. His father was a successful farmer but there were three sons and they couldn't all stay on the family farm. Derrick wanted to establish himself with land of his own. Margaret was so in love with Derrick that I think she would have moved to the moon with him if he'd wanted.

With the family's approval, a deal was struck and the newlyweds moved onto the farm in March of 1972. Derrick was anxious to be ready to put crops in that spring. He wanted to be sure the machinery was checked over and oiled up ready to go when the weather was suitable. I thought to myself how my father would have approved of his good work ethic on this point. Margaret and Doris were busy cleaning and painting a few rooms to make the place more suitable to Margaret's taste in decorating.

Margaret had applied for a teaching position in Weyburn and was able to secure a position in the music department. She also took on the position as organist at the Baptist Church that Mother had attended. I wished that Mother had lived to see this as I was sure she would have been very proud.

Doris and Sam decided that they wanted to be closer to Margaret and Derrick. Their sons were both married and busy with work and family responsibilities in Winnipeg. Doris felt close to her only daughter and Margaret seemed to need Doris's help with getting settled into her new home and new life as a working woman living on a farm.

Doris and Sam both loved gardening and Sam could help Derrick with things as well. So, they found a house in Weyburn to be close. It made it much easier for us to see them more often now too. Ethel was also pleased because now she could see more of Doris and the brothers, Sam and Jim, were also happy that they would be able to see more of one another. Cev was sorry to have Doris leave Brandon after all these years but she and Milt said they were happy that the farm was staying in the family and they promised they'd be making trips to join the family on the farm or at the lake whenever possible. Now that they were retired, it would be easy enough and Cev said she looked forward to spending time helping Doris decorate her new home.

The house they purchased was in need of some updating and they felt they should hire a carpenter to do the work as it was too involved for Sam to tackle alone. I told them I thought I could possibly help them find a suitable carpenter.

I had been thinking of my old friend, Joe and it was about time I looked him up.

ॐॐ

I called Joe one weekend. I wasn't quite sure what to expect. After all, it had been about 21 years since we had seen one another. I hoped he still remembered me. I was 41 now and Joe would be close to the same age. But would we even recognize one another?

"Of course I remember you," he said when I made the call. "I've wondered about you and last time I spoke with Martha she told me all about how well you were doing. I wanted to try to get in touch but I'm so busy with work here and I don't get up to Regina much unless I'm making a run in for some building supplies. But most of what I use is bought locally. I try to support the local lumberyards."

"I've thought about you too and I'd like it if we could meet for a coffee some time when I am in Weyburn. We get there quite often and one of my sisters is moving to the city.

Her daughter and son-in-law bought our family farm so I'm finally seeing more of my family."

"Well, that's great Don. Family is something we seemed to have lost when we were living in the hell hole. I never see my relatives but my wife has a sister in town and that is enough family for me," he chuckled.

"I am wondering Joe, if you might be interested in helping my sister and her husband with some carpentry work. They need to do some major renovations on the house they just bought. Also, their daughter may have need of some repairs at the old farm house, if you are interested."

"Sure, I can take a look and see what I think. Let me know where and when and we'll meet and discuss details and catch up with one another. I'd really like to see you again."

I was elated to know that Joe was in good health and doing fine. We met a week later and I took him to the new house for Doris and Sam and out to the farm as well. Doris and Sam were not completely moved into the house yet but they had moved a bed in and were sort of camping there while trying to help Margaret at the farm.

Joe looked the project over and told Doris and Sam he'd come back with an estimate for them. Doris would have hired him on the spot just because he was a friend of mine but Sam was more careful with his money than that. He'd wait for the estimate.

Joe was no longer that skinny kid that had been so sickly with TB. I didn't notice any freckles so much on his face anymore. He was tanned enough that they seemed to have all but disappeared; however, he still had that little scar on his chin. Seeing that brought a flashback of the day he tried to defend me in the fight with "Mr. Muscle Man", Art.

Of course, he had whiskers and a few deep lines at the corners of his eyes and around his mouth. He was a man now. Here we were two grown men who had survived something quite horrible as children but we were survivors. We sat in a little Chinese café on Main Street, called the Club Café, staring at one another over a cup of coffee. I realized I had never asked Joe about his story and how he had ended up in the Mental Hospital.

"Joe, I never asked you about your family or how you ended up in the Mental. I guess we were not as curious about how we got there as we were interested in how we were going to live there!" I mused.

"I've never talked about it to no one before. I did tell, Linda—that's my wife. We have two boys but I've never told them any of this."

"It's OK—you don't have to share it with me either if you'd rather not."

"I don't mind telling you. It's just that living here in Weyburn, well—I just feel it's safer not to have people know. There's a stigma about having spent time in there you know. Even if you were sane the whole time and never should have been there in the first place, people wouldn't believe you. They always assume the worst and it is just easier not to go there with people."

"I understand. I don't tell everyone I meet about it either. I've told my wife, Carol, of course, and we've explained things to our kids. They know I spent eight years there but they don't know all the gory details. We've got three daughters. We've shared with Carol's family, as well, but they don't question me about it. So, like you, it is rarely discussed. It seems to be a subject that makes people uncomfortable. They don't want to pry and, truthfully, I have felt shame and disgust even though none of it was my fault. So, I get the part about a stigma."

Joe nodded in agreement. "My parents were both hopeless drunks. Half the time Dad was out of work and out of town for days on a binge. Mom wasn't much better. She drank to fill her loneliness. I think it started during the war when Dad was stationed overseas. Dad learned to drink while he was in the military and probably did his own share of partying while over there. Mom got lonely and partied a little too much and brought home air force guys or any other guys willing to buy her drinks and keep her entertained while Dad was away. Mom left me and my little sister alone while she went out at nights and one night while we were sleeping a fire started from a cigarette Mom had left burning before she went out that evening. I managed to get out but my little sister, Katie, never made it out."

"God, Joe, I'm so sorry."

"Yeah, me too. Katie never deserved that and Mom drank all the more after that. She blamed me for not saving Katie. I blamed myself and still do at times if I let myself think about it."

He lit a cigarette and paused to suck in a deep inhale of smoke. He closed his eyes and put his head back and let the smoke drift in curls out his nostrils. I let him gather himself and almost wished I was a smoker so I could have shared a cigarette moment with him. I could feel his pain as he tried to get the story out.

"We needed help to bury Katie. Neighbours donated at a church to pay for costs to the funeral home. I was bouncing from one place to another. I got left at people's places while Mom tried to work cleaning shops downtown; but, she'd get drunk and forget where she'd left me. Sometimes, she'd get fired so there was no money and I was missing school. I wanted to go to school but it became easier to just stay away. Half the time my clothes were dirty and ragged. Kids at school picked on me and so I just gave up on school. One day, she just drove me out to the Mental with one of her drinking buddies and dropped me off without even looking back."

He looked down at his coffee cup and then drew another puff of smoke. Then, he looked at me with those eyes that told me there was a deep pain that went far beyond what we had experienced after we met. His pain started long before mine did. This man was my childhood friend but now I respected him more than ever.

"My Dad came home after the war." He flicked his ash off the end of his cigarette with his little finger. "When I got out of the Mental I tried to find them both. I asked around and found out that they'd split up. They were both into their alcoholism too deep and I guess they fought a lot and went their separate ways. I don't know where they are and I'm OK with that. I figured I was likely better off without them. When I got the opportunity to learn a trade and get working, I just immersed myself in work and tried to make a living for myself. I met Linda and when I knew I could trust her enough to share with her, I did. We have kept it to ourselves just because it is a painful story that doesn't need to be shared with our kids or any of the community."

"I understand. I've had my struggles over the years with this and I felt just like you. I didn't think I needed to tell anyone either. But, Carol could see that keeping this bottled up inside me was eating at me and it was even starting to affect our relationship. She is a very sensitive woman and she knows things about me before I do," I chuckled and Joe nodded knowingly. Man to man we both knew our wives were something very good for both of us.

"Carol convinced me that I needed to locate my sisters and my mother. It took some convincing and I had a lot of reservations about facing my mother. But, eventually, with Carol and our girls, I did make those contacts."

Joe lit another cigarette and the waitress stopped to refill our cups.

"How did that go?" Joe asked.

"Meeting my sisters and their husbands was good. They were all very happy to see me again and I did feel we had enough positive vibes between us to rebuild a connection as siblings."

"How 'bout your mother?"

"That was not a warm fuzzy reunion in the beginning. Carol and I drove into the farm yard and she came outside to talk to us and never even asked us to get out of our car. I just rolled the window down and spoke to her from the car. Can you believe it? She never even asked us inside and my kids were eager to meet their grandmother and that was the reception we got." Even though I had come to terms with all this and had forgiven my mother, it still stung as I explained it to Joe.

"I see. So, you don't have any connection to her now after all that I'm sure."

"Actually, after a time, we did manage to connect again when she needed the help of family. The guy she'd married was losing his mind and became violent toward her.

We managed to reconcile when she was on her death bed. I feel like it took a lifetime for me to work through it all and to be able to forgive," I admitted to him.

"Something should have been done about what was happening to us kids, Don. It just wasn't right for us to end up in that place. No kid should be put there mixed in with adults who are insane. What happened to us? Why us?" Joe butted his cigarette and had to blow his nose. I saw tears glimmering in his eyes. He cleared his throat and took a drink of his coffee. From the expression on his face and the obvious pain his story still caused him, I suspected that he wasn't really being totally truthful when he told me that he was OK with not knowing where his parents were. But I understood how he may have chosen to try to bury his feelings and just move forward in life.

"I know, Joe. It was the times and the circumstances that were stacked against us. It wouldn't happen to a kid today. Things have changed and it's all improving with more education and understanding about the needs of children in similar cases to ours. There are more social services and child services being made available today. It's a long road we've traveled but I have managed to put things into a better perspective with time. Finding my family and facing my mother has helped but it wasn't always easy. Believe it or not, I've even found some positive things worth mentioning that happened while I lived in the asylum. One of those positive things, Joe, was having you as my pal. I have not forgotten how you stood up to the bully, Art, that day. I see you still have the scar to prove it! I have something for you that I hope you'll accept."

I reached into my brief case and pulled out my book. I placed it on the table. It had just been published.

"What's this?" Joe reached for the book and took a look at the cover. He read the title out loud, "A Normal Boy by Donald Johanson. That's you!"

"Yes, it's just been published and I want you to have the first copy. This is another one of Carol's ideas to help me face my demons and to get this stuff out. It's my story and yours and Martha's as well. But, of course, I've changed the names and some of the details to protect our privacy. I hope you'll read it and share it with your wife. I'd like very much to meet her one day. I think maybe after you read the book we should connect again."

"You bet Don. I'll read it for sure and I hope writing this has helped you. I guess we handle our demons in different ways but we get through life the best way we know how. I was always glad to have you and Martha as my friends while we were growing up in that place."

"Me too, Joe."

"Oh, and speaking of how we handled our demons— do you remember this?" He stood up to show me the rabbit foot hanging from the belt loop on his blue jeans. "I've always kept it and worn it for good luck like you told me to. Maybe it worked, hey?" He laughed. We shook hands and had a man hug once we were out on the street.

As I drove home to Regina, I felt that one more piece of my past could be put to rest. I took comfort in knowing that Joe was a good man who had accomplished having his own business. He had a loving wife and two sons. Life had dealt him a lot in the beginning. He had suffered great losses and enough sorrow for 10 people let alone one little boy. He had surely felt unloved and certainly he was unprotected by an alcoholic mother and an absent father. But, here we were—two normal little boys who had suffered a very abnormal event in our childhood and, yet, life still had good things to offer us and we were living that life.

Life was good and Martha, Joe and I were all living a life worth living.

The last words in my book were, *The best things and most beautiful things in life are not seen or touched but are felt with the heart.*

My heart was at peace.

Made in the USA
San Bernardino, CA
04 March 2020

65091205R00210